FOR
YOUR
OWN
PROTECTION

ALSO BY PAUL PILKINGTON

FOR
YOUR
OWN
PROTECTION

PAUL PILKINGTON

Published by Thomas & Mercer, Seattle

www.apub.com

Amazon, the Amazon logo, and Thomas & Mercer are trademarks of Amazon.com, Inc., or its affiliates.

ISBN-10: 1542048125
ISBN-13: 9781542048125

Cover design by Tom Sanderson

Printed in the United States of America

For my family

PROLOGUE

The 4 x 4 took the corner at speed, before mounting the kerb and slamming into the cyclist. The bike was propelled for many metres, skimming along the road like a polished stone on a calm lake. The man rolled over the bonnet, smashed into the windscreen, and was lifted high into the air, over the roof of the vehicle, before crashing down on to the tarmac.

The vehicle did not stop.

Did not slow.

In his last moments, a strange thought came to the dying man.

My cycle helmet. Someone took it.

PART ONE

CHAPTER ONE

Matt Roberts flopped down, exhausted, on to the yellow sofa in the staffroom, and looked across at his younger sister, Amy. His head was still whirring from the exchange about firearms he'd just had with a six-foot-four-inch, twenty-year-old youth, built like a boxer and with an attitude to boot.

'So, how did I do? Terrible, or just mildly awful?'

Amy smiled. She looked down at the clipboard that Matt suspected was only for show, to wind up her big brother. 'I thought you did great. Really great.'

'Even the bit about the guns?'

'Especially the bit about the guns.'

Harvey – sharp, razored Afro and all designer gear and bling – had been referred to the financial management class by his youth offending team caseworker. He'd replied to Matt's question about financial calculations with a question of his own: 'Sir, what do you get when you add one guy with a gun to another guy with a gun?'

Matt had glanced around the rest of the fifteen-strong Friday-evening class at the North London College of Further Education, unknowingly tracing his tongue over his top lip. Half of them were suppressing smiles, knowing what was coming. The remainder weren't even listening. 'I don't know, Harvey, what do you get?'

'One helluva firefight!' he said, slapping the desk in celebration of the joke.

The class laughed and groaned in equal measure.

'What?!' Harvey said, gesticulating to those who weren't laughing. 'C'mon, people, show your appreciation!'

Amy had been sitting at the back of the classroom, her face not revealing her thoughts. She hadn't made eye contact with Matt, but he'd known she was waiting for him to come up with a suitable response to this challenge.

He'd tried to channel one of his favourite teachers from school, who had never failed to deal with troublesome class members. 'Very good, Harvey. Maybe you should try stand-up, not shoot-'em-up.'

'Your response was perfect,' Amy said. 'A bit risky, running with the gun analogy, but you judged it well.'

'I've got to admit, in those seconds after the words left my mouth, until he smiled, I did wonder.'

'As I said, you judged it well. Harvey likes you, I can tell. You're building a relationship with the group, after just a few weeks. There's respect there already. I'm impressed. They're still testing you out, challenging you. But that's part of the process. They're engaging with what you're saying, which is a massive step forward for them, believe me. Most of those guys have never had a father figure in their lives, and those that have, well, that father figure hasn't exactly been a positive influence. For them, being able to look up to someone wielding a pen or calculator, rather than a gun or knife, is a real revelation.'

'It's not like where we came from.'

'And it's certainly a different world to your usual place of work. How are you enjoying it?'

Matt took a couple of seconds. 'More than I thought I would. It makes a great change from fund-managing.'

'So, are you not tempted to do this kind of thing full-time? Make a career out of it? Say goodbye to the bank and hello to the classroom?' Amy noted Matt's sceptical expression. 'You're a natural at it. And you always wanted to be a teacher.'

'I already have a career, Amy.'

Amy continued, undeterred. 'You could make such a difference to people's lives.'

'Aren't you being a bit melodramatic?'

'I don't think so. I'm just trying to make sure you can see the benefits, that's all.' She smiled as she took a sip of her peppermint tea, the label from the bag dangling over the side. 'Harvey in particular really respects you.'

'You think?'

'Oh yes. You should've seen how he was with some of the other tutors.'

'I'm not sure I want to know.'

'He's scared off three tutors in the past six months. He threatened to fist-fight the first one, after the guy made the mistake of singling him out in class. I won't tell you about what he did to the other two. It's possible they deserved it though. A lot of teachers can't really handle these kids. They have to be approached in just the right way, otherwise things can go badly wrong.'

'Are you able to tell me more about Harvey? His background?'

'Sure. His father left when he was eight. Mother struggled to cope, financially and otherwise, with a family of four. His older brother was killed three years ago in a gang-related incident – chased through Peckham and knifed to death. Harvey was already being drawn into gangs, most of those kids are, but he really went off the rails after his brother's death. Got involved in petty crime, then drug-running, then harassment, and finally an assault that left a rival gang member hospitalised.'

'Wow,' Matt said, thinking back again to the incident with Harvey.

'He's very intelligent though,' Amy added. 'But you already know that.'

Matt nodded. Harvey was by far the brightest in the class. 'He just needs to put it to good use.'

Amy nodded. 'He's ambitious too, but do you know, the week before you started, he came to tell me he was quitting. Said he'd got tired of it all.'

'So what changed?'

'New tutor, maybe?'

Matt somehow doubted that.

Amy continued. 'I think he'd lost confidence in himself a little after a couple of tough classes, but he seems to have gone from strength to strength since. You think in a few weeks' time he'll be ready for the assessment?'

'I hope so. I'm not sure who's more nervous about this – them or me.' Passing the exam would give the students academic credits, which they could use to build up to a higher qualification.

'You'll do fine.' Amy smiled. 'If you decide to stick around a while longer, maybe take another class. The guys can continue to help you, too.'

'Help me?'

'I've not seen you this positive in a long time,' she replied. 'You seem happy in a way that you haven't been since . . .' Amy trailed off.

'Since I split from Beth,' Matt finished, with some reluctance. His relationship with Beth had ended eighteen months ago, following a gradual yet apparently unstoppable decay in relations that began after the death of his father from a heart attack, just six months earlier. He had tried to drown his grief with his job. But while ever-longer hours worked wonders for his career, winning him promotion at UGT to manager of the bank's premier ethical-investment fund, it had soured his relationship with Beth.

'I meant since Adam died.'

'Oh.' Matt's face darkened.

'I know you still blame yourself. But you shouldn't.'

Adam Thomas, a young co-worker whom Matt had mentored during Adam's first few months with the company, had fallen to his death from an apartment balcony during a party for UGT employees. Tests had shown traces of cocaine in his system. Matt felt tremendous guilt at what had happened – he was well aware of how hard the company pushed new recruits, how stressful that could be, and that drugs or alcohol often emerged as a coping mechanism. After all, he'd been through it himself. He should have done more to protect Adam.

'And what you did afterwards, you weren't your normal self.'

'I still cheated on Beth, whatever the circumstances.'

In the midst of what Matt now recognised was severe depression had come a transgression that to Beth was unforgivable – a drunken one-night stand with a colleague, Jessica Summers. Thrown out of the family home, and sinking deeper into mental distress during a torrid six months in which Beth began a new relationship, he had been given permission to take unpaid leave for an initial twelve-month period. Now, with the year almost gone, he was feeling a lot better and looking to return to the fray. Taking the voluntary teaching opportunity offered by Amy was a step towards that, and nothing more.

'I can see the old Matt,' Amy said. 'The Matt who dreamed of making a difference.'

Matt smiled tightly. Amy trying to steer him back to his original path was nothing new. His childhood dream had been to teach, following the careers of his parents.

'I think Beth would approve,' Amy noted.

'I doubt she'd notice. Although things seem a bit better between us recently.'

'I still hope you and Beth might sort things out.'

'She's with James now.'

James Farrah, a colleague at UGT and rival fund manager. Rival because there was always competition at UGT – the company encouraged it.

'Maybe she's with him to make you jealous?'

Matt shrugged. 'Who knows?'

Beth had history with James Farrah. James had shared a house with Beth's older brother Sean at university in Durham. Beth, two years his junior, had met James during one of her visits to see Sean, and they'd dated long-distance for a time back then. By chance, housemates Sean and James had both been signed up by UGT. Some years on, it was at one of Sean's house parties that Matt, by then also a UGT employee, met Beth. Only later would he discover that the man whose conversation with Beth he had interrupted, whom he already disliked, had once been her lover.

'Anyway, I've got more pressing relationship worries at the moment.'

'Catherine?'

He exhaled. 'I've decided to end it, but I want to tell her in person. I'm meeting her for lunch tomorrow.'

'The Last Supper?'

'I can't say I'm looking forward to it.'

'You still think she might be a stalker?'

'I know you think I'm crazy – maybe I am – but I'm sure she's been following me.'

Although they'd only been dating for eight weeks, it had been an intense, whirlwind couple of months – they'd seen each other nearly every day since that first meeting, and it had felt great. But Matt had become increasingly uncomfortable. He'd been getting the strange feeling that Catherine had been watching him when they weren't together. He didn't have any proof, but several times when walking among the London crowds, he'd thought he'd spotted her. And then there was the time he'd bumped into her on Oxford Street. He hadn't challenged her on it, and had only confided in Amy.

It did seem faintly ridiculous.

'That's not why I'm ending things though,' he clarified. 'It's been fun, and she's really nice, but I don't think it's going anywhere. I don't want to waste her time.'

'Fair enough. For what it's worth, I still think that Beth is the only girl for you.'

Matt headed home on the bus. He thought about Harvey. It would be good to get to know him better, to try to understand what he wanted.

He was enjoying the teaching more than he could have imagined. And it had awakened something in him. But it was merely a temporary diversion, not a new route in life.

Five minutes from home, his mobile buzzed in his pocket.

It was a text from Beth.

Hi Matt. Can we meet first thing tomorrow? Nine o'clock at Giuseppe's? Need to talk to you about something really important.

Matt was surprised by his emotional response to the cryptic message.

He felt hope.

CHAPTER TWO

Matt tried to dismiss any potential significance in Beth's chosen location for their meet-up. Giuseppe's had been a favourite haunt of theirs throughout the years they'd been living in Camden, north London. At this early hour on a Saturday morning, the cafe-bar was quiet. Beth was over in the far corner, her head in a book, with two drinks already on the table.

'Hi, Beth,' he said, approaching and feeling surprisingly nervous.

'Hey.' She smiled warmly, placing the book down on the table. Matt noticed it was a trashy thriller. She'd always been a sucker for that kind of thing. Matt tried to push away thoughts of whether she still read in bed as she used to, but with James now lying by her side.

'Take a seat,' she said, pushing strands of her brown shoulder-length hair behind her right ear. He had always loved the way she did that. 'I took the liberty of ordering you a mocha.' She studied his response, mistaking his nerves for dissatisfaction. 'You do still like mochas, don't you?'

'Yes, of course, thanks.'

Matt could see she was nervous, too. He was taken back to their first date. They'd gone to watch a movie and grabbed a coffee afterwards, finding their way through the conversation, making that initial, tentative connection.

Beth sipped at her drink. 'You still okay to have Charlie tomorrow?'

'Of course.'

Charlie – their four-and-a-half-year-old son. The lack of daily access to him was still a source of immense pain, even though visitation rights were as good as could be expected.

'Swimming and the park,' Matt said. Charlie was a real water baby, and delighted in the trips to the local children's pool, with its inflatables and water jets. And the new toddler-friendly, sit-on zip wire in the park across the road from the swimming pool was a total winner.

'Sounds good,' she said, stirring her coffee absent-mindedly.

'You off out with James?' Matt ventured.

She nodded, and for a moment looked as though she was going to elaborate. But she then didn't offer anything further, and Matt didn't pursue it. After all, it wasn't really any of his business.

Matt looked off towards the counter, where a girl was preparing supplies for lunchtime. He wondered what this meeting was all about, but was prepared to wait until Beth was ready to explain. Then, through the windows, he caught a glimpse of someone walking past the cafe. It looked like Catherine. If he wasn't sitting with Beth he'd have leapt to his feet and run after the woman. He needed to know whether Catherine was following him – and if so, why. So far, he'd never quite been able to shake off the suspicion that it was just his mind playing tricks.

'How are you, anyway?'

Matt brought his attention back to the table. 'I'm okay, thanks. Good, pretty good.'

Beth was really looking at him, in a way she hadn't done since things had started to go so terribly wrong. 'I hear you're seeing someone.'

'How did you—'

'Sean mentioned it to James. Sorry, I didn't realise you wanted to keep it secret.'

'I didn't. It's just that, well . . . It doesn't matter.' Matt wasn't happy about Sean, who was his friend, blabbing about his private life to the man who was now dating Matt's ex-partner. He'd have to speak with Sean about it.

'That's great news,' Beth said. 'I'm happy for you. We both need to move on.'

Matt searched Beth's face in an attempt to determine whether she meant what she said. He was disappointed to find that her sentiments appeared genuine. He considered telling her that by this evening the relationship would be over, but injecting that piece of negativity didn't seem appropriate or particularly helpful.

'I also hear you're volunteering at the local college.'

Sean again!

'Just the past month or so. Amy asked me to help out with a financial management class for these guys who've been in trouble with the authorities. I'm teaching them some basic maths and accounting skills.'

Beth looked genuinely impressed. 'So how's it going?'

'Really well, actually. Really well.'

'You always wanted to be a teacher,' she said. 'Do you think you might not return to UGT?'

A mischievous thought crossed Matt's mind. 'James hasn't put you up to this, has he?' He felt his face flush. 'Trying to find out if I'm returning to the company? Wanting to see whether the way is clear for him further up the ladder?'

'Matt, how could you think that? Of course not.'

'Because I *am* coming back, in the next month or so.'

Matt simmered.

'I can understand how you feel about James and me being together, but please, try to be happy for me and Charlie.' Beth's tone was conciliatory. 'Charlie gets on really well with James. He's happy.'

'He was happy with us.'

'Before things went wrong,' Beth countered. 'You know he was affected by the arguments, by the atmosphere.'

Matt conceded that point. 'You're right – of course you are.' Charlie had become withdrawn and anxious when they were splitting up. Now he seemed back to normal. Matt had never really thought about James's role in that. He hadn't wanted to think about James's role in Charlie's life, full stop.

Just then, Matt's phone vibrated. It was Catherine.

Looking forward to lunch xxx

Matt slid the phone back into his trouser pocket. 'I'm sorry, Beth. It's just that it's still hard, you know, seeing you with someone else.'

'But you are—'

'It's nothing serious,' he said, waving away the idea. 'Just a few dates. But you and James, it's obviously different. Even though it's only been six months, it seems serious. Are you living together?'

The directness of the question threw Beth, who immediately reddened. 'James . . . does stay over.'

'Most of the time?'

Beth sighed. 'Recently, yes. Most but not all of the time.' She gave him a look as if to say, *Are you happy now?*

Matt tried to look unaffected by the admission, even though the thought of James taking over his family and now his house wounded him deeply. What next? Charlie calling him 'Daddy'?

'How did it come to this?' he said quietly.

Beth, too, softened. 'You know how it came to this.'

'I still love you,' Matt found himself saying. 'You and Charlie, you mean the world to me.'

Beth shook her head. 'Don't.'

'Why?' Matt said, reaching out for her hand. She drew it away, but not before they touched momentarily.

'Because,' she said, looking down and closing her eyes briefly, steeling herself to say something. Then she stared directly at him. 'Because it makes this all the harder.'

'What? What is it?'

She swallowed. 'James has been offered a promotion. A transfer to UGT's Sydney office. It's just for two years in the first instance.'

The realisation of what she was saying hit home. 'No, you can't. Please, don't.'

'James wants me to come with him, and of course that means Charlie too.' Beth ploughed on, as if she were unable to stop the words from flowing, for fear that they'd be too hard to say once the momentum was lost. 'I'd need your blessing, to be able to go there with Charlie. After all, you're his dad. I couldn't take him there without you being happy with the situation.'

Matt struggled to contain his anger. 'Happy with the situation? Are you kidding me? Happy being thousands of miles away from my son, while another man brings him up?'

Beth bit her lip.

'No way,' Matt said, his raised voice drawing the attention of the girl behind the counter. 'No way will I give my blessing to that.'

'Just have a think,' she muttered.

Matt slid his chair back, scraping it along the tiled floor as he got to his feet. 'You tell James he's not stealing my son.'

CHAPTER THREE

Matt didn't stop to look back as he exited Giuseppe's, putting some distance between him and the cafe before pausing by a wall just outside a newsagent's. Already he felt some remorse for how he had reacted – the look of shock on Beth's face was not something he had taken pleasure in – but he was still angry.

He looked into the shop, and for the first time in many years felt an urge to smoke. Beth hated smoking, and Matt had quit within a month of their first date.

You'll never get Beth back if you start on those.

He turned away and pulled out his mobile, just in case Beth had sent a text message – although he didn't know what he expected her to say.

There were no new messages.

He circled around on the pavement, trying to think. Was it worth calling Beth and trying to continue the discussion, but this time more rationally? Maybe he could persuade her that the whole idea of Australia was a bad one. Beth wasn't fond of heat, or insects, or long plane journeys.

But she was fond of James Farrah, obviously.

Matt kicked at the low wall, then glanced at his watch. It wasn't even ten yet. There were another two hours before he was due to meet Catherine in central London. He pulled out his phone again and called Beth. Her mobile rang through to voicemail.

'Beth, I'm sorry I flew off the handle. It's just that it was such a shock. Can we talk some more about it? Are you still around? I can come over to where you are. I'm just down the street.'

He cut the message off there. He sounded desperate.

Then he called Amy and explained things.

'Go back there now,' she advised. 'You really don't want things to fester.'

'I'm still angry about it,' he said. 'Maybe I should wait until tomorrow morning, when I pick Charlie up.'

'You don't want to have that kind of discussion with him around. Go back there now; maybe you'll catch her.'

'Okay.'

'Oh, Matt, before I forget. Harvey wants to talk to you.'

'One to one?'

'Yes, after tonight's class, if that's okay with you. I said it was okay.'

'What about?'

'He didn't say.'

'It's fine. Look, I'd better get back to Giuseppe's. Although she's probably gone by now.'

'You might get her at home then.'

'Maybe.'

Matt jogged back to Giuseppe's, and he was surprised to see Beth through the window, still sitting at the same table. He rushed into the cafe, unable to slow his pace.

'Beth,' he said, approaching the table.

She looked up from her novel, shocked to see him back. Her face was puffy, and he knew she'd been crying.

'Look, Beth, I'm sorry for reacting the way I did . . .'

She seemed uncomfortable with his presence. Her earlier smile had gone. Had his outburst affected her to such an extent?

18

She shifted in her chair. 'Matt, maybe we'd better . . .' Then her eyes slid across to her right as someone approached from behind where Matt was standing.

'Matthew,' James Farrah said, with a confident, relaxed smile. He must have just emerged from the bathroom. 'Good to see you again,' he added, proffering a hand.

Matt made the split-second decision to accept the gesture, holding his own in a too-tight-for-comfort grip that lasted long enough for the two men to eyeball one another across the table.

'And you,' Matt managed.

James looked like he was dressed for work, in an expensive dark suit, with a blood red tie and white shirt. Matt felt self-conscious in his scruffy jeans and polo shirt, as James gave him a quick once-over. 'Enjoying the teaching career?'

The words were deliberately targeted.

'It's just temporary. Personal development before I return to UGT.' Matt glanced at Beth, who was still the only one of the three who was seated. She didn't raise her eyes from the table, and looked the picture of discomfort.

James then seemed to notice, dampening any combative attitude. 'Good. It will be great to have you back, Matt.'

'Thanks.' Matt, too, thought of Beth, and chose not to say what he really wanted to say: that there was no way in hell that James was going to take his son away from him without a damn good fight.

Beth looked up from the table, directing her attention at Matt. 'Maybe we'd better talk about, you know, another time. You probably need a chance to get your head around the idea.'

'You're right. I'm sorry I upset you.'

'When you pick Charlie up tomorrow,' she said. 'We can talk then. Is that okay?'

Matt nodded as James looked on in triumphant silence.

CHAPTER FOUR

The location for the break-up was deliberately low-key. Matt figured it wouldn't be a good move to do the deed in some swanky restaurant, where it might be difficult to 'end' the lunch easily. So he had chosen a small pub just off Trafalgar Square called The Admiral. He'd decided against doing it in private – back at his flat, for example. It might have been the kinder option, ensuring that there was no danger of spectators, but in truth there was a reason for the public place: it was security for him. What if he was right about her being a stalker? At least in public there was less chance of this taking any kind of sinister turn.

He scanned the pub for Catherine. There was a smattering of patrons in the bar off to the left, mostly men in their fifties and sixties. A younger man was playing the slot machine to the right. This wasn't a place that any of his colleagues at the bank would be caught dead in – not exclusive or expensive enough. But it suited Matt fine.

Not seeing Catherine around, he ordered a glass of lemonade, deciding it was best to keep a clear head, and took a seat at one of the tables near to the entrance. It would give her the option of a quick getaway.

He brooded over thoughts of Beth moving to the other side of the world, frolicking on golden Australian sands with her lover, perhaps never coming back, and leaving him with no connection to the son he so deeply loved and needed.

He sipped at his drink.

'Matt!'

He was taken by surprise, so lost in swirling negative thoughts that he hadn't noticed Catherine arrive. 'Catherine.' He managed a smile, and she brushed her lips against his cheek before taking the seat opposite. She looked stunning, with her blonde hair tied back in a short ponytail.

'How are you?'

'Great, thanks,' she beamed. 'Just been out in St James's Park for a really hard session with a new client. A businessman from Paris, over here for a few months.'

Catherine was a fitness fanatic, and worked as a personal trainer to a number of super-wealthy people in the capital. Unlike Beth, Catherine could never be described as curvy. She was angular, as if she'd purged any hint of excess body fat with exercise.

At twenty-eight, she was ten years younger than Matt and full of enthusiasm for life. As well as the niggling paranoia he felt concerning her, the age gap was a reason why Matt had decided the relationship, for all its fun, didn't have a future. In their case, the generation gap did seem to matter: they had few common reference points.

Matt decided he'd wait until after they had eaten before announcing his intention to end things. It didn't seem right just to come out with it at the outset. He thought back to Amy's comment about 'the Last Supper'. Maybe she was right.

He ordered food at the bar, looking over at Catherine, who was busy on her mobile, most probably scrolling through her Twitter feed. Her obsession with exercise was nearly matched by her obsession with social media, and she was always checking various apps. As if she sensed his gaze, Catherine looked up and smiled, then her head went back down to the screen.

Matt spotted a man sitting off to the left of Catherine, over by the window. The middle-aged guy was staring at her over his pint glass. His gaze only wavered when his eyes slid across to Matt. Holding the look for a couple of seconds, the man seemed to chuckle to himself as he looked away and downed the rest of his pint.

Matt returned to the table and relaxed into conversation, almost forgetting what was about to come. The man who had been leering at Catherine had ordered another pint at the bar and returned to his position, just a few feet away from them but out of earshot. He was still sitting on his own, but when Matt looked across at him, his attention no longer seemed fixed on either of them.

Matt and Catherine finished their lunch of baguettes and salad. Matt's insides churned as crunch time neared, and he felt the urge to pee. He was at the urinal when the man who had been looking at Catherine from the nearby table entered. Matt looked straight ahead at the white tiles of the wall. They were the bathroom's only two occupants.

'So, are you the real lover, or just another sucker?'

Matt took a moment to glance across, not quite wanting to believe that the man was talking to him.

The balding man, who must have been in his early to mid-fifties, was staring straight back at him, a slightly drunken smile on his face.

'Excuse me?'

'I said, are you the real lover, or just another sucker?'

Matt zipped up his trousers and stepped back towards the bank of sinks. 'I don't understand.'

'That girl you're with, is she your girlfriend?'

'Yes, she is,' Matt replied, addressing him via the mirror as they both washed their hands. He didn't particularly want to engage this man in conversation, but to just blank him would have been uncomfortable.

The man smiled again. 'Your girlfriend. She doesn't recognise me – looked right at me a few minutes ago, didn't even register. I've put on a little weight, let my beard grow. But I recognise her.'

Matt decided against spending time at the dryer. His hands could air-dry. 'Sorry, I have to get back . . .' He reached for the door handle.

'What name did she choose for you?' the man said, straightening up as he shook the water on to the floor.

'Excuse me, I don't understand . . .'

'She was Kirsten with me. What's she with you?'

'Catherine. Her name's Catherine.'

The man smiled knowingly. 'For you, yes. Why don't you ask her what her real name is?'

'Why would she lie about her name?'

The guy seemed to take pleasure that Matt had finally taken the bait. 'Ask her yourself.'

Matt shook his head. 'I've really got to go.' He didn't want to listen to any more of these ramblings.

'She'll ruin you. Get rid of her now, if it's not already too late.'

Matt pulled the door open, annoyed by the games. 'Thanks for your relationship advice.'

'Just ask her!' the man shouted as Matt exited. 'And see the reaction. Then you'll believe me. But whether you do or you don't, take it from me – you're in big trouble.'

CHAPTER FIVE

Catherine looked up from her phone and smiled warmly as Matt returned. She placed the phone on the table, with the screen side down, just as one of the bar staff came across with two coffees.

'I thought you'd appreciate the caffeine,' Catherine said, nodding at the large cup of flat white.

Matt rubbed at his eyes, which suddenly felt heavy. 'Do I look that bad?'

'Maybe,' she smiled. 'A little tired. Stressed?' She sipped at the drink without taking her eyes off him.

'Possibly.'

'What is it? Anything I might be able to help with?'

Matt thought back to what the man in the toilets had said: *Why don't you ask her what her real name is?. . . And see the reaction.*

He turned around, but the man was nowhere to be seen. Should he ask her? Had the man been telling the truth? What would he gain out of lying? Maybe it was just a case of mistaken identity, or possibly he was just a bitter drunkard out to cause trouble with an apparently happy couple.

'You seem really distracted,' Catherine continued. 'You don't have to tell me what's bothering you, but it might help. A problem shared, and all that.'

Matt felt strangely guilty as he returned her kindly smile. This wasn't going to plan at all. He decided to park the idea of breaking up and instead come clean about what was top of his worry list. 'It's about Beth and Charlie. Beth wants to move to Australia with James.' He dragged a hand across his face. 'And of course, that means Charlie too.' He was met with sympathetic eyes. 'She says it's for two years, but you just don't know, do you? Once you make that move, if it goes well, the likelihood is that temporary becomes permanent. Charlie is at the age where he'll feel it's his home: he'll be settled in a school, have friends. I'll hardly see him.'

Catherine reached out to take his hand. 'I'm so sorry, Matt. Can she just do that?'

'With my permission. Which is what she asked for.'

'And what did you say?'

'I said no way.'

Catherine didn't say anything.

'Do you think I should agree to it?'

'I don't know. It's very difficult. I'm not sure what I'd do if I was in your position. I know how much you love Charlie.'

'I didn't handle it well,' Matt admitted. 'I guess it took me by surprise.'

Matt gazed at her. Suddenly, the idea that she was some kind of stalker, or a woman going under a false name, seemed absurd. Maybe the real issue wasn't Catherine at all. Maybe it was him. He was looking for an excuse to end the fledgling but promising relationship, because he didn't want to admit the truth – that he still loved and wanted Beth.

She seemed to read his thoughts. 'This isn't just about losing Charlie, is it?'

Matt shook his head. 'I still love her. And I want her back. I'm pretty sure she doesn't want me, but I need to try.'

'I understand.'

'I'm sorry, Catherine. I really don't want to mess you around.'

But she was no longer listening. She was looking towards the exit and the man standing at the doorway – the man from the toilets, who was looking back at her, smirking. As he left the pub, Catherine continued to gaze at the spot where he'd been, as if lost in thought.

'Catherine?'

She snapped out of her reverie, but she was clearly rattled. She tried a smile. 'Sorry, what was it you were saying?'

Her face seemed drained of colour, and although she was doing her best to look interested, Matt could see she was still processing something.

The man was not a stranger to her, and Matt had to ask the question. 'The man at the door, who is he?'

'Sorry?'

'The man – you know him.'

'I don't know who you mean. Someone in here?' Her eyes swept the room, but it was just an act.

'He approached me in the toilets,' Matt revealed, trying his best not to sound confrontational. 'He said you knew one another.'

Catherine stayed silent and placed a hand on her downturned phone, as if readying herself for an exit.

'I dismissed him. He was drunk. But you do know him, don't you? You recognised him just then.'

She shrugged it off. 'He seemed familiar, but I couldn't place him.' Now her cheeks were reddening. 'I think he may have been a client a few years back.'

Matt wondered whether to stop there. It seemed they had almost reached the desired destination – breaking up – so he could just walk away and get on with trying to win Beth back. But he felt an irresistible urge now to find out whether Catherine was who she said she was, and if not, why she had lied. 'Is your name really Catherine?'

She tried to hide her reaction. But the micro-expression, a flash of guilt, told Matt what he wanted to know.

'Why?' he asked. 'Why lie about your name?' And then suddenly everything made sense. 'You're already married. This is an affair, right?'

She didn't deny it, instead keeping her head down. 'I'd better go, Matt. I'm sorry.'

She made to stand, so Matt stood with her. He kept his voice even, determined not to make a scene. 'Am I right? You're already married? That man, have you had an affair with him in the past? Is that how you know one another?' He tried to read her. Now he had vocalised it, that explanation didn't seem to fit somehow. She hadn't denied his accusation. But somehow it didn't seem right.

'I should go,' she said. Matt allowed her to pass by and head out of the door. But he followed her out on to the pavement, turning left towards Westminster. She'd set off at a quick pace, determined to outwalk his questioning, and he struggled to keep up.

'Catherine, please.'

'Matt, just leave it.' Her speed increased. He stumbled slightly, and she took the opportunity to scoot across the road through a gap in the traffic. By the time Matt tried to follow, he was left stranded, only able to watch as the woman he knew as Catherine jogged off down the street.

CHAPTER SIX

Rachel Martin took a sip of tepid water and found herself gagging. She managed to limit the damage to several stifled coughs, but it was still enough to draw a number of inquisitive looks from those crowded into the front room.

Wakes were, by their very nature, strange events. The idea of burying her boyfriend one minute and eating finger food the next struck her as repugnant. She would have avoided the wake altogether, but for the fact that Hilary, Alex's mother, had specifically asked her to be there. Rachel hadn't felt able to refuse.

Alex had been killed just over two weeks ago in what the police described as 'an apparent hit and run incident'. Two officers had knocked at the door, faces serious, to deliver the grim news: he'd been found lying dead on the road, just a few minutes from their home.

Rachel, utterly devastated, knew her life had been changed forever.

The funeral itself had been a blur. She remembered arriving at the church just outside the centre of the city; she remembered seeing the hearse pull up, with the light brown coffin in the back; and she remembered watching as the coffin was heaved on to the shoulders of family members clad in black. Events inside the church were harder to recollect: there had been the music, deliberately upbeat but still haunting; the readings by Alex's father and brother; and the eulogy. She'd wondered beforehand if she'd have the strength to look at the coffin, but once it was there, she couldn't take her eyes off it. Her eyes traced the grain of the oak panels around the gold handles they'd be using to lower it into the freshly dug grave. On several occasions, Rachel thought she saw the lid move slightly, minutely. Her heart had literally missed a beat, but the lid remained firmly closed. She had watched the coffin up until the point when it disappeared into the ground. Then, forcing herself to turn and walk away, she had headed straight for the car park. She hadn't looked back.

Rachel glanced around self-consciously, meeting the now-embarrassed stares. The watching guests returned to their protective huddles and resumed their polite, if uncomfortable, conversations. She'd hardly spoken to anyone in the thirty minutes she'd been here, and hadn't touched any of the food laid out so impressively in the front room. It must have taken Hilary hours to prepare.

'Rachel, how are you?'

She turned and smiled as Hilary approached, squeezing herself through the crowds of smartly and darkly dressed mourners.

'Not hungry?' Hilary said. Rachel had to admire her strength: she was putting on a brave face, but the strain behind her blue eyes betrayed her inner torment.

Rachel shook her head. 'I can't eat,' she said. 'I just feel sick.'

'Me too,' Hilary said, looking across to the food. 'To tell you the truth, I haven't touched so much as a crumb.'

Rachel smiled faintly.

'At least it gave me something to do,' Hilary said, exhaling. 'And at least some people are enjoying it.' She looked over at a large man whose plate was piled high with food, and for a moment Rachel sensed she and Hilary were wondering the same thing: *Have people forgotten Alex already?*

'I'll never forget him,' Rachel said, as Hilary turned back towards her.

Hilary's face had dropped its defences and her muscles had sagged, revealing a woman in mourning. 'Thank you, Rachel,' she said, squeezing her hand gently. 'I know how much you meant to Alex.'

What Hilary didn't know is that just four days before his death, Alex had proved his love for her by proposing. Rachel had accepted without hesitation. She knew she wanted to spend the rest of her life with him. Somehow, she had sensed it from their very first meeting in a West End pub, just two years ago. Now, though, the opportunity of a life with Alex had been ripped away from her, and it was hurting like a raw, open wound.

'Have you spoken with your parents recently?' Hilary said, regaining some of her earlier composure.

Rachel was thinking of happier times. 'Pardon?'

'Your parents, have you spoken with them much? It must be hard to deal with this, being so far from home.'

Rachel nodded. It was difficult. Except for her work friends, she was alone. Her parents were back in her home city of San Francisco, along with her long-time girlfriends. Three years ago, her employer, the marketing company VisiON, had offered her a transfer to the new European HQ in London. She had instinctively backed away from the move: she loved her family, and America, and was unsure about whether life in England would suit her. But it was a fantastic opportunity, and one she decided to accept. Rachel soon grew to love her new life. Now Alex was dead, however, the pull of home was strengthening with each passing day.

'I spoke with them last night,' Rachel said. 'They want me to come home, at least for a few months. But I'm not so sure.'

'Whatever you think is best, Rachel,' Hilary said, placing a comforting hand on her shoulder.

'I'll be fine, Mrs McKenzie, honestly.'

'Call me Hilary,' she said. 'I do think of you as one of the family . . .'

She trailed off, and Rachel wondered whether she was thinking about what might have been: all those avenues that were now closed off because of that fateful night. Hilary might not have known about Alex's proposal, but she must have imagined Rachel as her future daughter-in-law.

'Thank you.'

'And do pop by anytime,' Hilary continued, delicately dabbing a tear in the corner of her eye. 'I'm sure Alex would have wanted us to keep in touch.'

Hilary looked expectant, and Rachel nodded.

'It's good to see so many of Alex's friends here,' Hilary said, taking a sip of white wine from the glass cradled in her hand. Rachel noticed it was shaking as she brought it to her lips.

'Yes, Alex had a lot of friends,' Rachel said.

The funeral was packed. But she'd noted one significant absence: Michael Thornbury. Michael had been a close work colleague and friend of Alex's for years. She and Alex had often socialised with Michael and his long-term girlfriend, Annabelle, and had even taken holidays together as a foursome. But not only had Michael been out of contact since Alex's death, he then hadn't turned up for his friend's funeral.

'Hilary.'

Alex's father Stephen bore a remarkable likeness to Alex, and Rachel found it difficult to see him and not think of how Alex would have looked in thirty years' time. Stephen smiled at Rachel, then whispered something in Hilary's ear. Mouthing a last 'take care', Hilary drifted away towards the kitchen.

Alone again in the crowd, Rachel felt a desperate need for Alex. She looked around from her secluded corner by the bookshelf, feeling more vulnerable than ever: all of these strangers, eating, talking, even laughing. Suddenly it felt as though everyone was watching and talking about her. The cumulative volume of the room had increased to the point where it had begun to hurt her ears. The middle-aged man standing by the door, the old woman sitting in the comfy chair, the young boy kneeling on the carpet, they were all scrutinising her, burning holes through her with their eyes. She had to get out.

She left without goodbyes, quietly retrieving her coat from the pile in the back bedroom. She caught a bus back home, choosing to sit next to a teenage girl wearing headphones and reading a book. She wouldn't have to make polite conversation with her.

As the bus edged through the city centre traffic, Rachel decided: she had to find Michael Thornbury and discover what had kept him from the funeral of his good friend.

CHAPTER SEVEN

Matt stood staring at Catherine as she hurried away. She had made it clear that she didn't want to talk. But still the words of the guy in the toilets nagged at him. He'd call Catherine later and hopefully get some answers.

If only he could have another chance to question the man himself.

On a whim, he made his way back to the pub. Maybe the man was a regular, and if that was the case, the staff might know something about him. Or at the very least, they might suggest the best time to catch him there.

'Hi,' Matt said to the barman, who was busy wiping down the surface of the bar with a damp cloth. 'There was a guy in here a few minutes ago. Sitting over there,' he said, pointing over to where the guy had been. 'Balding, mid-fifties, I think. Do you know who he is?'

The barman continued cleaning. 'Why are you asking?'

Thinking on his feet, Matt pulled a ten-pound note from his wallet. 'I think he dropped this in the gents.'

The barman seemed unconvinced, and maybe a little amused.

Matt felt himself flush. 'He was in there before me, and I found it on the floor after he left. I stuffed it in my pocket, meant to ask him about it, but I had other things on my mind and forgot.'

The man shrugged. 'Give it to charity.'

'So you know who he is?'

'Oh yes,' he said. 'Eddie's a regular, unfortunately.'

'Unfortunately?'

'He brings in the cash, drinks this place dry, but I don't like to see it.'

'I don't understand.'

'My dad was an alcoholic. Used to practically live in boozers. And when he wasn't there, he was at home, slapping us around or shouting the house down. Eddie brings back too many unhappy memories. When I see him leave, pissed again, I wonder what he's going home to, and who's there to pick up the pieces. And I know the irony, me working in a pub, but hey, a job's a job, right? I've got a wife and young child.'

'So he comes in here often?'

'Most days, for most of the day.'

'You don't have any contact details, do you? A telephone number? Address?'

He laughed. 'I'm a barman, not his social worker.'

'But if I come back here another day, I'm likely to see him?'

'Definitely. And if you don't see him, then ring around the morgues. The way he knocks them back, I don't think he's got long left.'

Matt had just exited the pub when Sean Carey called.

'Matt, how's things?' He sounded bright, as usual. Definitely a glass-half-full type of guy. Sean was not only Beth's older brother, and godfather to Charlie, he was also a senior colleague at UGT and had been incredibly supportive of Matt since his arrival at the firm as a new graduate. Sean was a bright star in the company, having recently been promoted.

'Things are a bit weird,' Matt replied, stepping aside to allow a group of Japanese tourists past as they meandered along the pavement, cameras focused in all directions.

'Oh?'

'I've just had a very unusual experience with Catherine.'

'Really? You lucky sod.'

'Not like that.'

'Pity.'

'We've broken up. I think.'

'You think?'

'Well, it all went a bit strange. It's probably easier to explain in person.'

'That's why I was calling. Fancy meeting up this afternoon?'

'Yeah, okay. Where?'

'The King of the City, at three?'

'The King of the City?' The pub was just opposite the UGT offices, and a favourite haunt of many of his colleagues at the bank. 'Tell me you're not working on a Saturday?'

'Just need to pop into the office to pick something up.'

Matt shook his head. Sean could be described as a workaholic, but despite putting in a huge number of hours a week, he somehow managed to maintain a life outside the office. He was up at five to go to the gym, partied more than anyone Matt knew, enjoyed a weekly gamble at Samson's, one of London's premier casinos, and left some time for travel to far-flung places at least once a year. The sheer volume of life Sean packed in sometimes left Matt feeling inadequate. But he comforted himself with the knowledge that Sean didn't have family responsibilities – he was a confirmed bachelor – so that explained at least part of it.

'So, how about it?'

Matt hesitated. The King of the City wouldn't have been his first choice for a meeting place.

'There shouldn't be anyone from the bank there,' Sean said, interpreting the silence correctly. 'And if there is, they'll know better than to disturb us. Especially with my serious business face on.'

Matt couldn't help but smile. 'Okay. See you at three.'

CHAPTER EIGHT

Sean was sitting at the far end of the pub, and had already ordered two pints of Guinness. He raised a hand as he spotted Matt.

'Told you it would be UGT-free.' Sean smiled, as Matt took the chair opposite. Sean took a sip from his pint and let out a satisfied sigh. 'Hey, I was wondering if you fancy going out tonight for a few drinks with some of the lads.'

'You not going to the casino?'

'Nah. Taking a break for a while.' Sean clamped his hands behind his head and reclined, as if he was sunning himself on a beach.

'I'm teaching.'

Sean was aghast. 'A class on a Saturday night? That's harsh in the extreme – for all concerned.'

'It's a one-off, to make sure we get through the syllabus before the exam.'

'Maybe next time then,' Sean offered.

'Yeah, maybe.' As much as Matt was planning to return to the company in the near future, he still felt some reticence about diving back into the UGT social circle.

Matt took a look around. 'Just promise me, if you see Gabriel, warn me so I can hide.'

'Oh?'

Gabriel O'Connell, Matt's senior line manager and the head of fund management, was on the board of the company.

'He left a voicemail a few days ago, inviting me to come and see him to discuss returning to work.'

Sean sat back upright, confused. 'But that's great. Isn't it?'

'Yes.'

'You don't sound convinced.'

'No, I am convinced. But I haven't got back to him yet. I feel bad about it, and I don't want to see him face to face without having had a chance to reply.'

'You haven't had a chance?'

'Okay, yes, I have had a chance, but . . . Oh, I don't know – he called in the middle of the evening class I teach.'

'You do still want to come back, though, don't you? You'd be a big loss, Matt.'

'I don't know about that.'

'Don't undersell yourself. With your results, you're worth a lot to the company.'

'Is that what it's all about? The money? Don't you ever wonder, though, if there might be more to life?'

'Like what?'

'Helping other people?'

'You mean like sick animals and children? That sister of yours, has she finally got to you? Is the teaching going *that* well? You're getting me worried here.'

'You don't need to worry. But yes, it's going really well. I think I'll really miss it.'

'Rather you than me. Are you sure you're not going to do a Carla Conway on us?'

'I don't think so.'

Carla Conway had been an executive director of UGT. Tipped for a prestigious move to their global headquarters in New York, Carla had shocked the company by announcing her departure to take up the position of chief executive at Guy's and St Thomas' NHS Foundation Hospital Trust.

'Now, tell me about Catherine. What happened? You broke it off?'

'Kind of. Well, neither of us actually said it was over, but I think it's over.'

'Clear as mud.'

'It's a lot less clear than that. You know how I thought she might have been following me?'

'Not this again.'

'Now I think she may have been using a false name.'

Sean looked sceptical.

'I know you think I've got a paranoid streak,' Matt said, 'but while we were in the pub having lunch, some guy accosts me in the toilets.'

'Whoa . . .'

'Not like that. This guy, he said that Catherine wasn't who she said she was. Said she'd ruined his life. And that if I didn't do something, I'd be in trouble.'

'Wow. So what did you do?'

'I asked her if it was true. She didn't deny it. But she didn't say it was true, either. She just said she had to leave. Pretty much ran off.'

'You've not spoken to her since?'

'No. I thought I might give her a bit of time.'

'False name . . .' Sean shook his head at the thought. 'Sounds a bit fanciful. Why would someone do that?'

'Maybe if they were having an affair. Wanted to keep their identity secret.'

'Yes, I suppose.' Sean thought some more. 'The guy who told you, you believe him?'

'Not at first. He was drunk. But then, the way Cather— the way she reacted, I'm not sure.'

'You accused her of lying, of pretending to be someone else. Maybe she was just upset and angry. It'd be understandable.'

Matt hadn't really thought of it like that. That kind of reaction would have been reasonable. But she had recognised the man, he was sure of it. Or was he? Now the seed had been planted that he might have jumped to a conclusion, the doubt grew. 'I'll call her later. Give her a chance to explain.'

'Good idea. I know you don't know Catherine that well, but the guy in the toilets – hey, you said yourself, he was drunk. He may have spotted you with this beautiful girl and decided to try to cause trouble.'

'Except we were going to break up anyway.'

'That's not the point.'

Matt looked off to his left, suddenly feeling aggrieved that he might well have been taken in.

'I think you shouldn't be too hasty in ending the relationship,' said Sean. 'Things were going well until you started getting those silly ideas that she was stalking you.'

'Who says they were silly?'

'Well, you never actually saw her following you for certain, did you? You just thought you might have seen her a few times, out of the corner of your eye.'

Put like that, it did sound somewhat lame.

'I thought she was really nice. And you seemed good together.'

'You didn't say this before now.'

'I didn't want to interfere.'

'But now you've decided to?'

'Because I don't want to see you make a mistake.'

Something didn't seem right. 'Why are you so keen on this?'

'It's just good to see you happy. Moving on from—' Sean stopped himself, but it was too late.

'. . . Beth,' Matt finished. 'Moving on from Beth. And from Charlie too? Is that what this is about, Sean? Encouraging me to pursue a new life, so I'll agree to my son being taken thousands of miles away?'

Sean ran a hand through his hair defensively. 'You know I always hoped you two would patch things up.'

'But now you think it's a lost cause?'

Sean couldn't find the words, as Matt made to stand.

'And, Sean, please, don't go updating Beth about what I'm up to. I don't want James Farrah knowing intimate details about my life. Time for me to go.'

'Matt, don't,' Sean said. 'Beth might be my sister, but I love both of you guys. I've never taken sides in all this. I just want what's best for you all.'

'I really wish I could believe that.'

Matt headed for the exit.

CHAPTER NINE

'Michael.'

Michael didn't acknowledge her arrival. He sat clutching a glass of whisky, his tangled mass of dark brown hair falling down over his stony face. He stared down into the drink as if trying to read his own fortune. Michael's past drinking problems were well known. He'd once told them all about his battle with alcohol, which had begun in his late teens, increased through university, and peaked in those first few years of employment, fuelled at first by the lust for fun and latterly by the stress of his job. But shortly after meeting Annabelle three years ago, he had turned a corner and, as far as Rachel knew, had been dry ever since. But now here he was, sitting alone in a bar with a drink in his hand.

Rachel slid into the seat opposite. 'Michael, where have you been? I've been looking for you all day.' With neither Michael nor Annabelle answering their phones, she had visited their flat before scouring all the local haunts around Camden. Finally, she had struck lucky in a pub just down from Euston station. It was a place they sometimes frequented, but it had seemed a long shot at that time of the day.

Michael's hands stayed tightly wrapped around the glass and his head remained bowed as if in prayer. Rachel glanced at the adjacent tables, but no one else was taking any notice. She turned back towards him.

'Michael, why weren't you at the funeral?'

There was still no response.

'I was worried. I thought something might have happened to you.'

Michael raised his head slowly and their eyes met. She couldn't disguise her shock at his appearance. His eyes were fiery red and seemed to have shrunk back into his skull. His face was drawn, pale, and unshaven. He said nothing, instead bringing the glass up to his mouth in an almost automated, robotic movement. As he drank, his eyes shifted from Rachel to the diminishing liquid. He then brought the glass down hard on the table, as if he had misjudged the distance.

'I'm sorry,' he slurred. 'I'm sorry I couldn't be there.'

'Sorry? Is that it? You and Alex have been good friends for years, and that's the best you can come up with? Why weren't you at the funeral, Michael? And you've started drinking again. What's going on?'

Michael paused, looking down at the dregs of his whisky.

'I wanted to come, but I just couldn't.'

Rachel softened, her frustration quickly turning to concern. If he felt in any way the same as she did about Alex's death, which he surely did, it was understandable if he just hadn't felt able to be there. Maybe it was his way of trying to shut out the reality of what had happened.

'You didn't feel able to come? You're too upset?'

He shrugged. 'I need some time on my own, Rachel.'

'Please, Michael,' she said. 'I know you're suffering as much as I am. You don't need to do this on your own. We've got to support each other.'

Michael shook his head, lamenting some unspoken thought. 'You don't know.'

'Don't know what?'

'It doesn't matter,' he said.

She decided to let the strange comment pass. 'I've been trying to get in touch with you for days. You're not answering your phone, and work didn't know where you were. I couldn't even reach Annabelle.'

'We've split up.'

'What? When?'

'Yesterday. She's moved out.'

'But . . .'

'Took all her stuff. I'm not sure where she's gone. But she won't be back. That's the end of it. The end of us.'

Annabelle and Michael splitting up? This was yet another shift in what just a short time ago was their unshakeable world. Two weeks ago, the four of them had been out on a double date in Soho. It had been a fantastic evening. Four friends with the future ahead of them, and few cares to restrict the view. Yet now only two of them were left standing. 'But you and Annabelle, I thought . . .'

'So did I. We'd always be together.'

'I don't understand, Michael. What happened?'

'Things haven't been good for a few months,' he said. 'Something to do with this, possibly.' He smiled sadly as he raised the glass.

'So the drinking, it began some time ago?' Rachel had assumed it was Alex's death that had thrown him back into the grip of the demon drink, but it didn't look like that was the case now.

'Two months ago. I really don't want to talk about it. I'm far too pissed.'

But Rachel was undeterred. 'Annabelle left you because of your drinking?'

'Annabelle is far too good a woman to have to spend her life with a drunkard. So I broke things off.'

'You ended it?'

'Yes.'

'But it's not what you want, is it? You don't really want that. You're just trying to protect her from getting hurt.'

He snorted. 'You know, Rachel, you really don't know how right you are about that. Alex, he'd have done anything to protect you, wouldn't he?'

Rachel nodded.

'I'm sorry I couldn't protect him.'

'There was nothing anyone could have done,' Rachel replied. Although she didn't truly believe that. Why had the offending vehicle not seen Alex? Why had the driver fled after the collision, instead of trying to save Alex's life? And why had Alex not been wearing his cycle helmet? Maybe it wouldn't have made a difference, but without it there had been no chance of surviving the impact.

'I want answers,' Rachel continued. 'I know it won't bring Alex back, but if I can just try to understand what happened, it might help us all come to terms with it. Maybe I could even get to speak to the driver.'

'Not a hope in hell,' Michael said, with a surprising strength of conviction.

'You can't know that. They might come forward. Their conscience might be pricked.'

Michael shook his head. 'People like that don't have a conscience.'

'Driving off was a horrendous thing to do, but maybe they just panicked and now really regret it. It doesn't necessarily mean they're a bad person.'

Michael put a hand to his head, kneading his temple to fight what Rachel assumed was a growing headache. 'You don't understand, Rachel. You haven't got a clue.'

'About what?'

'It doesn't matter.'

'Michael, you're not making any sense.'

'Please, Rachel, just leave me alone.'

CHAPTER TEN

Matt didn't have much time for dinner, as the class started in just over an hour. He threw in a microwave meal for one and stared at the rotating plate, thinking about the day's events. Maybe he'd been hasty to think the worst about Catherine.

He ate quickly and hungrily, hardly even looking at the pasta before forking it into his mouth. Eating alone night after night was no fun.

Matt pushed aside thoughts about Catherine, and Beth's proposed move to Australia, and instead turned his attention to the coming class. He wondered what mood the group would be in tonight.

'Matt . . .' Amy smiled as he entered the staffroom. 'All ready for another character-building experience?'

'Kind of,' he said, pulling out a circular from his pigeonhole. It was from the teaching union, promoting an upcoming vote on strike action.

'That's the spirit,' she said, deadpan. 'Seriously, what's up? You feeling bad about the Beth/Australia thing?'

'That's part of it,' he said, glancing at his watch as he deposited the circular in the recycling bin. There were a couple of minutes still until kick-off.

'We can catch up later,' Amy said. After all, she'd been the one to warn him how tricky things could get if the teacher arrived late.

'I might have to rush off afterwards.' He was considering visiting Sean to apologise in person.

She looked disappointed. 'I think Harvey was hoping to catch you for a chat.'

'Oh, sorry, you did say he wanted to talk. What about?'

'Not sure. But it would be good to give him some time. If you could?'

Matt nodded. 'No problem. I can stick around.' Talking to Sean could wait.

Amy beamed. 'You're a good man.'

The evening's class was the best yet. The group was a bit lighter on numbers than in previous sessions, with only ten attendees, down from the usual fifteen. Matt hadn't been too worried about the drop-off, as Amy had predicted as much. And what the group lacked in quantity, it made up for in quality. There was the enthusiasm and clear desire to learn that had been bubbling under the surface throughout the previous classes. Harvey in particular was on good form.

By the time the class had finished, with Harvey hanging back while the rest of the group said their goodbyes, Matt's spirits had been raised in a way that he hadn't thought possible.

Matt gathered his papers from the desk, glancing up at Harvey, who looked like he was being deliberately slow getting his belongings together.

'Enjoy the class?' Matt ventured.

'Not too bad,' Harvey said, as he hoisted his bag on to his back with a grimace.

'I'll take that as a compliment.'

Harvey smiled. 'You do that.'

Matt smiled back, wondering whether Amy had got it wrong about Harvey wanting to chat. 'See you next time, Harvey.'

'Yep.' Harvey paused at the door. 'Mr Roberts?'

'Matt. Please call me Matt.'

'Matt. I was wondering – could we have a quick chat?' He held up his hands and took a small step back out of the room. 'It's okay, you know, man, if you're too busy.'

It was a novelty to see this imposing figure of a young man, who so often projected power and confidence, looking uncertain, even nervous.

'Of course, Harvey. Amy did mention that you wanted to chat. I'm happy to talk.'

Harvey relaxed. 'Great, Mr . . . Matt, great. Thanks, man. I mean, where should we go?'

'How about here? There's no other class due.'

'Sure.'

They pulled out two chairs at the front of the classroom, and Harvey dumped his rucksack on a nearby table with a heavy thud.

What the hell is he carrying in there?

For a couple of seconds, they just sat looking at one another.

Matt broke the silence. 'So, you wanted to chat?'

'Yeah. I wanted to apologise, you know, for last night. What I said about the guns. It was disrespectful. And stupid. So, I apologise.'

'Thanks. But really, it was okay. Did Amy—'

'Hell, no, she didn't tell me to do nothin', if that's what you think.' Harvey looked offended that his apology had been thought in some way forced.

'Well, thanks.'

'Cool. So that's sorted.'

Matt sensed that Harvey wanted to say more. 'You're doing really well, Harvey.'

Harvey looked unconvinced. 'For real?'

'Yes, for real. I'm really impressed.'

The youth laughed and shook his head in disbelief. 'You know, I don't hear that too often. I wasn't top of the class in school, let me tell you.'

'But I bet you could have been.'

Harvey deflected the compliment with another laugh. 'I guess Miss Roberts didn't tell you about my history?'

'I know you've been in trouble with the police.'

A genuine smile, showing unfeasibly white teeth. 'Well, I wouldn't be here otherwise, would I?'

'I guess not.'

'I've been in lots of trouble,' he said. 'A lot, man. I've done some bad things. Stealin', drugs, beatin'.' He searched Matt's face for a reaction.

'And how about now?'

'I want to be better, bruv.'

'That's good.'

He looked down towards the floor. 'I just don't know if I can.' He locked eyes with Matt. 'What do you think?'

'I think you can,' Matt said, without hesitation.

Harvey didn't look particularly convinced.

'Whatever you've done in the past, none of that matters now.'

Harvey laughed to himself. 'You think so?'

'You've been punished for what you did. And now you're putting things right.'

'Man, you and me, we live in different worlds.'

'How d'you mean?'

'What's your definition of success?'

The depth of the question took Matt by surprise. 'Well, being happy, content.' Just saying that, the fact that it had been so instinctive, made him feel sad. That's how he used to feel. Before everything went so wrong.

'Not money?'

'Not really, no.'

'You told us you work for a big bank in the City. Must pay well.'

'It does.'

'But bein' paid a load of money isn't your definition of success?'

'I suppose it was.'

'Where I come from, success is about money too. That ain't no different. But it's also about respect, and respect is about fear. My brother, he was the big success in our family.'

Matt kept quiet. He knew about the fate of Harvey's brother, of course.

'Do you know how he became so successful?'

'No.'

'Through terrorisin' people. He weren't a bad person, he just did his best under the circumstances to be a success.'

Matt didn't really know what to say.

'He died with a knife through the heart. Ran for over a mile to get away, but they caught him, sliced him up, and left him to bleed all over the playground. That's where he died – in a children's playground, by the slide. They've closed it down now, grassed it over. None of the parents wanted to use it no more. It was the bloodstain. They couldn't get rid of it.'

'I'm really sorry.'

Harvey shrugged. 'The police, social services, they think that's what really turned me. The shock of what happened, the grief of losin' my brother, the anger. They think it was the definin' point for me. But they're wrong.'

'Something like that happening, I can understand how it might change things, make someone do—'

'No,' Harvey interrupted, pushing himself upright in the seat. 'No excuses. I chose that way. Free choice. The same when I was younger. When my dad ran out on us, left us without a goodbye, my mum, my teachers, counsellors, they made excuses for me. I was the kid who was sufferin', the poor kid whose dad had upped and left.'

'I think maybe you're being a little hard on yourself.'

Harvey got up and paced to the front desk, tracing his fingers across the whiteboard. 'I'm not a victim.' His eyes burned with passion and determination.

Matt was beginning to understand. Harvey was being hard on himself, that was certain. After all, who wouldn't react to being abandoned by a parent and seeing your brother murdered? But he could see where he was coming from. This bright, articulate, thoughtful young man didn't want to be labelled a victim of events, at the mercy of factors beyond his control. And yet as Matt looked into his eyes, he could see a certain helplessness, a need for something.

But could he give it to him?

'Why are you doin' this?' Harvey said, turning his chair around and sitting back down with his legs either side of the backrest.

'What?'

'Teachin' us lot. You don't need to, do you?'

To feel valued? 'I guess not.'

'It can't be easy, with us.' Harvey smiled.

'I enjoy it.'

'I know you do. You can tell. Those other tutors, they were here for the money, to pay their bills and mortgage. I could see it.'

'Is that why you took against them?'

He grinned. 'So you *do* know what happened.'

'Amy told me you scared off a few of the tutors. She didn't give any details.'

'Maybe she was afraid of scarin' you off?'

'Maybe.'

'I'm not proud, really, of what I did. But it was for the best.'

'What did you do?'

'Enough.'

'You were careful not to go too far,' Matt noted, 'because you didn't want to be kicked off the programme.'

Harvey smirked. 'You might be right.'

'So, why do you want to do this?'

Harvey paused to think. 'Because I'm sick of definin' my success by how many people fear me.'

Matt nodded. 'Do you know what you might want to do?'

'Maybe I can be a rich banker like you.'

He misread Matt's negative facial expression.

'What, man, you don't think I could do it?'

'No, it's not that.' Matt searched for the right words. 'There might be better things to aim for in life, that's all.'

'So that's why you're doin' this, teachin' us – aimin' for something better?'

'Maybe I am.'

'Funny,' Harvey said, musing on Matt's response. 'We're both in a similar situation.' He thought of something. 'It must be tricky, doin' this on top of your day job. I thought you guys, the suits in the City, work long hours?'

'They . . . we do.' Matt wondered how far to go with the explanation. But Harvey was opening up to him, so he should at least meet him halfway. 'I've been on a break from work.'

'Suspended?'

'Thankfully nothing that exciting.'

'So why the break?'

'I wanted to take some time out, do something different.'

There were limits to how much he was prepared to tell Harvey about the most traumatic of times. 'Nice watch,' he noted, nodding towards the Rolex dangling loosely from Harvey's wrist.

'I bought this, you know.' The young man's brow knotted defensively. 'It's not stolen.'

'I didn't say it was.' On reflection, it probably had come out sounding a little bit like an accusation. 'I didn't mean anything by it.'

Harvey straightened the watch on his arm, its diamonds catching the light. 'Bought it in a store, opposite the Ritz. You wanted to see their faces, man, when I walked in. I could tell what they were thinkin'. They had a security guy on the door, face like a pit bull. Don't think he wanted to let me in really. There weren't no other customers.' He was still looking at the watch as he spoke. 'Then the assistants, two old women plastered in make-up, I could see them stiffen. Probably thought I was going to pull out a gun.' His mouth twisted at the thought. 'I asked about the watches, tried on a few. Dogface from outside came in, stood at the entrance, puffin' out his chest. Assistants probably had their hands hoverin' over the panic button. I asked for some more expensive options, and they brought out this little beauty. Knew I had to have it. So I pulled out the cash, slapped it down on the counter, and the watch was mine.'

'It's impressive.'

'Damn right it is.' Harvey's features clouded over as he gazed at the watch's face. 'You know, those shop assistants, I'm sure I had no more respect from them after I left than when I arrived.'

Matt felt he was beginning to understand Harvey's motivations. 'Try to ignore people like that. They're not worth it.'

Harvey seemed to like that. 'Thanks. Sounds like good advice. So,' he continued, 'why teachin' then, bruv?'

'Amy asked me. Told me she thought I might really enjoy it, find it rewarding. And I have.'

'Maybe I should be a teacher then. Follow your sister.'

'I think that might be a better idea. What would you teach?'

Harvey thought for a second. 'Art, maybe.'

'Art?'

'I like to draw. Sketchin'.'

There was definitely more to Harvey than met the eye. 'What do you sketch? Anything in particular?'

'Urban landscapes. I try to capture the grimness, the gritty reality of what it's like to live in this city for most people. Not the places the tourists see, Buckingham Palace or Big Ben, or Canary Wharf or the Shard or all that shiny shit. I draw real London.'

'You should bring in some of your work, show the class.'

'You're shittin' me! No way, man.'

'Why not?'

'No way, bruv. I'll show you, but not them.'

'Show me, then. And Amy.'

'You're serious?'

'Completely. I'd love to see your stuff.'

'Okay, I will. Next session, I'll bring some. You really are cool, man.'

'You got rid of the other tutors. Why not me?'

''Cos you're Amy's brother. And Amy is the coolest person I know. She's helped me so much, cut me slack when others would've just stamped on my face. I thought, well, Amy's brother deserves a chance, right?'

'So I have her to thank.'

'At first. But after that, you had to convince me.'

'Convince you of what?'

'That you were worth my time.'

Now Matt laughed.

'Man, I don't mean no disrespect, but if I want to achieve, I need to put my energies into the right things. Those other tutors, they were wastin' my time. They didn't believe in us like Amy does, or you do.'

'How can you be so sure that I believe in you?'

'I can tell. You do, don't you?'

'Yes. I believe you can all achieve things.'

'First time I met Amy, she said that everyone has the potential to better themselves. That really spoke to me, you know – *really* spoke to me, right deep down.'

Before Matt could reply, Harvey's phone rang.

'Sorry, man,' he said, peering at his top-of-the-range gold iPhone. 'Got to get this.'

He dismounted from the chair and slipped out of the room. Matt could see Harvey in the corridor, animated in conversation. He was gesticulating, throwing his hands up in the air, putting his hands to his head and pacing around. Then a noise shocked Matt back from his thoughts about who Harvey might be talking to.

Harvey's weighty rucksack had toppled from the table on to the floor. Matt leaned down and tried to lift it with one hand, straining to pull it off the ground. There was no chance – it was just too heavy. He got up and hauled the bag on to a chair. It was certainly some weight – the kind of weight you imagine Marine commandos lugging around on outward-bound exercises.

Matt had hold of the bag when the thought arose. He turned to look at Harvey, who had his back to him, still gesticulating. And then, without any more thought, he pulled at the bag's zip.

The glint of metal caught the light.

The bag was full of knives.

CHAPTER ELEVEN

'Hi, Matt.'

Matt stood on the threshold of what still felt like his family home, despite the fact that it had been invaded and colonised by his great rival. 'Hi. Is James—'

'He's popped out to get a newspaper. Would you like to come in? Charlie's just finishing off a Thomas movie.'

Sunday was Matt's favourite day. It was his day with Charlie, a day he treasured more than anything.

Charlie was lying on the sofa, one of his arms draped over the side.

'Hey, Charlie, how are you?'

'Huh?' he said, raising his head in Matt's direction. Lost in the movie, he smiled in surprise, only just realising that Matt was there. 'Okay, thank you, Daddy.'

'Ah, *Day of the Diesels*. That still one of your favourites?'

Charlie nodded absent-mindedly, his focus drawn back to the television. Matt tried once more. 'You looking forward to swimming?'

That did get his attention. 'Yes! Swimming – I *love* swimming.' He sat up and pumped his fist comically. 'Are we going today?'

'Yes, we are,' Matt smiled, 'and afterwards the park. Is that good?'

'Yes!'

'The zip wire?'

Another fist pump. 'Yes! Zip wire! Wheeeee!' Charlie mimed himself flashing past on the sit-on rubber ring.

'Just be careful,' Beth said softly from behind Matt's shoulder, trying to avoid Charlie hearing. 'I'm not sure about that thing. If he falls off . . .'

'I *won't* fall off, Mummy!' Charlie replied. He had the hearing of a bat. 'I promise I won't fall off.'

'Okay,' Beth conceded. 'Just make sure you take care,' she added, directing her comment at Matt more than their son.

'We will,' Matt reassured her.

Matt took a seat next to Charlie, who smiled and shuffled over. On screen, Thomas the Tank Engine was talking with his friend, the green engine Percy. Matt had seen this movie more times than he cared to remember, so he knew at a glance that there were only about five minutes left. The film brought back painful memories of the three of them, happy together, before it all fell apart.

'Are you okay if I just nip upstairs?' Beth said. 'Just got to finish off my make-up.'

'Of course.' Matt turned to Charlie. 'We're okay, aren't we?'

Charlie nodded enthusiastically.

'Off anywhere nice?' Matt said. She had been uncharacteristically cagey about her and James's day.

Beth hesitated. 'We're going to see someone, about our plans.'

'About Australia.'

'Yes.' She flushed.

Matt had always found that extremely attractive.

He was thinking of a reply when Charlie jumped in before him. 'Australia! I *love* Austrayliaaa! We're going there, Daddy, on a big plane, do you know that?'

He couldn't find the words as his stomach went into free fall.

'Honey,' Beth said. 'Why don't you tell Daddy about what you did at school this week, while I go upstairs for a few minutes.'

Matt chewed on his lip and resisted the temptation to throw an accusing glance at Beth. 'What have you been up to, Charlie?'

'Nothing.' Charlie was typical of most four-year-olds. Most of what happened at school stayed at school. But he could be cajoled and coaxed if he was in the right mood.

'C'mon, Charlie. You can tell Daddy,' said Beth over her shoulder as she headed upstairs.

'I made that,' he said, pointing over at a piece of paper on the table.

'A painting? Let me take a look.' Matt reached across and took in the splashes of bright colour. He could make out some smiling faces among the technicolour splodges. 'Nice faces. Who are these people? Your friends from school?'

'Nah!'

'Who are they then?' Matt could make out three faces. 'Is one of them you? That one there, with spiky orange hair and red eyes. Looks just like you.'

Charlie giggled. 'Daddy, you're so funny!'

'Glad to hear it.'

He was back to watching the film.

'C'mon, tell me who they are then.'

Charlie let out a dramatic sigh of exasperation, then jabbed at the crinkly paper. 'Me, Mummy, and James.'

'Right . . .'

'Going to the airport – to Australia.'

'Okay.'

'And there's you,' Charlie added, pointing to the far side of the painting. 'You're at the airport too, but you're not coming on the plane with us. That's why you're sad.'

There *was* a face he hadn't noticed, looking on from afar. That face, an impressionist representation of him, was wearing a frown. Matt felt a lump in his throat, and for one horrible moment he thought he might burst into tears. He tried desperately to hold back the rising river of sadness.

Oblivious to his father's torment, Charlie continued enthusiastically. 'Do you know, Daddy, Australia is very far away. You get there on a plane. You can go there by boat, but it takes a long, long time, so you go there by aeroplane. The plane goes whoooosh!' He demonstrated the take-off using one of his hands. Matt watched in horror at the spark of excitement in Charlie's eyes. 'I'm a bit scared of heights, Daddy. That's why I'm going to sit in the middle of the plane, just in case. I'm not going to look out of the window. No, it's too high. Daddy, if there are clouds in the sky, can the plane hit them?'

Matt ran his hands through his son's brown hair and swallowed down his feelings. 'No, the plane flies straight through the clouds. It goes through them and then there's blue sky above, and the clouds below. So it looks like you're floating on top of the clouds.'

'Wow. Have you been on a plane, Daddy?'

'Lots of times.'

'Cool! Did you like it?'

'Yes, it's pretty cool. You know, one time, we were flying right over London, and I saw Big Ben.'

'Big Ben?! That's cool! I like Big Ben.'

Matt squeezed Charlie. 'I know you do. Do you remember the day we went on the boat, on the river, and we sailed straight past Big Ben just as it was boinging?'

Charlie laughed. 'Yes! Yes! It was *boinging*! One, two, three, four, five, six, seven, eight, nine, ten, eleven, twelve.'

'You're right. Twelve o'clock. There's nothing wrong with your memory, little man.'

'I remember that, Daddy.'

'I know, you're good.'

'I am.'

Matt laughed. 'And modest.'

'Yes, I am. Daddy, would you like to come with us, on the plane, to Australia?'

Matt tried to bite his tongue. 'I won't be able to, Charlie.'

'Oh! Why not? You'd like it, in Australia.'

'I don't think I'm invited.'

'Yes, you are! You are invited, Daddy! Please come with us. It'll be great!'

Matt couldn't bear puncturing his son's excitement, but he also didn't want to lie. 'We'll see what happens.'

'Australia is brilliant! There's beaches, and sharks, and kangaroos that hop, hop, hop, hop! And cola bears.'

'Koala bears.'

'Yes, cola bears.'

Who has been telling him all this?

'Matt.' He hadn't noticed Beth had come back downstairs. He wasn't sure how long she had been standing there at the door, but it was obviously long enough, judging by the look on her face. 'Can I have a word for a minute?'

'Sure.'

The Thomas movie's end credits were rolling. Charlie slid off the sofa and began playing with his Lego bricks. 'I'm going to build a plane, Daddy, to take us all to Australia!'

'That's good, honey, you have a play while I just speak with Daddy. We'll only be next door, in the hallway.' Beth looked like she wanted the ground to open up and swallow her.

'I'm sorry, Matt,' she said, in a hushed voice. 'I'm really sorry about all that. I know it must be difficult. I do understand.'

'You've been talking to him about Australia. Before anything has been decided.'

Beth flushed again.

Matt pressed home his advantage, although he wasn't particularly enjoying making Beth squirm. 'Before you told me?'

She shook her head. 'It was James. I told him not to say anything to Charlie before we had a chance to speak with you, and to decide whether this was something we really wanted to go for. But a couple of weeks ago, we were talking in the house, and Charlie overheard a few things. You know what he's like. He started asking questions about Australia. I think they'd done something in school about the countries of the world where they'd mentioned it, so he was interested. Later that day, James told him we might be going to visit, and he's been asking questions ever since. I had a right go at James about it, told him he shouldn't have mentioned anything – that he should have waited, and left it to me or you to explain things to Charlie. I'm sorry, Matt.'

'Charlie doesn't know it's not just for a holiday?'

'No.'

'He invited me to come along.'

'I know. I heard.'

Matt pinched the bridge of his nose. 'This is terrible. Just terrible.'

'I'm sorry, Matt. I really am.'

'Not sorry enough to change your mind though?'

Just then James entered the house, newspaper under his arm. 'Oh, hello, Matt. I thought . . .'

'I might be gone by now?'

'Well, yes.' He looked at both of them, caught mid-conversation in the hallway, with a slight air of suspicion.

'We were just talking about what Matt had planned for today,' Beth said, also picking up on James's reaction.

James smiled tightly at Matt. 'Anything nice?'

Matt had to admit it felt good to be part of the mini-conspiracy. 'Park and swimming.'

'Great,' he said, seeming totally uninterested. 'Sounds great.'

'We'd better go,' Beth said, noticing the time. 'We're supposed to be meeting the guy in twenty minutes. Matt, are you okay to see yourself out?'

'But—' James began.

'It's fine,' Beth interrupted. 'Matt knows his way around, don't you, Matt?'

Matt had to fight hard not to smile. He exchanged a knowing glance with Beth. 'We'll be fine.'

CHAPTER TWELVE

The night had been like all the others since Alex's death.

Rachel had slept for only three of the six hours she had lain in bed. The early morning in particular had passed painfully slowly while her mind spun with visions of the funeral and thoughts of her conversation with Michael.

She showered and pottered around the flat. It was good that work had been so keen for her to take compassionate leave, but maybe being busy, losing herself in her job, would have been better. Sure, colleagues would have found it weird (and no doubt uncomfortable) for her to appear in the office just a day after his death, but so what?

After an hour of trying but failing to get on with some housework – as if vacuuming the living-room carpet was important under the circumstances – she decided to escape the flat. It was another gloriously sunny day, casting a brightness on anything and everything that in no way matched Rachel's mood. There was solar-powered happiness all around. Yet she longed for it to rain so she could hide under her umbrella and cry.

As Rachel neared her destination on Camden High Street – her favourite bookshop, Page One – she felt utterly alone. As she entered the store, she gratefully inhaled the comforting smell of ageing paper. She had first visited the bookshop just a couple of days after arriving in London. She'd been finding things tough – suddenly transported to an unfamiliar continent, with an unfamiliar culture and unfamiliar accent.

She'd been wandering around Camden, pondering how many days she'd last before jumping on the next plane home, when she'd noticed the window display. It had appealed immediately.

The owner of the shop also happened to be an exiled American. Jim was from the East Coast – New York – and had married an Englishwoman more than thirty years earlier. They'd lived in Camden for twenty of those years, buying the bookshop and running it ever since. Rachel had formed an instant friendship with Jim. And after that first visit, she'd returned to the shop at least once a week. Sometimes, when business was slack, Jim would offer her a cup of coffee: *real American coffee*, as he said.

'Rachel,' Jim said, standing up from behind the oak desk. 'How are you?'

'Oh, you know, pretty bad,' she said, closing the door behind her.

'Still not sleeping?'

Rachel shook her head and was surprised to find tears filling her eyes. It was the first time she had cried since Alex's death.

'Cup of freshly brewed American coffee?' Jim offered.

Rachel nodded, wiping the tears away with her finger. She managed to regain her composure, not wanting to lose it completely. She knew she needed to cry, to vent her emotions, but not yet.

The coffee was great. And the conversation helped, too. Jim was a good listener and was suitably comforting.

'Do whatever you think is best,' Jim told her, pushing an open packet of biscuits across the desk. 'Oh, and keep quiet about the cookies. We've got a strict no-eating policy in here.' He winked and smiled weakly, unsure whether his humour was appropriate.

Rachel smiled back to reassure him that it was. 'Thanks.'

'Just promise me you'll think carefully before you do anything,' he said. 'Things are really bad at the moment, but they will get better.'

'I know,' Rachel said, finding the cliché hard to stomach. She stared into the bottom of her mug.

'Now,' Jim said, 'did you just come here for a drink, or are there any books I can tempt you with? After all, I do run a business, you know.'

Rachel managed another smile.

'Any interesting books come in?'

'Early copy of *Alice in Wonderland*, decent condition. Also, we've got two Graham Greene novels, first print run, from a collector in Brighton. Very apt, eh?'

Rachel nodded without smiling.

'Better get in there quick, before the rest of the locals get out of bed.'

'Yeah, I'd better.'

Rachel finished the dregs of her coffee, wincing slightly at the harsh taste, then rose from the desk. 'Thanks, Jim. You've been a real help.'

The second-hand section was in the basement. It was her favourite part of the bookshop. Over the past few years she had spent hours down there, hunting through the books with all the excitement of a small child looking for buried treasure. And there was treasure indeed. The collection of second-hand books was astounding. Wall-to-wall stacks of shelves reached from ceiling to floor, lining the room like fancy wallpaper. The stock was always changing, too. Books came in each week from collectors and book sales all around the country.

Rachel stepped on to the polished wooden floor of the basement. Down here, away from the contamination of the street outside, the smell of paper was intense. She looked down the tunnel of books that stretched out into the near distance. She had the floor to herself.

Rachel had always loved books, for as long as she could remember, and her room when she was growing up, although not quite as remarkable as this place, was certainly impressive in its own way. Her childhood friends had often referred to it as the library, as there were so many books crammed in – on shelves, in drawers, under the bed.

She moved across to the 'C' shelf and quickly found the copy of *Alice in Wonderland* to which Jim had referred. It was in perfect condition. Carefully turning over the first few pages, she read the faded message that one of its owners had penned:

To my darling Emma. Many happy returns. Love Father.

Rachel ran a finger over the ink, feeling for any bumps like a blind person reading Braille. She tried to guess how old Emma might have been when she received this gift. It was a loving message, preserved within fiction. The message had become part of the book, and now had as much right to be there as the White Rabbit or the Mad Hatter. As Rachel began to leaf through the rest of the text, she thought of her family back home. She did miss them terribly. Phone calls, emails, and Skype were okay, but nothing could match real face-to-face contact.

Rachel placed the book carefully back on the shelf. Sometimes she bought things, but often she'd just browse. And when she did buy a book, in a funny way she almost felt guilty for taking it away from what she saw as its rightful place on the shelf. She moved over towards the 'G' section, which was situated some way along. As she passed the staircase, she heard the ring of the bell. Someone else had entered the shop. Jim greeted the person with a friendly hello, but Rachel didn't hear the visitor respond.

Just as Rachel was pulling out the copy of *Brighton Rock*, she heard the familiar creak of the wooden stairs. She had her back to the staircase, and immediately felt the need to shift her body slightly in a clockwise direction, to afford herself a better view of who might be coming down. A man who looked to be in his mid-thirties entered the room. Rachel's eyes shot down to the book in her hand as the man turned briefly towards her. She felt uncharacteristically uneasy.

Rachel had never seen him before. Or at least had never noticed him. And she'd surely have remembered a man of such towering stature. He must have been pushing six foot five, and as she ventured to raise her eyes from the book, she noted that his shoulders spanned nearly half the length of the bookshelf he was now facing. He was dressed casually, in a blue T-shirt and khaki trousers. The shirt clung to his body, defining the contours of the well-developed muscles along his neck, shoulders, and arms. She noticed a pair of wraparound shades hanging from his back pocket.

The stranger was probably a tourist. Although the shop survived mainly through its local clientele, the tourist trade provided a welcome boost during the spring and summer months. The Americans and Japanese were especially fond of the shop, which was mentioned in a few London guidebooks.

Rachel returned to flicking through the book in her hands. Her concentration had returned enough for her to be able to digest at least some of the text. She had read *Brighton Rock* in college, and had been captivated by the town it described, with its Mafia-style gang warfare and the backdrop of the English seaside. It had inspired her to take a day trip to Brighton with Alex last summer. They had caught an early-morning train from Waterloo and arrived at the coast before lunch, before spending a fun-filled day enjoying the pier and the beach.

'Excuse me.'

Rachel flinched, nearly dropping the book.

'Sorry. Didn't mean to startle you.'

She had been daydreaming and hadn't noticed the man was so close. His accent was South London, if she wasn't mistaken.

The guy was right in her personal space, up against the bookcase, just inches between them.

'It's okay. I'm fine,' she said, resisting the urge to take a step back. 'I was daydreaming. You know, away with the fairies.' She managed a laugh, but it came out all wrong: its strained nature screamed out nerves and even fear.

But the man didn't back off.

Rachel's eyes met with his for a split second, before she returned to the safety of the novel.

'Murder is a worrying thing, don't you think?' the man said, trailing his fingers along the spines of the books on the neighbouring shelf.

Rachel's heart began pounding, and a stab of nausea welled up from her stomach. She didn't know how to respond, although she wanted to run. She wanted to push past this mountain of a man and sprint up the stairs to safety. Rachel looked at him, and he smiled.

'That book,' he said, still smiling. 'It's awash with murder. Gave me nightmares when I read it for the first time. Then again, I was only twelve.' He smiled again, and this time Rachel managed to smile back. Her body stood down from panic stations.

'Yeah, murder,' she said, with a barely disguised note of relief. She held the book out towards him. 'You want to look at it?'

The man took it, reaching out with his bear-like hands. He flicked through the first couple of pages, but he didn't really look interested in its content.

'Do you know what I love about this book?' he said, fixing Rachel with an intense stare.

Rachel shook her head.

'The beginning of the novel: the way Hale is stalked through the crowds of tourists. He knows he's going to die. It's just a matter of time. They're on his case, and there's nothing he can do about it. Only run.'

'I like it too,' Rachel said, now stepping back slightly from the man. She hoped he wouldn't notice her subtle manoeuvring.

He snapped the book shut.

'But you can only run for so long,' he said, passing it back to Rachel.

Rachel nodded, smiling weakly. She cradled the book in her arms before placing it back on the shelf. She wanted to leave, now. This man was freaking her out. He was talking in riddles. And he was still standing too close.

'I have to go,' Rachel said, avoiding eye contact. 'Nice meeting you.'

She headed towards the stairs, forcing herself not to run. She'd look stupid. The man would think she was some kind of nut. He was probably only being friendly.

'Nice meeting you too, Rachel,' he said, as she reached the bottom step. And that's when she ran: bounding up the stairs to the ground floor and dashing past Jim, who was reading an imported copy of the *New York Times*.

'Rachel?' she heard Jim say as she flew out of the door on to the street. 'You okay?'

She didn't stop to answer, instead running across the road and straight into the path of an oncoming bus. The screech of brakes was followed by a symphony of horns as the bus and the vehicles behind it vented their anger. The whole traffic flow, on both sides of the road, had stopped. Rachel staggered to a halt, facing the front of the bus. The driver leaned out of his cab window and shouted something, although Rachel couldn't make out what it was. She looked back at the bookshop, then turned and hurried across the road. Once she reached the other side, the traffic restarted and she broke into a sprint, dodging and weaving through the crowds. Her breath was shallow and she was tired, but fear, no matter how irrational, drove her on.

As she approached her flat, she began to relax, even chiding herself for being so silly.

But then she noticed her front door was ajar.

CHAPTER THIRTEEN

The swimming pool was always packed on a Sunday morning, rammed with parents and their children, keen lane swimmers, and boisterous teenagers. Matt and Charlie had been going to this leisure centre for almost twelve months now, and Matt prided himself on the fact that it was only because of him that Charlie was now confident enough to swim without needing to be held by anyone. He still had to use armbands, of course, but to swim on his own, with only the armbands, was a huge step forward. He knew James had never taken him swimming, and Beth only a handful of times.

'Daddy! Let's go in here!'

Matt held on tightly to Charlie's hand as he strained to break free. 'Don't run, and careful you don't slip.'

'I *will* be careful, Daddy!'

They entered the shallow warm water of the toddler pool. In front of them, parents and children frolicked and splashed among the various water spouts and jets that burst forth from the pool's sides and bottom. It was particularly busy today, and must have been close to capacity.

'Daddy, I want to go on the slide!'

Matt nodded and waded across with Charlie to the steps that led up to the water slide. It had taken Charlie numerous aborted attempts before he had mustered up the courage to slide down it, but now he had broken through that mental barrier, there was no stopping him. On one visit, Matt counted that Charlie had been down the slide twenty times in just under an hour. The slide itself was safe for young ones, being not too high, and impossible to fall off, with its concave shape. It was out of bounds for adults, so Matt would often accompany Charlie to the steps, before dashing out of sight to the foot of the slide. Charlie would be at the top, waiting impatiently to come down, and would direct Matt to hold out his hands before going for it.

'You go to the bottom,' Charlie said, pointing out where Matt should go, as if this were his first time.

Matt watched him climb the first couple of steps before making his way to the foot of the slide.

'Daddy! Hold your hands out!'

Matt crouched down and spread out his hands in a welcoming embrace. Charlie nodded his appreciation before launching himself down the slide.

Matt and Charlie laughed as they were both sprayed with water.

'Again!' Charlie giggled, wiping the water from his eyes. 'I want to do it *again!*'

Matt made to go with him to the steps.

'It's okay, Daddy, you wait here.'

Matt hesitated. Last week, for the first time, he had let Charlie return to the slide on his own. He had been out of sight for no more than thirty seconds, but it had felt infinitely longer. Matt now examined his son's expectant face. It wasn't just that he wanted another go on the slide. He wanted to do it on his own, to exert his independence. Matt had noticed in recent months how Charlie had grown up. Yes, he was still only a young child of just over four years of age, but he could see the grown-up waiting to emerge inside, the man he would be and wanted to become. That reality saddened him. His little baby had gone. A week ago, Matt had been backing up his computer files and had found himself looking through the photos of Charlie's first year. There were hundreds and hundreds of images – mostly of Charlie, but some of the three of them, of Beth and him, proud new parents. It had been the best of times.

Charlie cocked his head as Matt stared down vacantly into the water, gaze lost in the bubbles from the jets below. 'Daddy, can I go on my own?'

'Yes, okay, but be careful. And make sure . . .' But Charlie was already splashing off. 'Make sure you come straight down!' Matt shouted after him, though he probably couldn't hear over the general noise anyway.

Matt waded back towards the bottom of the slide, waiting impatiently for Charlie to appear at the top. Two larger boys splashed down in quick succession, and a small girl came next, coaxed down by her mother. Matt got ready to open out his arms in anticipation of Charlie's appearance.

'C'mon, Charlie.'

Where is he?

A young boy appeared. But it wasn't Charlie. Matt stepped back as the boy flew down the slide and splashed off for another go.

'*C'mon*, Charlie, where are you?' It had only been just over a minute. But Matt was already beginning to panic. He stood his ground, goose pimples forming on his damp arms and legs as his body cooled outside the water. He debated whether to go around to the slide's entrance, in case Charlie had got distracted by something. The danger was, if he left his station just as Charlie made it up the slide, they might miss one another.

The boy who had just slid down appeared again and whooshed down. He was probably just a little bit older than Charlie.

'Have you seen a little boy on the steps? Brown hair, red shorts?'

The boy shook his head, looking a little worried. His parents had probably given him the same 'don't talk to strangers' lecture that Matt and Beth had delivered to Charlie. Matt glanced around, self-conscious that the parents, who must surely be nearby, might think him a danger to their little one. But the boy merely splashed back around to the start of the slide.

Matt looked back up. This was starting to feel desperate. He should never have let Charlie go off alone. Matt waded towards the steps up to the slide with some urgency, having to negotiate infants, babies, and parents who were busy enjoying themselves. Rounding the corner, he caught his breath. Charlie wasn't anywhere to be seen. He splashed back over to the base of the slide and looked up. Charlie wasn't there. Turning, Matt scanned three hundred and sixty degrees, desperately hoping to catch a glimpse of him. But there was no sign of his little boy anywhere among the crowds of swimmers.

'Please, no.'

Maybe he's sitting at the top of the slide, just out of sight, waiting for his daddy.

Matt ignored the 'No Adults' warning and ascended the steps, earning a rebuke from one of the young lifeguards. The steps turned around the corner just near the top, which gave him hope that Charlie might be there. But he wasn't. Neither was he in the water below. 'Charlie, where the hell are you?'

'Excuse me,' the lifeguard said, now appearing at his shoulder. 'You're not allowed up here. Children only.'

Matt, lost in terrible thoughts, failed to reply. His lack of recognition of the lifeguard's presence seemed to unnerve the young man.

'Sir, you've got to come back down,' he said, almost apologetically. 'It's just for children.'

Finally his words got through. 'My boy, Charlie, he's missing.'

'Oh, right, okay. We'd better get a call out.' The lifeguard pulled out a walkie-talkie from his waistband. 'We've got a child missing from their parent. His name's Charlie.' The youth addressed Matt again. 'How old is he and what does he look like?'

'He's four, four and a half. Wearing red swimming shorts, with red armbands. Dark brown hair, brown eyes.'

The lifeguard repeated the words to his colleague on the other end of the line. 'Where did you see him last, and when?'

'He was going to go on the slide, I was waiting at the bottom. It was three, four minutes ago.' As Matt said the words, the guilt was there. He had let him go off alone in a way that Beth would never have allowed. If anything were to happen, she'd never forgive him. And he'd never forgive himself.

'Please, please help me find him,' Matt pleaded.

'We'll find him,' the lifeguard replied, as they came back down the steps and over to the pool's edge. 'This kind of thing happens every day. We always find them.'

'Thanks.' His words were reassuring for a second or two. But as Matt continued to scan the pool, feeling increasingly helpless and hopeless, the words felt hollow.

'We've got staff on all the doors,' the lifeguard explained. 'No one can get out without us knowing about it.'

Almost immediately a sickening thought swelled to the surface. What if in those few minutes before the alarm was raised someone had already taken Charlie out of the centre?

'Cameras,' Matt said. 'Can you look at the cameras?'

'Well, yes, I guess so. We haven't had to do that before, as far as I know.'

'Please,' Matt said. 'Get someone to look at the cameras.'

The lifeguard nodded and reached for his walkie-talkie again.

Matt moved forward, back into the shallow water, still scanning the pool. Charlie had disappeared. *Shit.* He felt so helpless and longed to do something proactive. He ran through the conversation he might need to have with Beth, and shuddered. He looked around again, this time trying to think more logically where Charlie might be. And then came what should have been an obvious thought. *The toilets.* Charlie was great when it came to taking himself to the toilet. He might have been caught short on the way to the slide, tried to find the bathroom on his own, and got lost.

'You okay, sir?' the lifeguard asked as Matt rushed past him.

Matt didn't answer. He took the corner of the pool at speed, his legs sliding from under him, just managing to stay upright with the help of the wall.

He ran into the communal changing area, narrowly avoiding a woman leading a young girl towards the poolside.

He didn't stop, heading for the toilets and shower area. He darted inside the toilet block and pushed at each of the cubicles in turn. Of the four doors, three swung open to reveal they were unoccupied. The fourth was locked.

'Charlie? Are you in there? Charlie?'

He went to crouch down to try to look underneath the door, but checked himself. What if it wasn't Charlie? He'd risk the wrath of the adult behind the door, or worse still, the accusations of the parent whose child he had just disturbed. And either of those would hinder his search for his boy.

'Charlie?' he said, a little less forcefully. 'Is it you in there?'

'Please, leave me alone,' a voice whispered, almost like a soft prayer. 'Please, bad man, leave me alone.'

It was the voice of a little boy. But it wasn't Charlie. Matt's skin prickled in horror at the thought he was scaring some child half to death. 'I'm really sorry, I thought you might be my son Charlie,' he said, trying his best to sound friendly. 'I didn't mean to scare you.'

There was no reply as Matt raced out of the bathroom and turned a hard right into the shower room. There was a man on the far side, lathering up his hair. He turned to acknowledge Matt's arrival, but almost as soon as their eyes met, Matt was out of there. He burst back into the changing area, looking in every direction. He raced down one of the aisles, a bank of lockers to his left, changing cubicles to his right, and emerged at the side of the main pool. Serious swimmers were shearing through the water in lanes, while a small area was roped off for informal swimming. In this section, a mixture of families and slower swimmers battled for space. Charlie would know better than to go into this pool unaccompanied, but it was worth looking, just in case. Matt's eyes swept the whole pool. Charlie was nowhere.

Matt glanced over at the windows that showed the street outside. Again that horrible thought came to him: that someone might have taken Charlie. He could be anywhere by now – led down the road into town, in the back of a van, dragged into a . . .

Matt turned and headed for the reception. He ignored the calls of the lifeguard patrolling the edge of the wet zone. She shouted something about not going dry-side wearing swimwear. Not that Matt had remembered he was only wearing shorts. He rushed up to the front desk. There was no queue.

'My son,' he said to the grey-haired woman behind the desk. 'Have you found him?'

'Your son?'

My God, they said they'd informed the front desk!

'Yes, my son Charlie. He's been missing for about ten minutes. Weren't you told to look for him? The lifeguard – he said he'd tell you.'

'I'm sorry, I'm not normally on here. I'm just covering for a few minutes while my colleague nips to the toilet.'

Matt shook his head, incensed. 'A four-year-old boy has gone missing from one of your swimming pools. *Everyone* should know about it!'

She reddened. 'Yes, of course, I'm sorry.'

Matt was growing more frightened with each passing second – fate seemed to be conspiring against him. 'How long have you been on the desk?'

'Er, two minutes or so.'

Matt put a hand to his head. 'He could have walked out of here any time in the past few minutes, and you wouldn't have known.'

'I . . . I'd have seen a child, a four-year-old, walking around on their own. I'd have spotted that and intervened, I'm sure I would have.'

'But what if they were with an adult? What if he's been taken? They said they'd give his description to whoever was on the front desk. Four years old, brown hair, brown eyes, red—'

Matt was cut off by the leisure centre manager striding towards him. 'Mr Roberts. We've found him.'

Matt could hardly take it in. 'You've got him? Thank God. Where is—'

'He's in the staffroom, with Nikki, my deputy, enjoying a cup of orange juice and a biscuit.' He noted Matt's expression, still full of concern. 'Don't worry, he's fine. Come on, I'll take you to him now.'

'Where did you find him?' Matt asked as they made their way through the double doors, back to the wet zone.

'Someone handed him to Alice, one of our lifeguards.'

'Someone?'

'A woman. She said she'd found him wandering around the ladies' loos.'

So I was right to investigate the toilets. I just got the wrong ones.

'Daddy, where have you been?' Charlie chastised as Matt entered the room. Charlie placed the plastic cup of half-drunk orange juice on the table, crunched on his digestive biscuit, and eyed Matt for an explanation.

Matt ran over and hugged him tightly. He had never been so pleased or relieved to see anyone in his life. He felt like crying. 'I was waiting for you, Charlie, to come down the slide. But you never came back. Where did you go?'

'Toilet,' Charlie said, rather sheepishly. 'Needed a wee.'

'You should have come back to me. I'd have taken you. I was so worried, Charlie. You know not to go off on your own. Mummy and Daddy, we've told you bad things can happen if you walk off like that.'

Charlie hung his head. 'I'm sorry, Daddy. I won't do it again, I promise.'

'Good boy,' Matt said, placing a comforting hand across his son's back. 'You're lucky that nice lady saw you and helped you.'

'Yes,' Charlie said, brightening as he snapped off another piece of biscuit. 'Lucky that Aunty Cath saw me.'

'Pardon?'

'Lucky she saw me.'

Matt made sure Charlie was listening. 'Charlie, you saw Aunty Cath?'

Charlie put a hand up to his mouth, theatrically wide-eyed. 'Oops. I wasn't meant to tell you that, Daddy.'

CHAPTER FOURTEEN

Rachel moved towards the door, her body tense and fearful at the thought that someone might have invaded her home.

Could she have forgotten to close it?

It seemed highly unlikely. Normally her problem was controlling her OCD, which made her check multiple times that the door was locked.

She pushed at the door, her hand shaking. 'Hello?' she shouted, a warning wrapped as a greeting: if there was a burglary in process, she'd rather the perpetrators escape out the back now than face her down. 'Is anybody there?'

But as she edged through the open doorway, there was no response, and no other sounds of life coming from within the flat.

Maybe she had just left the door open after all.

Then Rachel put a hand to her mouth. The entrance hallway was strewn with coats, which had been yanked recklessly from their hooks. She stepped over the items, her heart pounding. 'My God!' The living room had been turned upside down – an indoor tornado of destruction. Drawers had been flung open and lay upended on the carpet, their contents littered around. The bookcase was empty, with books flung in every direction. The kitchen had been attacked, with plates smashed and cutlery everywhere. In the bathroom, the cabinet had been ripped off the wall, taking a sizeable chunk of plasterboard with it; shards of splintered mirror speckled the floor and bottles spilled out their contents. But her bedroom was the worst – her and Alex's most private possessions violated.

Rachel turned and fled the flat, half stumbling in her panic to escape the scene. She dialled 999 before she even reached the pavement.

Rachel waited outside until the patrol car arrived. The two female uniformed officers offered to conduct their initial questioning of her in the vehicle, but Rachel felt it best to get back inside the flat – after all, it was just putting off the inevitable, and whoever had done this was now long gone.

'Looks like they popped open the door with a crowbar,' the older officer noted. 'See these marks here,' she said, pointing at two dark scuffs on the white doorframe. 'They use the crowbar to push the door sideways in its frame, and if the full lock isn't on and the door has a bit of give in it, then it just pops open. That's why you should always double-lock these doors. See the extra hook locks here, top and bottom? If they're engaged, then the door will hold firm.'

'I usually do that,' Rachel replied, cursing herself silently for not doing so this time. What were the chances that the one time she didn't engage the full locking mechanism, she'd be targeted by burglars?

'It happens a lot,' the officer said, noting Rachel's displeasure with herself. 'One of those things, unfortunately.'

But was it just one of those things? Rachel wasn't so sure. She thought back to Michael's coded warning. And the creepy man in the bookshop.

Could it all be connected?

They entered the living room.

Rachel realised there was nowhere to sit, as the sofa and chairs were covered with debris. 'I'll just clear this,' she said, snatching up as much as she could hold and dumping it on the corner table after righting it.

'It's okay, Rachel, really,' the second officer said. 'We can stand.'

'No, no, sit down.'

There was now space for them, and they took their seats, surrounded by the wreckage of Rachel's home.

'Have you noticed if anything is missing?' the older officer asked, her eyes sweeping all four corners of the room.

'I haven't,' Rachel replied. 'Not yet, anyway.'

'Of course,' the officer said. 'I realise you haven't had much time. But there's nothing obviously missing then? Car keys, car, purse, cash, electronic equipment?'

'I'm not sure. I haven't been around the house yet. But my iPad is over there, with the TV, they haven't been taken.'

'Is it okay if we have a look around?' the same officer said, already making to stand as Rachel began to nod. 'Please, you can wait here. We'll only be a minute.'

Rachel waited in the armchair as the two policewomen stalked around the flat. She heard them muttering from the bedroom next door, but couldn't make out what they were saying.

They re-entered the living room and settled back down on to the sofa.

'They really turned the place upside down,' the younger of the two officers noted, her only words since she'd first introduced herself. She looked to be in her early twenties, probably close to Rachel's age, with mousy brown hair with blonde highlights, and very blue eyes.

Rachel picked up on her surprised tone. 'Is that unusual?'

'It's a little bit unusual.'

'In what way?'

'Well, house burglaries fall into several main types. There's the opportunistic break-in, where an offender might notice a front door open and do a smash and grab. Then there's the variant, where the offender might know a potential weakness, such as with your door. Again, it's usually a smash and grab, sometimes targeting car keys that are often left by the entrance. They exploit the weakness, grab the keys and car, and they're gone. And then there's those who are prepared to spend more time in the property. They're still looking to be inside for as little time as possible, but it could be some minutes as they move about, taking as much of value as they can.'

She let the silence settle.

'But this doesn't fit any of those,' Rachel said, filling the void.

'No, it doesn't.'

'So what type of break-in is this?'

With a glance between them, the older officer picked up the conversation. 'Rachel, when we see such destruction, in our experience there is often just one explanation: the perpetrators were looking for something.'

'Looking for something?'

'Do you have any idea what someone may have been looking for? Do you have anything of special value in the flat? I don't mean just financially. Do you have anything here that someone else might want to get their hands on?'

Rachel trawled her mind for an answer. It seemed ridiculous to think that someone had targeted the flat for something in particular. 'I can't think of anything.'

'What do you do, Rachel, for your work? Anything dealing with sensitive information?'

'I work for VisiON, the marketing company. We work on quite commercially sensitive projects, of course, but I don't think someone would go that far. I've never heard of it happening to anyone before.'

'Do you work on the projects at home? Store things on your home computer, for example?'

'Sometimes. But we're limited to what we can work on outside the office. If it's something deemed highly sensitive, like when we were involved in the run-up to the London Olympics, then we can only work at work, if you know what I mean.'

'What about your partner? We saw the photo in the bedroom,' the officer explained, registering but unable to read Rachel's expression.

'Alex. He died two weeks ago.'

'Oh, we're so sorry.' She looked down at her notebook. 'May I ask how he died?'

'A traffic collision. It was a hit-and-run, so there isn't much information, but the police think it was a four-by-four of some kind.'

'I'm really sorry, Rachel.'

'You think all this might be connected?' The question had burst its way out of her and the sinister, deadly serious insinuation clearly threw the officers a little, who took a few seconds to consider their response.

'You think the break-in might be connected to your partner's death?' the officer said. 'What makes you suspect that?'

Rachel shrugged. 'I honestly don't know.'

'Is there any reason to believe that your partner, Alex, may have had anything of value in the flat?'

'I don't know.' Rachel put a hand to her head. 'This is all just so . . . crazy. I don't know what to think anymore.'

'It's a lot to deal with, Rachel. Have you seen one of our support officers?'

Rachel nodded. The liaison officer, a very nice lady, had been around the day after Alex's death. She'd returned a few days later, and had offered continued support by phone. But what could she really do that would make it any better? She couldn't change the awful truth.

'Well, don't be afraid of calling on them again. You may want to talk about what has just happened. It's up to you, of course. We'll send someone to advise about security, though, and in the meantime, get the locks changed. One of the team will be in touch. Should be today or tomorrow at the latest. Do you have family or friends you can stay with?'

Rachel was surprised. 'I was planning on just staying here. You wouldn't recommend it?'

'Again, it's up to you. The front door still works, so there's no reason why you can't stay. It's just that after something like this, some people need to get away for a day or so.'

'I think I'll be fine.'

'Just make sure you engage the double locks. Also, keep a key in the lock, just in case.'

'In case what?'

'In case the thieves have taken a set of keys. That way, even if they have a key, they won't be able to open the door.'

The thought of them having a key and returning gave a fresh perspective to Rachel's thoughts of remaining in the flat. 'You think they might come back?'

'Very unlikely. It's a big risk to return to the scene of a break-in, particularly so soon after the event.'

'And usually they already have what they wanted,' the other officer added, 'so there's no need to come back.'

Rachel was troubled by a terrifying thought.

What if they hadn't found what they were looking for?

CHAPTER FIFTEEN

Matt turned to Nikki, the deputy manager of the leisure centre. 'Did you get a description of the lady who found Charlie?'

She looked confused as to why he was asking the question. 'No, I'm sorry, I didn't. Why?'

Matt hesitated. How could he explain? Especially with Charlie sitting there, listening. And he *would* be listening. 'I just think it might be important. I might know her.'

'Oh, right,' she said, her face clouding over with concern. 'I thought it was just someone who happened to spot your son. You think there's something to worry about here?'

'Maybe,' Matt replied, checking whether Charlie was taking any notice. Thankfully his attention had been diverted by a toy Minion he had spotted on one of the shelves – he was straining his neck to get a better look. Matt moved a little closer to the woman. 'I've been having some problems recently with a woman I was in a relationship with. I'm keeping a record of when things happen. That's why it's important to know whether it was her or not.'

She nodded. 'I can call Alice in. She'd be able to describe her for you.'

'What about the CCTV?'

'Non-operational.'

'You're kidding me?'

'We had some technical issues six or seven weeks ago, and it's been offline ever since. To be honest, in all the time I've been here, we've never actually looked back at any of the footage, so we haven't been in a rush to get it replaced.'

Typical.

'If you could ask Alice then, that would be great.'

She radioed through, and Alice appeared at the door.

'Alice, the lady who brought Charlie to you, could you describe her?'

Alice, a sporty-looking teenager with tied-back red hair, seemed thrown by the question. 'Er, yes, I guess. She was about my height, blonde hair in a ponytail. Pretty.' She looked between the deputy manager and Matt. 'Why, is there something the matter?'

'Everything's fine,' Nikki said. 'Thanks, Alice, you can return to your station now.'

The girl nodded, looking somewhat confused, before disappearing.

'Does that help?' the woman said to Matt.

'Yes, I think so. Not that there's any real doubt,' he added. 'Charlie is very rarely wrong. If he said that it was Aunty Cath, then it probably was.'

◆ ◆ ◆

'Daddy, look at me! I'm tall!'

Matt smiled as Charlie stood at the summit of the climbing apparatus, both arms stretched up into the air. The playground across the road from the leisure centre was themed around pirates, and currently Charlie was perched up in the crow's nest of the pirate ship. He had developed quite an obsession with all things pirate over the past couple of months.

'Daddy! I'm going to walk the plank!'

Matt watched as Charlie whizzed down the slide, then immediately sprang up and ran around to climb back up the rope netting.

Charlie was showing no after-effects of the drama just an hour earlier. Unlike Matt, who couldn't shake the terror he had felt over losing Charlie. During lunch at the leisure centre cafe – chips, sausage, and baked beans for Charlie, and a sandwich for Matt – he'd tried but failed to recover. His unease was heightened by the fact that he seemed to have got his son back with the help of the woman who was quite likely stalking him.

What would he tell Beth? She'd freak out if she knew he had lost Charlie for almost ten minutes. At the very least, it would put a new strain on their relationship. At the worst, it might jeopardise the current access arrangements, or even strengthen her resolve to relocate to Australia.

'Daddy! I'm going to walk the plank again!'

Again, Charlie whizzed down the slide.

Even if Matt decided not to tell Beth about what had happened at the swimming pool, there was no guarantee Charlie himself wouldn't mention it. He was now at the age where he passed messages, news, and secrets between his parents.

A few weeks ago, he had revealed to Matt that James had bought Beth a 'special ring'. Matt hadn't brought the subject up with Beth, and hadn't seen the ring – she certainly hadn't worn it during his pick-ups and drop-offs – but he did wonder, with some horror, whether it had been an engagement ring.

Except it couldn't be, could it, considering Beth's aversion to marriage?

Beth's parents' toxic relationship – a marriage built on sand mixed with broken glass – had shaped and warped her view of the ritual. Only two dates in, she had been upfront with Matt about her feelings: marriage, to anyone, was off the table, and there would be no changing her mind, no negotiation in future years. To Beth, commitment was about proving yourself with deeds over the long haul, not a shiny ring and paperwork.

But still, you could never say never, could you?

The thought made him feel nauseous.

Charlie slid down the slide for the umpteenth time, but on this occasion he raced over to Matt, who was still dwelling on whether to come clean with Beth. 'Daddy, I want to go on the rocky, wobbly pirate ship!'

'Okay, mate,' Matt said, as Charlie sprinted off to the see-saw.

'Excuse me.'

Matt turned to see a young woman. She was holding a baby against her chest, rocking from side to side as she looked up at Matt. 'Hi,' he said.

'Aren't you the guy who was looking for his son in the swimming pool?' the woman asked.

'Yes. That's me.'

'I just wanted to say, I was so happy you found him. I was near you, at the water slide, when you first lost him. I was in the pool with my little girl, and when I heard you talking to the lifeguard, I actually went to look for him myself. I'd been watching him going down the slide, so I knew what he looked like.'

'That was really kind of you. I really appreciate it.'

'I know what it's like to be in that situation. It's just so horrible. I lost my eldest once; he was three at the time. It was only for two or three minutes, but it felt like a lifetime. And when I got him back, I just didn't want to ever let go again.'

'But you have to, don't you?' Matt said.

'Yes, you do. At least he doesn't seem any the worse for it,' she said, watching Charlie, who was giggling as the see-saw bounced up and down even harder than before.

'No, *he's* fine. It's me who needs a lie-down.'

'I bet you do. I was nearly the one who found your son,' she revealed. 'We'd looked around the toddler pool, and the bigger pool, and we were just about to enter the ladies' loos when I saw him coming out with another lady. I was so happy to see him – I recognised him immediately – but then I suddenly wondered, what if that woman actually took your son? What if she hadn't just found him, and she was taking him away? I feel a bit bad for thinking that now, but you just can't be too careful these days, can you?'

'No,' Matt said, thinking that this woman didn't know how close to the mark she possibly was.

'Anyway, because I had those doubts, those suspicions, we followed them, past the changing rooms. I thought at first they were heading for the exit, and I was trying to think of what to do to stop her. But then I realised she must have just been looking for a member of staff, because she walked right up to one of the female lifeguards. As soon as I saw that, we went to get changed. Like I said, I felt a bit guilty about jumping to the wrong conclusion. But I felt better once I had a chat with her.'

Matt nearly didn't take in that last sentence. 'A chat? You saw her?'

'Yes, just before I saw you, actually. I thought maybe you might have seen her too.'

'Here? You saw her here?'

The woman seemed a little startled by Matt's horrified reaction. 'Yes, just over there.' She turned to her left and indicated the picnic area. 'She was sitting down at one of the tables, just a few minutes ago. I happened to spot her as we were walking past.'

Matt looked over at the picnic tables. There was no sign of the woman he knew as Catherine. But if she had been watching Matt and had seen the young woman who'd spoken to her now talking to him, she would surely have got up and left. Maybe she was still close by. His eyes swept across the wider area of the park.

And there, in the middle distance, was Catherine, walking away.

'Are you okay?' the woman said, interrupting Matt's thoughts.

If he set off at a pace, he'd catch up with her in less than a minute.

But he wasn't on his own – could he run while holding his son?

Maybe he could ask this woman to keep an eye on Charlie?

He quickly dismissed that idea – he couldn't believe the thought had even crossed his mind after what had just happened.

He looked across at Charlie, then again at Catherine, who was getting further and further away.

'Are you alright?'

There has to be a way.

'I'm okay,' he said finally. He went for his phone and stepped away from the woman. It was worth a shot.

He dialled Catherine, and watched her in the distance.

The call rang through. He saw her stop.

'C'mon, pick up, pick up.'

He glanced at Charlie, to check he was still okay. Then back to Catherine, who was still stationary. Just as he thought the call would go unanswered, it connected.

'Catherine?'

Silence.

'Catherine. I know that's not your real name. But it doesn't matter. I just want to know what's going on.'

More silence.

'Why are you following me?'

No answer.

'And why run away yesterday and ignore my calls?'

No reply. But at least she was listening. Matt checked on Charlie again. He was still engrossed in his play.

'Please believe me,' she said finally. 'Everything I've done, it's for your own protection.'

And then the line went dead.

PART TWO

CHAPTER SIXTEEN

Matt dropped Charlie back with Beth. He'd made the decision not to tell her about what had happened at the swimming pool. There was a risk that Charlie himself would let it slip, but he hadn't mentioned it on the way home. He'd been too busy enthusing about the pirate ship.

Matt thought back to what Catherine had said.

Everything I've done, it's for your own protection.

What was that supposed to mean?

By the time he reached his flat, he'd decided to confront her face to face. As he neared her apartment block, located on a busy junction on Seven Sisters Road, he rehearsed how the conversation might play out. It could go terribly wrong, but at least it was better than leaving things hanging.

Matt pressed the intercom buzzer for Flat 5. No answer. He pressed the button once more, but again there was no reply. He stepped back and looked up at the building, to the windows of Catherine's flat. There were no signs of movement, but it was distinctly possible that she'd had the chance to peer out, see him, and decided to ignore his presence. He called her again on her mobile, but it rang through.

He was just about to leave when he saw a man at Catherine's window. The guy's face was only there for a second or two.

Several thoughts pinged around Matt's head.

Is that her partner?

Or maybe another lover?

Or something more sinister?

Just a few weeks ago, Catherine had told him about a break-in in the block. The elderly lady in Flat 3 had returned home to find her place turned over. Somehow, someone had got into the block and then forced their way through the flimsy front door.

Matt didn't stop to think too much. He punched in the entrance code Catherine had so trustingly provided him with and ran up the stairs.

He took a steadying breath and knocked on Catherine's door.

He could hear movement. It sounded like sliding furniture.

'Catherine, it's Matt.' He was surprised how nervy his voice sounded.

Still the sounds within the flat continued. He knocked again.

This time the door opened.

'Hello. Can I help you?' the man said, in accented English. He looked nervous, holding on to the door as if it were a shield.

'I'm looking for Catherine Smith.' Matt couldn't resist the urge to peer around the man, in case he caught a glimpse of her.

'Sorry. She's gone,' the man replied, in what Matt detected was an Eastern European accent. Possibly Polish or Romanian.

'Gone?'

'Yes. Gone. Today.' He seemed to relax and released his grip on the door.

'She's moved out?'

'Yes.'

'Do you know where she's gone?'

He shrugged. 'Sorry. I don't know any more than this. I'm just here to clean.'

'So you work for the owner?' Maybe if he spoke to the owner, he could find out where Catherine had gone.

'No. I work for agency. Agency calls and tells me where to go. I go.' The man smiled sadly.

Matt nodded. 'Thanks for your help. I'll let you get on with your job.'

◆ ◆ ◆

The woman called out just as Matt reached the top of the stairs.

'Excuse me? It's Matt, isn't it?'

He turned to find Mariana, Catherine's next-door neighbour, approaching. They'd passed each other in the corridor a number of times since he and Catherine had begun dating, and had been introduced just last week. She was a strikingly pretty Spanish doctor, studying infectious diseases at the London School of Hygiene & Tropical Medicine. She was holding a book.

'Mariana.'

'Is it true Catherine has moved out?'

'Apparently. Didn't she tell you?'

'No.' She looked a little hurt. 'She didn't say a thing.' Her brow knotted as realisation dawned. 'Not even to you?'

'I'm afraid not.'

'Oh,' she said, looking down at the book, which dangled limply from her hand. 'I was hoping you could give her this back.' She passed him the Agatha Christie novel.

'It's mine,' Matt said. 'Thank you.'

'Oh, good. Well, there you are.' Her smile was dazzling. 'I really enjoyed it.'

'So you didn't see her leave?'

'Unfortunately not. I came home from town an hour ago and spoke to the cleaner.'

Why the secrecy and urgency?

'Did Catherine ever have male visitors?' Matt felt awful asking the question, both for putting Mariana on the spot and for doubting Catherine again, but he needed to know.

'Not that I saw. Only you.'

Matt nodded to himself.

'I hope things work out with you both,' Mariana said, interpreting Matt's surprise at Catherine's disappearing act as symptomatic of a relationship breakdown. She smiled sympathetically. 'If I see Catherine, I'll tell her you were looking for her.'

'Thank you. But I don't think she'll be back.'

CHAPTER SEVENTEEN

Rachel gasped for breath as her eyes opened. She turned over, expecting to see intruders, but there was no one. She was alone in her bedroom. A glance over at her bedside radio told her it was just gone ten o'clock in the morning. Her body was drenched with sweat, although the temperature of the room felt cool on her skin. She thought back to the previous day.

What a nightmare.

Rachel brushed her hair and went to the bathroom to shower.

She'd just dressed when the landline, located in the living room, began to ring. The bell had never seemed so sinister.

'Hello?'

Just silence. But someone *was* on the other end of the line.

'Hello?'

The break-in.

Driven by fear, she slammed the phone down on to its holder.

The phone rang again.

Rachel just glared at it, willing it to stop.

And then that horrifying thought returned.

What if they hadn't found what they were looking for?

Rachel swiped her keys from the kitchen table and hurried back through to the living room. She paused only to grab the police contact card off the arm of the sofa, stuffing it into the back pocket of her jeans. She burst out of the front door, fumbling with the lock, and sprinted down the stairs and off down the road, in the direction of the high street.

◆ ◆ ◆

Something had stopped her from calling the number on the police contact card. Instead, she called Michael.

But he didn't pick up.

She tried again, but still without luck. In desperation, she called through to his office, but the receptionist came back with the news that he'd called in sick.

It was like he'd just dropped off the planet.

But why?

Rachel headed for the bookshop, and the only person this side of the Atlantic with whom she felt safe – Jim. She'd tell him everything, call the police, and wait in the shop with him for them to arrive.

As soon as Rachel turned the corner on to the high street, she saw the ambulance and police car parked right in front of the shop.

She froze, and was suddenly jolted from behind as a man collided with her before offering his apologies and hurrying on his way. Rachel hardly noticed, staring in horror as two green-clad paramedics unloaded an empty stretcher from the back of the ambulance. A group of onlookers had positioned themselves just outside the shop door. Rachel brought a hand up to her mouth, as if that would keep the emotion in. She went to move forward, but found that her body resisted. Instead, it was begging her to do the opposite: to turn and run.

Is this all connected?

She gasped as the paramedics brought someone out through the door of the shop on the stretcher. She couldn't see from this distance what state the person was in.

Was it Jim?

The memories from Alex's funeral came crashing back, just as her mobile shrilled. She brought it to her ear with a shaking hand.

'Hello?'

No answer.

The line went dead. She stumbled backwards, her head spinning, and met a brick wall, which slammed into the back of her head. She grabbed on to the wall to steady herself. The world was spinning dangerously out of control. And she had to get away.

'You okay?'

A concerned passer-by reached out with a hand. Rachel couldn't tell whether it was a man or a woman; she couldn't focus through the tears and the shock. She shook her head but found she was pushing the arm away, rejecting the assistance. Who was this person? Were they really here to help? Rachel took one last look at the ambulance as it drove away.

No sirens blaring or lights flashing.

Is that significant?

'I think this lady is unwell,' Rachel heard a distant voice say.

She staggered forward, pushing past several bodies, none of whom resisted. Suddenly her vision cleared slightly, but significantly, and she could once again see the world around her. She didn't look back at the crowd, or at those trying to help her, or at the bookshop.

She just ran.

CHAPTER EIGHTEEN

Catherine's disappearance had been bothering Matt all evening and the following morning.

Why would she clear out of her flat so quickly?

It's like she was running from something. Or someone?

He'd tried her mobile countless times, but with no joy. To take his mind off the mystery, and faced with an empty day ahead of him, he changed into his jogging kit. He'd try and outrun his concerns.

The buzz of his mobile interrupted his plans. He stared at the caller ID, debating whether to leave it to ring off.

It was Sheila McIntosh, from UGT.

Matt paused, thinking things through. He knew he'd soon have to face the world of work again, but part of him didn't want to.

Could he do this now?

He took a deep breath and answered. 'Hello, Matt speaking.'

'Matt, it's Sheila here, from Gabriel's office.' Sheila was always very matter-of-fact, very professional, with a clipped tone. She could sound unfriendly, but Gabriel's assistant of over ten years was actually a very nice lady.

'Sheila, lovely to hear from you.'

'You too, Matt. Is now a good time to talk?'

Matt kicked off his shoes. It wasn't.

'Sure.'

'Gabriel would like to see you this afternoon.'

That brought Matt up short. He hadn't expected that and didn't feel ready. But, coming from Gabriel, he knew this was a demand, not a request. 'No problem.'

'Perfect. If you come over to the offices for four, that would be great.'

◆ ◆ ◆

The UGT offices were situated in the heart of the City of London. Matt gazed up the twenty storeys of piano-black tinted glass. The impressive and imposing structure, just four years old, projected money and power. He couldn't help but think of the decaying building that housed the North London College of Further Education, and the constant fight for funding just to ensure that the students could study without the threat of the ceiling leaking on to them.

Matt was met with a warm smile at the reception desk. 'Mr Roberts, lovely to see you.' Holly was one of the smiliest, happiest people in the building. 'Are you here to see Gabriel?'

Matt nodded.

'Sheila let me know you'd be arriving,' she explained. Her brightness dimmed slightly. 'I'm really sorry, but you'll have to sign in as a visitor. Sorry.'

'No worries.' Matt's ID had been retained on leaving the company twelve months ago. He completed the requisite boxes.

Holly brightened again. 'Fantastic. Here's your visitor's pass. The meeting is on the top floor, room 20Z. If you wait there, Gabriel should be along with you shortly.'

◆ ◆ ◆

Matt stepped out of the lift on the twentieth floor. Room 20Z was empty, save for a tray with coffee, tea, and biscuits placed in the middle of the oval table. Matt loitered at the window, looking out across London and the River Thames, waiting nervously for Gabriel to arrive.

His thoughts turned back to Catherine, and the mystery that surrounded her.

'Who are you?' he asked the world below.

'That depends,' came the unexpected reply.

Matt spun around as James Farrah approached, his smile professional and his palms outstretched.

James looked pleased to see him.

Matt looked over James's shoulder, to see if Gabriel was with him. He wasn't.

'Gabriel's meeting is overrunning,' James explained, reading his thoughts. 'He asked me to swing by and make sure you're okay.' He glanced at his watch. 'He should be along in the next five minutes or so.'

Matt watched as James circled the table, settling by the window. He, too, admired the view, but seemed preoccupied. Matt wasn't sure why he was hanging around.

James tapped on the tinted glass. 'Look, Matt,' he said. 'I know things have gone downhill between us in recent years. But it doesn't have to be like that. I was hoping we might be able to start afresh.'

Matt didn't want to point out that things had never really been good between them. 'It's okay, James. You don't have to do this.'

'Yes, yes, I do. I have to. *We* have to do this. For Beth's sake.'

'Beth?' Just hearing James say Beth's name was enough to put Matt on edge. He didn't think he'd ever get used to discussing Beth with him.

'Yes. You must know how much it's affecting her, you and I being so off with one another.'

Matt said nothing. The fact that James now had more of a handle on what Beth was thinking and feeling, when that had been Matt's preserve and pleasure for so long, was painful.

'We need to sort things out, be more amicable,' James continued. 'Would you like a drink?'

'I'm okay,' Matt replied. He was thinking through what James had just said. Had he been so blind as not to notice how his behaviour towards James was affecting Beth?

James poured himself a coffee from the steel urn and stirred in two sugars. 'Look, Matt, I know things aren't easy right now for you, with the news the other day about Australia, but it's just so important to Beth that she knows you're happy with it all.' He took a sip from his cup, but kept his eyes on Matt for a reaction.

Matt tried to think of a way of putting his feelings into words. As much as he didn't want to discuss his innermost thoughts with James Farrah, there was no avoiding it. 'I love my son more than anything in the world,' he began. 'I'd do anything for him.'

James nodded his understanding, but he didn't have children of his own, so how could he possibly understand?

Matt continued, hoping that he wasn't about to lose grip of his emotions. 'The thought of losing him, it makes me feel sick. Physically sick.'

'But you wouldn't—' James interjected.

Matt put up a hand. 'If he goes to Australia, I'd lose him. I wouldn't see him.'

'We would FaceTime.'

'I'd be a face on a screen. It's not the same.'

James didn't deny it.

Matt held James's gaze as he tried to get him to truly understand. As James stood there, attentive, there suddenly seemed a purpose to this conversation – maybe Matt could change James's mind, if only he could find the right words.

'Charlie is four and a half now. He's changing so much, growing up. If you take him to Australia, then he will grow up without me.'

It sounded selfish, but didn't he have a right to be selfish when it came to his own son?

James ran a hand across his face. 'I do understand, Matt, I truly do. I may not be a father, but I can understand. That's why I turned down the Sydney job offer initially.'

'You turned it down?'

'Yes. Twice. And you know how much Gabriel likes to be turned down.' His smile was tight. 'He wasn't particularly happy, but I decided I couldn't do it to you. Not after what you've gone through.'

Matt found James's empathetic statements hard to believe, but maybe he was being too cynical. 'So what changed?'

There was a telling pause. 'Beth convinced me to go for it.'

It felt like a low blow to the stomach. 'Beth convinced you?'

'She said it was too good an opportunity to turn down. And . . . and it would be good for Charlie to experience a different culture.'

Matt found himself shaking his head in a mixture of disbelief and anger. He closed his eyes and pushed down hard on the words he wanted to release.

James stepped towards him. 'Beth said she wanted to make sure you got to see as much of Charlie as possible. You're free to come over to Australia and visit whenever you like. You can stay at our place, no problem.'

Matt was hardly listening.

'Beth was concerned about how it might affect you.'

'Just not concerned enough,' Matt let slip. The sense of betrayal was palpable and wounding. They might not be together now as a couple, but surely they'd always be together as a family?

'Look, Matt—' James was interrupted by his mobile. He stepped back towards the windows. 'Hi . . . Okay, sure. Will do.'

'The meeting is still overrunning?'

'No, it's finished. But Gabriel's just had to leave for an unscheduled meeting at the Bank of England. I'm afraid he's going to have to postpone.'

Matt was glad. 'I'd better be going then.'

'Wait,' James called, as Matt headed to the door. He pulled out an envelope from his jacket pocket and handed it over. 'Gabriel wanted me to give you this, in case he didn't get the chance to tell you himself.'

Matt left the letter unopened until he'd exited the building.

It was a personal letter from Gabriel.

He wanted him back with the company, one and a half weeks from now – accompanying him on an important trip to New York.

There was an offer of immediate promotion. And a salary increase of 25 per cent.

Matt had to give his answer by 9 a.m. tomorrow morning.

CHAPTER NINETEEN

'Matt. I wasn't expecting to see you.'

Amy welcomed her brother into her small rented flat in Stoke Newington early on Tuesday morning. The place was tiny, just a small bedroom with an adjoining kitchen/dining/living room. But Amy had done her best to make it pleasant, decorating it with paintings, pottery, and beautiful throws.

'Cup of tea?' she asked, already filling the kettle.

Matt nodded. He stifled a yawn.

Amy eyed him. 'You look terrible.'

'Thanks. I didn't sleep too well.' His mind had been racing with thoughts of Gabriel's offer, and of the revelation that Beth had encouraged James to take the Sydney position. He'd finally given up on sleep at 5 a.m., and had instead gone for an early-morning walk to try to clear his head.

'So, what's up?'

Matt had run through his explanation during the walk. But the carefully crafted lines had deserted him. 'I'm returning to the bank.'

'Oh,' Amy said, looking momentarily quite disappointed. She recovered almost instantly. 'Well, if that's what you want to do, then that's great. Really great. I'm pleased for you.' She patted him on the arm, then turned her back as she popped a couple of teabags into the pot.

Matt watched her back, wondering what she was thinking. But really, he knew.

'I let Gabriel know first thing this morning. I'm sorry, Amy.'

She took a couple more seconds to turn back round, her smile quite sad. 'You don't need to say sorry, Matt. You really don't.'

'Gabriel wants me to start back in just under two weeks' time.'

'Right . . .'

'He's invited me for dinner tonight at Eden to discuss my return.'

'Sounds cool.'

'I want to carry on teaching the evening class until then. I don't want to leave you in the lurch.'

'That's good.' Amy nodded. 'The guys will appreciate it.' She seemed troubled, frowning at some thought.

'Will you be able to get a replacement with a fortnight's notice?'

She nodded. 'We'll find someone. It's just . . .' She hesitated.

'The assessment,' Matt finished. 'The assessment is the week after that.'

'You can't delay returning to the bank?'

'Gabriel wants me to accompany him on a trip to New York that week,' Matt explained. 'I don't think I could get out of it.'

'Of course,' Amy replied.

'If there was another way, I'd do it. I feel bad about it all.'

'Don't worry, it'll be fine. We'll find someone.'

'And Harvey?'

'I'll speak to him, explain things. He'll understand. You've got him to such a great place, and he's got real momentum behind him going towards the assessment. I think he'll be okay.'

Matt could see the doubt in Amy's eyes, and he swallowed down his feelings of guilt.

'I hope so, Amy, I honestly do.'

Matt walked back home via Regent's Park, mulling over his decision to accept Gabriel's offer, the implications for the class at the college, and Amy's reaction. It had been muted, but he knew her too well not to have seen the disappointment.

Matt sat on a bench and watched the people stroll by. He began to think about Beth and James Farrah.

Could he really deny Beth what she wanted? After all he had put her through?

He came to an uncomfortable yet firm conclusion.

After a few minutes, his mind turned once again to Catherine. He needed to find out the truth. And with Catherine not answering her mobile, and clearing out of her flat, there was only one person who offered the possibility of finding out more.

Eddie – the man from the pub.

CHAPTER TWENTY

Matt entered The Admiral. It was only eleven in the morning, but the barman had said Eddie was there most days, all day, so Matt wasn't surprised to see the guy sitting over in the far corner, pint in hand, watching the football highlights. Matt exchanged a glance with the barman as he approached the bar.

'I guess you've already seen Eddie?' the barman said. 'Over in the corner.'

Matt nodded.

'What can I get you?'

Matt slid his eyes across the pumps. He wanted to say something like a fruit juice or cola, but even though it was a bit early for a beer, he thought it might go down better with Eddie. 'Pint of London Pride, please.'

'Sure. Good luck with the conversation,' the barman said, as he began to fill the glass. 'I hope you get what you want out of it. Eddie's not in the best of moods this morning. Already had to tell him off for shouting at another of our regulars.'

'Sounds great.'

The man smiled as he brought the pint down gently on the bar. 'If you bought him one of these, it might help things a little.'

Matt thought for a second. 'Go on then, two pints of London Pride.'

'Good man.'

Matt took both drinks and made his way over to Eddie, who didn't seem to have noticed his presence, such was his attention on the television.

'Eddie.'

He didn't move a muscle. Matt might as well have been invisible.

'Eddie. I need to talk to you. About what you said. You remember me, don't you?'

Still no movement. Not even the slightest tell that he knew Matt was standing there.

'Eddie?'

Nothing.

'I've bought you a pint,' he tried, holding up the drink in his right hand.

'Well, I guess you'd better sit down,' Eddie said, in a slow, deliberate drawl. He still didn't take his eyes off the screen as Matt took the stool opposite and placed both drinks down on the table.

'I've come to talk to you about what you said the other day, about Catherine.'

Now Eddie did turn his attention away from the screen. He smiled, and Matt realised he was already drunk. It was before midday and the alcohol was in command. 'Did you ask her,' he said, 'what her real name is?'

Matt closed his eyes briefly. 'I told her about what you'd said to me. That she wasn't who she said she was.'

Eddie looked smug. 'I *knew* you'd ask her.' He leaned forward as he slid the pint Matt had offered him over to his side of the table, next to a glass that was still half full. 'And what did she say to that?'

Matt didn't particularly feel like sharing all the details with this man. But if he wanted to get anything out of him, he couldn't really afford to be evasive. 'She refused to explain. She just left.'

'Ah,' Eddie said, sitting back, satisfied with the answer. 'So she got found out, and she went running off. You've not seen her since?'

'No. I went to her flat, but she's already moved out.'

'You know where her flat is?' he cried. 'That's more than I knew.' He smiled a tight smile. 'Little slapper didn't take me back to hers. Always wanted to go to hotels. I should have realised then that everything wasn't as it seemed.'

'What wasn't as it seemed?'

The man appeared surprised, then amused. 'You still don't get it, do you?'

'Get what?'

Eddie shook his head in disbelief. 'You really don't get it – Catherine, Kirsten, whatever she decides to call herself, she's into deceit. She's a deceiver. You've been set up, my friend. All those wonderful times you've had together, the walks in the park, the fancy meals in lovely restaurants, the sex – it's all lies.'

Matt's eyes narrowed.

'You've been set up, like I was, like the rest of those poor bastards whose lives have been ruined by that woman. Entrapment, they call it, don't they?' He lifted up the newly bought pint and poured the contents down his throat in one. Matt didn't even see him gulp.

Eddie brought the now-empty glass down hard on to the table. 'And there it is, my friend, you've officially been screwed. Congratulations.'

'She sets up men?'

'Give the man a prize! Yes, my friend, she does just that. She destroyed my marriage, my life. My wife, she paid her to seduce me – can you believe that? *My own wife* paid another woman to sleep with me. And for what? To prove I wanted more than she could give me? My God, she could have just asked that, and I'd have told her straight. If she'd actually given a damn, she'd have realised that for herself. But no, she pays that slapper to seduce me and report back, and then – *bam!* – that's it, she has everything and I have nothing. All those years on the road spent selling crap, for what? To feather her nest and then be kicked out into the cold. Is it any wonder I'm drinking myself to death? But

I'll tell you what, when I die, I'm coming back to haunt the witch.' He now picked up his original pint and downed that, too. 'So, who was it in your case? The wife?'

If it was as the man said, then Beth seemed the only candidate. Who else was there? But Beth paying that woman to seduce him seemed nonsensical. She was in a new relationship, which seemed to be going very well. Why would she be bothered? It would have made sense if they had still been together, given Matt's infidelity, but why do it now?

Unless there was another motive.

Maybe Beth wanted evidence to undermine Matt's case as a trustworthy father, in the event of a custody battle for Charlie. But then, he wasn't doing anything wrong by dating Catherine, or whatever her real name was, given that his relationship with Beth was seemingly dead.

It just didn't make sense.

Eddie was still waiting for an answer. 'So, who was it?'

'I don't know,' Matt replied.

Eddie laughed in disbelief. 'You don't want to tell me. Fair enough – that's your choice. I don't really care, to be honest. You know, I'm surprised she's still at it. I thought I might have put her off, when I rumbled her. I tracked her down, you see. She thought she was too clever for me, that she was untraceable. Except she wasn't. She'd mentioned her local supermarket – probably didn't mean to, but I remembered.' He tapped a finger against the side of his forehead. 'I remembered, and when I needed that information, it was right there, ready to use.'

Matt wanted to leave now, but it was too early to extricate himself. And maybe there would still be some useful information to be had from this vile man.

'It took three visits, but on the third I saw her, at the top of the aisle. She didn't see me coming, and before she realised, it was too late. I hit her with both barrels. Told her exactly what she was – a prostitute.'

In other circumstances, Matt would have argued that point, but it really wasn't worth it.

'Anyway, I said she was lucky I wasn't the violent kind. You know – she should look out for who she screws with, because some men in my position would talk with their fists.'

Matt didn't particularly want to meet this man's gaze – didn't want to be part of this conversation. He looked off towards the side exit. Eddie noticed.

'You know, you should be thanking me!'

Matt resisted saying what he really wanted to say.

'If it wasn't for me, she'd still be playing you for a fool, my friend.' Eddie thought of something and his eyes lit up. He clicked his fingers. 'Or maybe that's why you're not too happy with me – I shattered your illusion, your dream. I bet you miss the sex, eh? Not getting much in the way of bedroom action with your missus?'

Eddie had finally overstepped the line.

'You don't know a thing about me.'

'I don't need to,' he replied. He went to take another drink, before realising both his glasses were empty. He looked at Matt and glanced down at the untouched pint.

Matt pushed the glass across to him. Eddie took it without a word and gulped down a large mouthful.

'You really should stop drinking so much,' Matt said.

Eddie shook his head. He held up the pint. 'It's the only thing I've got left. I've lost everything but *this*.'

'Your wife, she left you?'

'Oh yes, she did. She was just looking for an excuse to get me out of the way. That's what I think. Do you know, I was hardly out the door before she had another man in there – in her bed, no doubt. And you know, the guy, I knew him. Her friend's husband. They'd had dinners at our house, we'd been out for lunch, we'd even been on holiday together. And then he screws me, and he screws her. Can you believe that?' He shook his head, eyes burning with rage. 'She set me up and got just what she wanted. It was probably all planned, by the two of them.'

Matt couldn't help but see his own situation reflected in that story. But the idea that Beth had paid this woman to seduce him still didn't ring true.

'Have you tried to get help? You know, about the drinking.'

Eddie smiled tightly. 'Look, are you going to let me watch my TV and drink my beer?'

'Okay,' Matt conceded. 'I'll leave you be.' He got to his feet, wanting to encourage the man again to get help. But as he looked down at Eddie, surrounded by empty beer glasses, transfixed by the TV screen, he was lost for words.

CHAPTER
TWENTY-ONE

After returning from the bookshop, Rachel had spent the rest of the day in her flat with the outer door locked and the landline unplugged. She didn't want to stay there, but she was more scared of being outside. The night dragged, her sleep fractured by fearful thoughts.

In the morning she stayed hunkered down, feeling safer behind the locked door. She looked around the bedroom, which she had at least cleared following the break-in – the other rooms were still a mess. She thought about Jim.

Am I overreacting?

Maybe it wasn't Jim on the stretcher . . .

The man in the bookshop and the break-in – they probably have nothing to do with Alex's death . . .

How she wished she could talk to Michael. But he was still uncontactable. She'd left him a message on his mobile, telling him about the burglary, but had had no response. Surely he'd have picked up her message.

Where the hell could he be?

She stared at her mobile before finding the number for the Page One bookshop online. Before she could change her mind, she keyed in the number and waited for someone to pick up.

'Hello, Page One.'

Rachel recognised the voice. It was Joanna, Jim's shop assistant. They had spoken about their shared love of Emily Brontë on more than one occasion.

'Hi, I was hoping to speak to Jim.'

'Oh, I'm afraid he's not here right now. Can I take a message?'

Rachel cursed herself for not being more direct. 'Sorry. Is he okay?'

A pause. 'Is that Rachel?'

'Yes.'

'Sorry, Rachel, I wasn't concentrating. I'm really sorry, but Jim's in hospital.'

'What happened?'

'Heart attack. He just keeled over in the store. Fortunately, he was serving customers at the time and one of them was a nurse, so they looked after him until the ambulance arrived.'

Rachel *had* overreacted. There hadn't been any suspicious circumstances. 'How is he?'

'He's doing well. I heard from Marge this morning, and she says he's in good spirits.'

'Thank God for that.'

'I'm seeing him this afternoon. I'll pass on your best wishes.'

'Thank you. Just tell him I'm so pleased he's okay. And get well soon!'

'If you're free and would like to go, I know there's no one there with him for the first hour of visiting this evening.'

'Really?'

'Yes. I know he'd love to see you. He's at St Barts. Visiting starts at seven.'

'Thanks for letting me know.'

Rachel's spirits were lifted by the news that Jim was fine and that her paranoia had just been playing tricks with her mind. The relief galvanised her to tackle the rest of the house, although it was hard work, such was the chaos the intruders had left behind. She'd have to get someone in to fix the bathroom plasterwork and fit a new cabinet, but with some effort, she cleared the floor. The living room and kitchen were easier, and it felt good to get back to something like normal. She treated herself to an hour on the sofa enjoying an episode of *Blood Red Horizon*, the smash-hit Scandi crime drama.

By later that afternoon, she had decided that she would visit Jim in the evening. She really wanted to see him.

He watched her flat from across the street, leaning back against the wall as he lit a cigarette and took a long drag. With the other hand, he held the book he'd purchased at the weekend.

Brighton Rock.

He decided to stay for another half an hour. But if she didn't venture out, he was happy to come back tomorrow. And the next day.

He was being paid handsomely for his time, after all.

And it was worth waiting for just the right moment.

CHAPTER
TWENTY-TWO

Matt exited the Tube at Embankment and approached Eden. The domed forty-first floor, the top and most exclusive section of the skyscraper, was where Gabriel had chosen to meet.

Matt entered the building, all silver metal and mirrors, and checked in with reception. They had his name down on their electronic register. 'Welcome to Eden, Mr Roberts.' The glamorous-looking receptionist resembled one of Matt's colleagues, Michelle Lo, a very talented trader from Singapore. 'I can see from our records that it's your first time with us.' She smiled. 'I'm sure this will be the first of many visits. Please, the express elevators are over there to your right. You'll be heading for Floor 41. I'm sure you must have heard about how amazing the floor is. But it really has to be seen to be believed.'

'I've certainly heard good things.'

'If you want the best view, choose the elevator on the left.'

Matt followed her advice, watching as the doors slid shut. There were no buttons to press, because you couldn't choose your floor – that was done by the girl at reception. The tight control of visitors to Eden had fuelled rumours about what the owner, Australian billionaire Jerry Turner, was doing with the building.

The lift began its rapid ascent, and Matt was filled with awe at the view, despite the nerves he had about the meeting with Gabriel. Matt brushed down his dark grey suit collar and straightened his tie. He had dressed not to impress, but to fit in. The lift slowed to a stop and pinged as the doors slid open.

'Mr Roberts,' the awaiting attendant said, smiling politely. His accent was French. 'Welcome to Floor 41, the heart of Eden. Mr O'Connell is just on his way, so feel free to get a drink at the bar and explore the surroundings. Your table is ready, but you may wish to take some time to soak up the atmosphere.'

'Thank you.'

Matt took a few steps out of the lift, stunned by what he saw ahead of him. The lifts were at the highest point of the floor, along with a bar area. A terrace slightly further down housed the restaurant. Both of these high balcony levels looked out over what could only be described as a small forest, housed under the gigantic transparent dome.

Matt gripped the barrier that ran across the bar. The air was warm, but not uncomfortable. Up above, the blue sky seemed to wrap itself around the building, and the sun blazed. But the roof must have had some form of protective coating, because even with the full-on sun, it wasn't hard on the eyes.

'Matthew, so great to see you.'

Matt turned at the sound of the soft Irish lilt to see Gabriel O'Connell striding towards him, arms open wide in welcome. Gabriel patted him warmly on the shoulder in greeting, his glacial blue eyes examining Matt closely.

'You look well, Matthew. Very well indeed.'

'Thank you. I feel good.'

'Excellent,' Gabriel replied, giving a final pat. 'Now, come on, let's get to the table – it's got the best view in the place. You been here before?'

'No.'

'It's my sixth or seventh time,' Gabriel said, as they headed for the steps that led down to the restaurant. 'To be honest, the first time I was invited here, I'd convinced myself it was going to be so tacky that it would be my only visit. But it's just such an architectural triumph, and so immersive. The stream down there, it's heated and full of the most amazing range of tropical fish. You really need to go and take a look.'

'I will.'

'You know,' Gabriel added, 'I don't really like Jerry Turner, he's got an ego the size of Jupiter, and he can be a real pain in the rear, but he's really achieved something special with this.'

They were shown to their table overlooking the forest. They ordered – Gabriel had the crayfish, and Matt the steak – and made polite conversation, about sport mainly.

'So, Matthew, it's great news you've accepted my offer.'

'It was a very generous offer,' Matt said.

'Well, it's excellent news indeed. Excellent news. I couldn't be happier. We've missed you, Matthew.' Gabriel chewed on a morsel of crayfish and washed it down with some wine.

Matt's phone buzzed. He glanced at the screen from under the table. It was a text from Amy:

I told Harvey you were leaving. He quit the course.

'Everything alright?' Gabriel arched an eyebrow as he forked some green beans.

'Yes, fine. Fine.' But Matt felt sick to his stomach. He hadn't expected Harvey to quit like that. And he hadn't expected to feel so responsible and terrible for what had happened.

He tried to continue the meal with Gabriel watching on, but felt he needed some breathing space. 'I've just got to visit the bathroom.'

In the gents, Matt stared into the mirror, his hands flat against the sink. The doubt about his decision had been growing with every passing minute since receiving the text. He pulled out his phone and typed out a hurried message:

Don't worry Amy. I'll sort it.

He returned to the table, still dazed from the news about Harvey.

'Everything okay, Matthew? You not feeling well?'

'I'm okay.' And then, in the midst of his turmoil, it just came out. 'I was wondering whether it was possible to delay my return to work?'

Gabriel smiled tightly. 'I'm afraid not, Matthew. I really need you to accompany me to New York.'

Matt wanted to ask why someone else couldn't go instead, but that wasn't the way to get anything out of Gabriel O'Connell.

'Something has come up,' Matt said. 'Something that means I need to be around here for the next few weeks.'

'Something?'

'The college class I teach. They have an important assessment, and they need my support.'

Gabriel was impassive. 'But you knew this when you accepted my offer, did you not?'

'Yes, yes, I did. But I didn't realise how much it would affect the students if I left early.'

'I'm sorry, Matthew. It's either now or never.'

'One of the students, he's got so much potential. He's been in trouble with the police, but he wants to do well. I know he can do well, but I've just found out he's quitting the course because I'm leaving.'

Gabriel didn't appear to be paying attention. 'Waiter, can I have another glass of the white, please? Thank you.' He turned back to Matt. 'Look, Matthew, you can worry about other people, or you can worry about yourself.'

As Matt struggled within, Gabriel continued eating. Maybe if there hadn't been a vacuum of silence to fill at that precise moment, Matt would never have vocalised his innermost thoughts. 'I've decided to resign.'

Gabriel continued eating, not missing a beat. As Matt watched his boss act as if he hadn't even heard what he'd just said, he felt the need to elaborate.

'I won't be coming back. I'm sorry.' Matt had in no way planned to say those words, but somehow, from deep down, they had escaped. His first reaction was to correct himself, but now it had been said, there was a surprising feeling of liberation.

Gabriel placed his knife and fork on the table, and ran his tongue across his teeth. He dabbed at his mouth with a napkin as Matt's pulse quickened in anticipation.

'I didn't mean to pressure you, Matthew. I don't want to push you into doing something drastic – something you might regret.' Gabriel fixed his blue stare on him for a few seconds, before carrying on with his meal.

Matt didn't really know what to say. Then he just opened his mouth and it all came pouring out. He told Gabriel about his increasing doubts about a career in banking since the split from Beth, and how his recent experience with teaching had reignited something in him that he wanted to grab with both hands. Gabriel let him speak, without interrupting. He just kept eating and drinking, sometimes catching Matt's eye and nodding to reassure him that he was still listening.

Matt eventually stopped, waiting for Gabriel's reaction.

'Matthew. You need to do what you think is for the best. But,' he added, pointing at Matt with his fork, 'you know what they say – act in haste, repent at leisure. You're one of the best fund managers we have, and we want you back working for UGT. But if you walk away now, there will be no coming back.'

'I understand.'

'Good. So, my advice to you, Matthew, is to think this through some more.'

'I think I've made my—'

Gabriel held up a finger. 'Matthew, stop, please. Go home. Think things through some more. Sleep on it. Use that analytical mind of yours to come to a considered decision. Then give me a call and we can take things from there.'

Matt wanted to press home his point, but Gabriel had stood up, put his napkin down, and was already walking away from the table.

CHAPTER TWENTY-THREE

Rachel arrived at St Bartholomew's Hospital for seven o'clock on the dot. Jim was in remarkably good spirits for a man who had suffered a heart attack just a day before. He already had a stack of books by his bed.

'Thanks so much for coming, Rachel. It means a lot to me.'

They chatted for over an hour, before Rachel made a polite exit when the nursing round began.

It was on the dark journey home that Rachel began to feel uncomfortable. She sensed she was being followed.

What the hell is happening to me?

Once the thought was there, it proved impossible to banish it.

As the Tube train rumbled beneath the streets of London, she couldn't help but glance around at her fellow passengers in the packed carriage. Everyone was minding their own business. With a shudder, she thought back to the opening of *Brighton Rock* and the man with whom she had discussed it in Jim's bookshop.

The man, Hale, being pursued to his death among the crowds of tourists . . .

Again she looked around.

She reached King's Cross, the interchange for her onward journey via the Northern Line. The doors slid open and the masses disembarked, brushing past those passengers waiting to take their places.

Rachel stiffened as someone pressed up against her. But it was just an elderly lady, struggling with her case.

'Are you okay? Would you like some help?'

Rachel carried the case along the platform and down to the escalators. She watched as the lady ascended, before rejoining the continuous flow of people as they headed towards the Northern Line platform.

Helping the old lady had taken her mind off things, but now her fears about being followed resurfaced. It was as though she could feel a man's presence – the man from the bookshop.

I'm really losing it.

She glanced behind her as she emerged on to the northbound platform.

C'mon, Rachel, pull yourself together.

She looked up at the information board. There was a train in two minutes. The platform filled with people like a pool fed by a stream, as the time indicated just one minute until the train's arrival. People were pressing tighter against her from behind as she found herself moving towards the platform's edge.

There were people all around her.

And for a second she thought she saw him.

It's just my imagination . . .

The strengthening rumble and whoosh of warm air signalled the train's imminent arrival. As the front carriage emerged from the tunnel, its lights blazing, she sensed him right behind her.

As the train bore down, he pushed hard.

There was nothing she could do.

CHAPTER
TWENTY-FOUR

The first person Matt called as he left the building was Amy.

'I've quit UGT. Call off the search for my replacement. I also need a favour . . .'

Amy was stunned.

As Matt headed for the bus stop that would take him to Peckham, he tried to call Harvey.

No answer.

By the time the bus arrived, just gone eight o'clock, darkness had descended and the rain was falling. Matt sat back in his seat and watched London pass by through the rain-splashed window, not quite believing what he had said to Gabriel. He had finally done it. As lucrative as it might be, it was a future he had come to realise he no longer wanted.

The bus pulled up to a row of shops that his phone's GPS told him was the nearest stop to Harvey's place, the address of which Amy had provided him with. He jumped off the bus, dodging the oily puddles. Three roads on, and there was Empire Lane. The road was flanked by mid-rise blocks of flats, with drab concrete walls and walkways past the doorways. He found Harvey's block and made his way up to the third floor, passing through two sets of doors, the internal glass shattered from some kind of impact and the woodwork flaking.

Knocking on the door of Harvey's flat, Matt had no guarantee he would actually be at home. If he was, Matt had decided to do whatever it took to persuade him to return to college.

Harvey opened the door almost immediately, all designer gear as usual, his mouth opening in surprise as he realised who was standing there.

'Thought I'd come and see this flat of yours.' Matt tried a smile.

For once, Harvey seemed lost for words. 'Mr Roberts. Matt. I didn't expect to see you . . . Hey, come on in, please.' He beckoned. 'You don't want to be hangin' around that corridor. Not lookin' like that, man. C'mon in!'

Matt followed Harvey into the flat. The place actually looked really nice inside – not at all what Matt had been expecting. It seemed to have been recently refurbished, with a shiny wooden floor, dark furniture, and a lot of high-tech gadgets on display – stereo system, wireless speakers, laptop, and a huge flat-screen TV.

Matt wondered where the money had come from for all this stuff.

'Just got this the other day,' Harvey announced, seeming to read Matt's thoughts and pointing at the TV. 'Top of the range – 4K display, whatever the hell that means. Wi-Fi enabled so I can watch Netflix, YouTube, other stuff. Cinema surround sound, good bass. My neighbours have already been complainin'.' He grinned mischievously. 'Got it for quite a bargain.'

Matt just smiled and nodded.

Harvey jabbed at the remote control and the screen burst into life, illuminating the room more effectively than the ceiling lights. It was on a music channel and the bass boomed, but Harvey still turned the volume up several decibels for the demonstration.

'I'm gonna live, as hard as I'll die, always gotta try, reach for the sky. Boom!'

Matt tried to hide his embarrassment as Harvey acted out the chorus. 'Nice one.'

Harvey switched the TV off, plunging the room back into relative gloom. 'I'm gonna have some fun times with that baby. Hey, sorry, man, take a seat.' He gestured towards the black leather armchair. 'It does massage. You press one of those buttons on the controller by the side there and it vibrates.'

Matt took a seat. 'I'll probably give that—'

But Harvey had already reached out and turned the chair on. Ripples of movement rolled up from Matt's lower back into his shoulders, before beginning again, like breaking waves. It was pretty forceful, and not particularly relaxing – the armchair equivalent of an overenthusiastic, slightly sadistic masseur.

'Not bad, is it, bruv?' Harvey said, searching for a reaction. 'You'll feel that in the mornin'.' He turned it off, moving over to the window. 'These blinds, and the curtains, they're automatic. You control them from your phone.' He slid out his iPhone and tapped at the screen. The blinds swivelled left to close, and then the curtains swooshed across to meet in the middle. 'Cool, eh? I saw them on TV, one of them shoppin' channels. They do stick sometimes,' he said, watching as the curtains struggled to return back to the original open position. He tapped away more vigorously at the phone's screen. Finally, they moved again, and Harvey turned back around to Matt for the final verdict.

Matt gave him what he thought Harvey wanted. 'You've got some great stuff.'

Harvey beamed. 'Thanks, man. I do my best to buy the best.'

It sounded like a slogan. Matt could see the pride on his face, like a little boy wanting validation from his dad about a painting he had produced or a goal he had scored. This demonstration, it wasn't about showing off, Matt could see that. Harvey was looking for something deeper – he wanted recognition and positive feedback from someone whose opinion he valued.

'It's a lovely place,' Matt said, as Harvey continued to watch him. 'You've done a great job on it.'

Satisfied by Matt's reaction, Harvey relaxed and flopped down on the seat opposite. 'So, Matt, you really came to check out my flat?'

Matt shook his head. 'Amy texted me earlier this evening. Told me you'd quit the course.'

'Yeah, that's right.' Harvey shifted in his seat. 'You know, time for other things. Lots of things to do with my life.'

'But I thought this was your priority.'

He smiled. 'I have lots of priorities.'

'I just think it's a shame. Particularly because it's only a couple of weeks until the assessment, and you've been doing so well.'

He shrugged. 'I wouldn't have thought you'd care, man.'

'Of course I care.'

Harvey gave an almost imperceptible, dismissive shake of the head. 'You lookin' forward to New York?'

The question was an accusation.

'I'm not going. I quit the bank.'

Harvey's mouth hung open in shock. 'You're kiddin' me.'

'No, I'm serious.'

'But . . . why?'

'Because it's not what I want anymore. I'm not sure it's what I ever wanted.'

'Man, I did not see that one comin'.' Then realisation hit. 'Does that mean you'll be stickin' around then, at the college?'

'Yes.'

Harvey didn't react.

'Under one condition. If I go back, you go back.'

A smile curled Harvey's lips. 'Sounds like a deal.' He held out his ring-adorned hand and they shook on the promise. 'Good on you, man. You're a natural teacher.'

'Thanks. I'm from a family of teachers. It must have rubbed off.'

'School put me off teachin', big time,' Harvey said. 'My teachers, they were really down on me, man – they wrote me off, just like those other tutors. Used to tell me I'd end up as a nobody. Told me I'd probably end up in jail.' He looked away, deep in thought, then chuckled. 'I guess those bastards were right in that respect.'

'Never let anyone else define you,' Matt said.

'Your sister said that to me once,' Harvey replied. He smiled. 'You two share notes?'

'It was something our dad used to say,' Matt said sadly.

'Your dad sounds like a clever guy.'

'He was. He died.'

'I'm sorry.' Harvey filled the uncomfortable silence. 'So what changed? Why'd you go into bankin'?'

'I went to my old school for a week-long placement before starting uni. The first morning, I was in the staffroom when my old form teacher entered. When I told her I was planning to train as a teacher, she just said, "What a waste," and left the room.'

'And that changed your mind about your career? Never let anyone else define you,' Harvey joked.

'Glad to see you've been listening.'

'I always listen. Hey, man, I didn't ask you if you wanted a drink.' He sprang to his feet. 'Tea, coffee, whisky, beer? Unless you want to go out. There's a club just down the road. I can show you some of the sights on the way.' He seemed to read Matt's reticence. 'Don't worry, man,' he said, looking at Matt's suit. 'They won't think you're a copper or anythin'. No plain-clothes copper in their right mind would walk around this place in a suit.'

'Er, okay.'

'Great. And anyway, I wouldn't be hangin' around with no police. People see you with me, they'll probably think you're my lawyer or somethin'.'

'Accountant, maybe.'

'Exactly, man! You're my big-shot private accountant. I like that. Nice idea. If anyone tries to start somethin' with you, blind 'em with numbers, yeah? C'mon, bruv, let's go.'

◆　◆　◆

'So is this place as dangerous as its reputation?' Matt said, as they paced along the poorly lit street.

'Murder capital of the capital,' Harvey quipped, always scanning around, scrutinising everyone who walked towards them and everyone on the other side of the road. They passed closed betting shops, launderettes, grocers, and a surprising number of Internet cafes. 'But a lot of it is imported crime,' he added, narrowing his eyes at a group of men congregating across the road. 'The people who live here, a lot of them anyway, they don't get into no trouble. They just want to get on with their hard lives, do the best they can. It's those who come in, the gangs, they bring in the violence. The real London is ugly as hell. You wouldn't wanna see it.'

Matt watched Harvey as they strode on. This guy was warning him against seeing the ugly side of London. But surely Harvey was part of that underbelly. Or he had been up until very recently.

'Stop!' Harvey said suddenly, thrusting his arm, barrier-like, across Matt's chest to bring him to a dead halt. 'That group over there – I know them. We need to be careful.'

Matt glanced across the street. It was the group Harvey had been looking at just a few steps ago. They had now started to walk in parallel with Matt and Harvey, just behind them, on the opposite side of the road. There were five of them, all in their late teens or early twenties. All wore jeans and dark leather jackets. Matt's first thought was that they looked to be of Turkish background. They looked uninterested, but Harvey's reaction was telling.

Harvey turned his back on the group. 'Just wait here a few seconds, hope they move on. You don't want them to come over. If they start to cross the road, I got a plan. Just pray you never find out what it is.'

Matt was terrified, while Harvey looked like he was enjoying the brush with danger.

'Don't look at them,' Harvey instructed, as Matt's eyes darted across to the group. They'd drawn level now, still looking uninterested in anything but their own business. 'Get your wallet out.'

'What?'

'Your wallet, get it out, bruv.'

Matt hesitated. 'You're . . .'

Harvey's eyes were insistent.

'Okay,' Matt said, taking out his wallet.

'Pass me across some notes. It don't matter how much.'

Matt picked out a twenty and handed it to Harvey.

'Good man. Here you go.' Harvey placed a bag of white powder into Matt's hand, closing his palm over it before Matt could reject the swap.

Matt looked at Harvey for further instructions, shocked at what he had been left holding. Matt had never taken drugs, although he had seen cocaine more times than he cared to remember. Smoking and drinking to excess were frowned upon at UGT, but cocaine use was more than tolerated.

'Put the bag in your pocket,' Harvey said, his back still to the group. 'Don't worry, we'll swap back in a few minutes. Just as soon as those guys go. Are they movin' away?'

Matt ventured a look across. 'Yes. They're walking off now.'

Harvey smiled. 'Excellent. Now you continue off down the road. The club is just on the right: the Underground. I'll be along in a minute.'

CHAPTER
TWENTY-FIVE

Michael Thornbury stood in his flat, staring at the ringing phone.

Unknown number.

He let it ring another ten times before answering. He held the phone to his ear, not saying a word.

'Check out the news,' the voice said.

The call cut off.

That voice. It was him . . .

His hands shaking, Michael opened up the BBC News app on his phone.

The breaking-news headline was chilling.

'Please, God, no.'

He clicked on the story, then sank to his knees, and burst into tears.

CHAPTER
TWENTY-SIX

Matt continued along the road, leaving Harvey standing on the pavement. Despite himself, he ventured another quick glance at the gang of youths, who had stopped again, some way back along the road. None of them seemed to be looking in his direction. He already felt under threat, just being here, dressed like the City banker he used to be. It shocked him just how uncomfortable he could feel in the city he called home. This place certainly seemed like another world to the one he knew: unfamiliar and threatening.

The club was guarded by a doorman, a big black guy with a scrutinising stare. Matt smiled self-consciously at him, expecting to be challenged, but the bouncer pulled open the door without question, letting the throbbing music out into the street.

Inside the club, Matt looked around. If he had felt uncomfortable on the streets, that feeling was magnified several times in here. Off to the right was a smallish raised dance floor, crammed with gyrating men and women, with lights pulsing to the beat.

Matt couldn't see any other white faces. Or anyone else dressed like a banker. But no one seemed to care.

'What can I get you?'

Matt turned to the woman who had shouted the question. For a split second, he thought he was being propositioned, but then he noticed the 'Underground' motif on her black T-shirt. She watched for a response through unfeasibly long, jet-black eyelashes.

Matt peered over towards the bar area. Except there was no bar. It was just a counter.

'We don't have no bar,' she explained. 'Drinks are in the back. Orders are from the floor.'

Without any of the usual visual clues – beer pumps, bottles of spirits stacked along the back wall – his mind was a blank. Then he noticed that nearly all of the revellers were drinking the same – something from a yellow-and-black-striped bottle.

'I'll have one of those.'

She nodded. 'You know what it is, yeah?'

'Not a clue.'

She smiled. 'We've got lager too. Bud.'

'No, I'll have one of those.'

She slapped him on the arm. 'Good man. I'll be right back.'

Matt waited self-consciously, alone in the energetic crowd as a river of people flowed past him on either side. He glanced over at the door, wishing Harvey would appear and rescue him from his social discomfort. But there was no sign of him. Matt wondered why Harvey had stayed outside. Was he planning to challenge the gang, to tell them to get off his turf?

The music seemed to increase in volume as a new track kicked in. The dancers were really going for it, and the dance floor itself was spreading out as people joined in.

'Here you go,' the woman said, handing Matt the bottle. 'That'll be five pounds.'

Matt delved into his pocket, only then remembering he was in possession of a bag of Class A drugs. A wave of anxiety washed through him as he imagined an imminent police raid – being caught with cocaine would stop any teaching career dead in its tracks. He couldn't get rid of that bag soon enough.

Where the hell is Harvey?

Matt found a fiver, and the woman stuffed it into the back pocket of her jeans.

'You're Matt, aren't you?'

'Yeah, how did you—'

'Harvey just texted. Asked me to look out for you.'

'That was good of him.'

She thrust out a hand. 'My name's Harmony. Harmony Taylor. I'm Harvey's cousin.'

He took her hand. 'Matt. Matt Roberts. Lovely to meet you, Harmony.'

'I only work here a few nights a week for the extra money, and 'cos I enjoy the vibe. Mostly 'cos of the vibe, 'cos the money's pretty rubbish. I run a beauty salon, on the high street.'

'That's great.'

'My parents own the shop – it used to sell bread, milk, fags, booze. But they wanted to retire, and last year I pitched the idea of a salon. It's doin' really well. You have a wife, girlfriend who might be interested? I can do a good discount for friends of Harvey.'

As ever when there was a reminder that he was no longer with Beth, he felt both sick and sad. 'I'm on my own at the moment.'

'We do men's treatments too. Though it's mostly women. You interested?'

'Maybe.' Matt smiled, and took a first sip of his drink. He grimaced at the sour taste. 'What is this?'

She grinned, as if she'd been expecting this. Maybe that's why she was hanging around. 'Bitter lemon and vodka.'

Matt inspected the bottle for the first time. It was called 'Lemon Blast' and there was a picture of a beach flanked by palm trees. 'It's very lemony.'

'Very vodkary too,' she joked. 'Don't drink too many too quickly. I don't wanna be havin' to pick you up off the floor. And I'm tellin' you, you don't wanna be lyin' on that floor – I have to clean it, so I *know*.'

Matt was looking at the ingredients on the back of the bottle. As well as vodka and lemon, it was also part energy drink. He looked over again at the heaving dance floor, a mass of human movement. No wonder they could keep that up.

'I'd better keep workin',' Harmony said. She looked at the door, an unspoken thought playing on her mind. 'Hopefully he'll be here any minute. In the meantime, enjoy the music.'

And with that, smiling at him over her shoulder, she wove expertly through the people, almost dancing as she went.

Matt felt alone again, and his mind returned to the thought of the cocaine in his pocket. He thought about bailing – abandoning his drink, walking out and going home. He could give Harvey his drugs back another day. But just as he considered his options, a hand took hold of his and tugged him forward.

'This way!'

Matt was too surprised to resist the pull of the woman, who led him to the dance area. There she looped her arms around his neck, dancing seductively. 'C'mon, mister, show me what you can do!' she giggled.

Matt began to move in time with the woman, or at least made an attempt to. The dance floor was so full it was hard to step more than a few inches without risking treading on someone's toes. The woman fixed her wide eyes on his, and he smiled back uncomfortably.

Where the hell is Harvey?

'You're not too bad at dancin',' the woman said. She leaned in close to his ear. 'You're quite cute, you know,' she whispered, her breath making Matt's skin tingle excitedly. 'The name's Rochelle.'

Matt felt himself flush, but then a large figure loomed in from the left, pushing at Matt's chest.

'What the hell, man? What the hell you doin'?'

The guy pushed him again, and Matt fell back into some dancers as he was caught off balance. 'Sorry, sorry,' he said, as the dancers glared at him before they shifted away from the trouble.

The man took a step forward, right up into Matt's face. His nostrils were flaring, his eyes wide and zoned in on his target. 'I asked you a question, man. What you doin' with my woman?'

'Oh my days, Tyrone,' the woman pleaded over the music. 'It was nothin'. Just a bit of fun.'

'Shut up,' he said, dismissing her. 'I'll deal with you later. Now I deal with him.' He jabbed a finger into Matt's chest. It felt as though an instant bruise was blossoming at the point of impact.

'Please, Tyrone, don't do anythin' stupid. You remember what happened last time.'

Matt didn't want to find out what had happened last time, and he definitely didn't want a practical demonstration. He searched desperately for a way out. 'Look, I'm really sorry. I'd better be going now.' He moved to walk past and, to his surprise, the man let him pass. Matt didn't turn around, and he didn't run. He took care to maintain an even, relaxed pace as he picked his way through the crowd, towards the exit. He thought he caught a glimpse of Harmony watching him, off to the right, but he didn't look round to check. He reached the door and stepped out into the night air, nodding a goodbye to the doorman and thanking his lucky stars he'd got out of there.

Matt looked left and right, then across the road. There was no sign of Harvey. What the hell had happened to him? Deciding it was best to put some distance between himself and the club, Matt hurried down the street.

Maybe it was the noise of the traffic that muffled the footsteps of his pursuer.

A large hand gripped him tightly around the back of the neck and pushed him violently down the dark side alley he'd been so unfortunate as to be standing next to.

The man from the club spun Matt around and rammed him into the brick wall. A wave of pain reverberated around Matt's head. 'You still ain't answered my question, man.'

'Please, she led me to the dance floor. I didn't speak to her. I don't know who she is.'

The guy didn't seem interested in Matt's explanation. His aggression was growing, and any reasoning seemed futile. There seemed a certain inevitability about what was going to happen, as if it had already been written. 'D'you know who I am, man?'

Matt shook his head, scared.

The man smiled. He had a gold cap on one of his front teeth. 'No, didn't think so.'

Matt heard a flick, and with some terror, saw the blade of a knife.

CHAPTER
TWENTY-SEVEN

Catherine caught the tail end of the breaking news on the radio. A woman had fallen in front of a Tube train this evening at King's Cross.

It piqued her interest enough to search for the story online on her phone.

Details were still coming through, but the police weren't ruling out foul play. Several witnesses had reported a man fleeing from the scene directly after the woman had fallen on to the rails.

Detective Inspector Paul Cullen from the British Transport Police had said it was a miracle the woman had narrowly missed the approaching train. He appealed for more witnesses and asked the public to study a series of CCTV images of the person of interest.

Catherine scrolled through the images.

She caught her breath.

Could it be?

CHAPTER TWENTY-EIGHT

Tyrone moved in even closer. Matt could smell alcohol and tobacco on his breath, could feel the man's spittle land on his own face as he said words that, in his horror, Matt could no longer hear. As if he was some kind of backstreet barber, the man brought the blade up against Matt's cheek and traced its cold edge along the side of his face. Matt screwed his eyes shut, trying desperately to think of a way out of this. Maybe Tyrone's girlfriend would follow him out of the club and plead with him to stop. But surely she'd be here by now. Maybe the guy was just trying to scare him. Maybe he wouldn't use the knife.

'I'm wonderin' just how much to cut you up.'

'Please, please, I'm sorry.' Again Matt ran through the options he had. Tyrone was standing really close – it might be possible to bring a knee up to his groin, inflict just enough damage for Matt to break free and flee for his life. But that was a high-risk manoeuvre. If it didn't come off, it would just make things worse.

But can things get any worse?

And then came an alternative idea.

'Harvey,' he spluttered, as the blade toyed with the soft skin underneath his chin. 'I'm a friend of Harvey Taylor.'

The man laughed. 'Shit, man. This just gets better. You his lawyer or somethin'?'

Matt shook his head. He longed for the blade to be removed. 'No, no. His teacher.'

Tyrone laughed again. 'Well, if there's one thing I hate more than Harvey Taylor, it's teachers. Made my life a misery, man. So thank you for making this all the sweeter.'

He withdrew the blade and slipped it back into his trouser pocket. Confused, Matt allowed a shaft of optimism to pierce the darkness. But that soon slipped away as the man turned briefly to his right, before winding up and letting fly with a crushing hammer-blow of a punch to Matt's abdomen. Matt opened his mouth, but nothing came out. He had never been hit so hard. He folded towards the ground, but was pulled back upright by his hair.

'Stay standin'. You're gonna take this like a man, you son of a—'

Tyrone didn't get to finish his sentence. From the darkness, a fist crashed into the side of his head, sending him staggering sideways in shock and pain.

'What the—'

Harvey closed the gap between them, and in one swift movement grabbed the man and threw him into the wall opposite. He hit the brickwork face first, almost bouncing off the surface. Harvey delivered another punch to Tyrone's head and swept his feet from underneath him. Matt watched, frozen to the spot, as Harvey kicked Tyrone several times in the gut. The man, so powerful just a few seconds ago, was curled up on the floor in the foetal position, begging for his life and holding a busted, bloody nose.

Harvey wiped his mouth and jabbed a finger down at him. 'Next time you mess with one of my friends, I'll kill you. You understand?'

Tyrone mumbled something.

Another kick, this time to his back. 'You understand?'

'Yes, yes!'

'Good.' Harvey turned to Matt. 'C'mon, let's go.'

Matt followed Harvey, but paused at the corner to check on Tyrone. He was still lying on the ground, but thankfully he was moving. Matt didn't want to think that this man, whatever he had been intending to do, would be anything more than temporarily hurt.

'C'mon,' Harvey repeated, pulling at Matt's shoulder. 'He'll be fine.'

Matt resisted the pull, still watching the man on the floor. 'How can you be sure? He might need medical attention.'

'*Matt.* Trust me. He'll be fine. If I'd have wanted to really hurt him, I'd have really hurt him.'

Matt nodded, and followed Harvey back around the corner. He was surprised when he was led back to the club. He just wanted to get away and get out of this place.

'Do you think this is a good idea?' Matt said, hanging back from the entrance as the doorman studiously ignored them. Given what had just resulted from his first visit, it wasn't a place he particularly wanted to return to.

Harvey moved back from the doorway and placed a hand on Matt's shoulder. 'It'll be fine, Matt, I promise.'

'But what if he comes back?'

Harvey laughed. 'Tyrone? Nah, man, he won't be back tonight.'

'You can't be sure though.'

'Oh, I can. He won't be back tonight.'

Harvey's certainty didn't have the desired soothing effect.

'I'm just not sure—'

'Trust me, man,' Harvey said. 'You said you believe in me. Prove it. I wouldn't take you back in there if I thought you'd be in any danger. In fact, it's probably the safest place for you.'

'Okay then,' Matt said, his resistance crumbling in the face of Harvey's insistence.

'Great, man!'

Matt followed Harvey through the door, but not without taking one last quick glance back down the road, in case Tyrone was following. Thank God, there was no one.

The place was still in full party mood, and Harvey seemed to inhale the atmosphere like a drug. 'People!' he shouted. 'A big welcome back to my good friend Matt, who successfully fought off a cowardly attack by the one and only Tyrone Edwards!'

Harvey pointed theatrically at him with both hands, and Matt wanted to curl up and die as half a dozen people turned to look at him.

'This is the main man, people!' Harvey shouted, bouncing up and down on the spot. 'Bow down to him!'

Matt caught a glimpse of Harmony, watching from the far side of the room. And then he felt a push in his back.

It was Rochelle, angry and agitated. She pushed him again, forcefully. Matt knew this had been a bad idea. He should never have listened to Harvey.

'Hey, what the hell have you done with Tyrone?'

Matt made to speak, but she wasn't ready to let him.

'Tell me what the hell you've done to him.'

'I—'

'Hey, Rochelle,' Harvey interjected. 'Cool it down, babe. Tyrone's fine. Nothin' that some superglue and a few dozen stitches won't sort out. You weren't plannin' on motherin' his children any time soon, were you?'

She turned on him. 'You better not have hurt him.'

''Course I did, sis, but only as much as I needed to.'

Matt wondered if he'd misheard the word with all the noise.

Rochelle is his sister?

Rochelle folded her arms across her chest, her lips twisting in anger. 'Where is he?'

Harvey pretended to think. 'Last time I saw him, he was on the floor in the alley next to the club.'

'Why, Harvey, why?' she cried. 'I know you and Tyrone don't get on, but why do that?'

''Cos he was about to cut my friend here. Look, Tyrone'll be fine. He's a big boy. I just did enough to protect my man. Have you met Matt?'

Matt smiled tightly, feeling the dictionary definition of uncomfortable.

'Yeah, briefly,' she replied. She looked Matt up and down, her face like stone.

'Matt's one of my teachers at college. I thought I'd show him some of the local sights.'

'Lucky him,' Rochelle deadpanned. 'Look, I'd better go and see how Tyrone is. Nice to meet you, Mr Teacher.'

'No,' Harvey said, reaching out. 'Don't go out there alone. Wait for me. I'll take you back to the flat, make things right with Tyrone.'

She smiled in disbelief and tried, unsuccessfully, to brush him off.

'I mean it, Rochelle. I don't want you goin' out there on your own. It's not safe.'

She fixed him with a hard stare. 'Why not?'

'I can't tell you, but just trust me, okay?'

'What you been doin'?'

'Rochelle,' he rebuked. 'Stay in the club . . .'

'But what about—'

'Call him if you wanna check he's okay. Tell him you'll be home in an hour, and that I'll be bringin' you back.'

She nodded. 'Okay.'

'Good decision.'

'Harvey, you said you'd stop gettin' involved in all that stuff.'

'I have, sis. I have,' he soothed. 'Don't worry.'

She looked unconvinced. 'I'll call Tyrone now. Nice to meet you, Matt. You watch that brother of mine, won't you?'

'I will,' Matt said, as Rochelle turned to head back towards the dance floor.

'C'mon, Matt, my man. Let's go upstairs.'

CHAPTER
TWENTY-NINE

The room was at the top of a dark wooden staircase. Overlooking the high street, it contained a round wooden table with eight chairs around it. The air smelled of stale smoke, and the deep bass was thumping through the floor from below.

'This is where the games are played,' Harvey explained. 'Poker mostly.'

Matt moved over to the large window that spanned the length of the room. He leaned against the windowsill, and gazed down at the peeling white paint that came off on his fingers as he tried to steady himself. Just a few short hours ago, he had been dining in one of the most exclusive restaurants in London, and now here he was, drugs in his pocket and a victim of assault.

What the hell am I doing here?

'You wanna drink?'

Matt was still lost in thought.

Harvey moved across to him. 'Hey, Matt, you okay?'

Matt clawed at his neck as he flashed back to the cold, razor-sharp blade tracing along his skin. 'Just a bit shaken. What would he have done if you hadn't come along?'

'I think he was just tryin' to scare you.'

'He succeeded.'

'Tyrone is an idiot. Still can't believe he's datin' my sister. But Rochelle has always liked bad boys.'

Matt couldn't help but see the irony. 'Have you fought with him before?'

'Loads of times. I can't see us makin' peace anytime soon, if he goes round threatenin' my friends.'

That word. *Friends.* Did Harvey really see Matt and him as friends?

'Rochelle seems like a nice girl.'

'She's nice, but she's sometimes her own worst enemy. See, tonight, like, I know what happened. Rochelle came on to you, started flirtin', usin' those hips, gettin' in close on the dance floor. Am I right?'

Matt flushed. 'I didn't do anything.'

'I know *that.* Don't worry, Matt, I'm not accusin' you of nothin'. I *know* what happened, 'cos it's happened before. Rochelle and Tyrone. They have one hot relationship, man. They fight a lot. He tries to control her, and she rebels.'

'So she was trying to make Tyrone jealous?'

'Her way of makin' a point.' Harvey set down two tumblers and filled them about three fingers deep with whisky. 'Get that down you. Help you get over the shock, bruv. I promise it'll do the trick.'

Matt took a sip. It was good stuff, warming the length of his throat like honeyed molten lava.

'So, what d'you think of the club?' Harvey asked, pulling out a chair and sliding into the seat. Matt joined him at the table.

'It's a great place.'

'My uncle owns it.'

That explained how Harvey had been able to commandeer the upstairs room without any question.

'Yeah, my Uncle Robert, he's one cool guy. He's actually more like a dad to me. When my real dad ran out, he did a lot for us. And he's always supported me. I'll have to introduce you to him some day. He's on holiday right now. I can introduce you to his daughter though, my cousin. She works here, and she's on tonight.'

'Harmony?'

'You already met? I did text her to look out for you. She gave you a friendly welcome, yeah?'

'She did. To be honest, if it wasn't for her, I might have turned around and walked back out the door.'

Harvey smiled, circling the top of his glass with his index finger. 'That's how I felt on that first night at college – right out of place. I was about to go when Amy talked to me. Don't tell her this, but Harmony, she's one of the reasons why I went for the college programme. I saw what she's done with her life. She's only young, man – nineteen – but, like, she's runnin' her own business.'

'It made you want to succeed in other ways?'

'Yeah, it did.'

Matt thought of something that had been troubling him. 'You warned Rochelle not to leave the club on her own. Said it was dangerous.'

Harvey just watched him.

'You said something similar to me – that it was safer inside the club than outside. What did you mean?'

'These streets can be dangerous, man.'

'But it felt like there was something specific.'

Harvey slugged back a finger or so of whisky.

'Is it Tyrone, or his friends?'

Harvey laughed at the suggestion.

'Or that group of men who were eyeballing us from across the road?'

Harvey bristled ever so slightly. 'Why you bothered?'

Matt gulped back his nerves. 'You realise what you did out there – to Tyrone – it could ruin everything for you.'

Harvey smiled ruefully.

Matt ploughed on. 'I know what it says in the good behaviour contract you signed with the college.'

Harvey glanced at the window, then fixed Matt with a hard stare. 'You won't tell Amy, will you? I did that to protect you. D'you think Amy would've wanted her brother cut up in a dark alley?'

Matt admired the way Harvey had tried to reframe the discussion. 'What did you do, when you told me to go into the club?'

'No comment, Your Honour. Look, Matt, what's this all about?'

And now for the real thing that had been pricking at him for the past few days. 'The other night, at college. What was in your bag?'

Harvey stared back at him, unmoving. 'Why d'you ask?'

Would it really be wise to admit that he'd looked inside his bag?

Harvey raised his eyebrows in challenge.

'It doesn't matter,' Matt said.

Harvey shook his head. 'I should probably say "none of your business", but what the hell. Knives. The bag was full of knives.' Harvey waited for a reaction. And when he didn't get one, he continued. 'Well, aren't you gonna ask me why I was carryin' a bag full of knives?'

Matt had lost the stomach for this conversation. But Harvey pressed on.

'The knives are mine. *Was* mine. A collection I'd built up over the past six, seven years. I handed them all in.' He downed his drink. 'There's an amnesty runnin' at the moment across the city. Part of Operation Blaze – targetin' knife crime. There are secure sites where you can drop weapons, no questions asked. I was meant to go there before college, but I missed my bus so I had to rush to class with all that stuff in my bag. A bit dumb, really.'

'So you've given away all your weapons?'

'I told you already, bruv. I've decided to take another path in life.'

'But you're still engaged in violence.'

'Shit, man. I'm tryin' my best. We can't all be perfect, Matt.'

'I'm far from perfect.'

'Oh, really?'

Matt gazed into his whisky glass, watching the amber ripples on the surface. 'My dad died of a massive heart attack two years ago. I could have prevented it.' He downed the rest of his drink. 'I'd been really busy at work that week, trying to impress the bosses. I knew Dad had tried to call a few times the previous day, but I assumed it wasn't anything important. I hadn't stopped to check whether he'd left any messages on my voicemail.'

'But he had?'

'Yes. Two messages, which I only picked up while we were at the hospital. In the first message, he said he'd been having chest pains while he was out walking in the park that morning. He wanted to ask whether he should mention anything to Mum – he was afraid he might worry her unnecessarily, and she's always been a big worrier. The second call he made at ten past seven. I was still in the office, completing a trade, and I missed the call somehow. He said the chest pains had come back again, and he was scared it might be something serious. He asked me again whether he should bother Mum. But he never got an answer, and he never told my mum. If I'd spoken to him, things would've been different. He would've got help sooner, and he'd probably be alive today.'

'You shouldn't blame yourself, man. I'm sure your mum don't.'

'She doesn't know about the messages. I never had the courage to admit what happened. I haven't told Amy either.'

'I can understand that.'

'If I'd been honest, then maybe things wouldn't have turned out the way they did. But keeping the secret, it turned me into something bad. I grew to hate myself, hate what I'd done, and I pushed everyone who cared about me away. They wanted to help, but I wouldn't let them because I was afraid they'd find out what I'd done. It was the same with Adam's death. He was a junior employee at UGT who I'd taken under my wing – died at a party after taking drugs. I blame myself for that too.'

'That's heavy stuff, man.'

Matt smiled sadly. 'And then I betrayed my family. Cheated on my partner Beth with a work colleague.'

'A one-off?'

'Yes. There was an office party.'

'But she found out?' Harvey shook his head. 'Man, you must be one careless mother.'

'I told her.'

'Really? You wanted your relationship over?'

'Not at all. It was the last thing I wanted. But the guilt was destroying me.'

'She didn't forgive you?'

'No.'

'Harsh, man. I mean, people make mistakes.'

'She had good reason.'

'Like what? You got a kid, haven't you? Surely for their sake.'

'Her father was a serial adulterer. He cheated on his wife multiple times, throughout a thirty-year unhappy marriage. She did it to protect herself – and more importantly, our son Charlie.'

'But you're not her father. Just because you made one mistake, it don't mean you'd do the same again.'

'She said she couldn't take the chance.'

'So that was it?'

'Yes, that was it. Eighteen months ago. She gave me two hours to clear my stuff and leave.'

'Shit. You don't think she'll ever forgive you?'

'Maybe. But it won't get me my family back.'

'How can you know?'

Matt smiled tightly. 'Beth is in another relationship now.'

'Who is he?'

'James Farrah. He works at the same place I work – well, used to work.'

'That must hurt, bruv.'

'It does.'

'So when did he and Beth start their relationship, if you don't mind me askin'?'

'A year ago.'

'Only six months after you split? Man, that's painful. You sure he's not just a rebound? Or maybe she's tryin' to make you jealous?'

'I'd like to think so, but no. It's serious.'

'How d'you know?'

'Because they plan to move to Australia together.'

'No way! But what about you and your son? Surely she can't do that – move to the other side of the world with your kid?'

'I have to agree.'

'You gonna say no though?'

'I'm not sure what I'm going to say.'

Despite his feelings, Matt now didn't know if he was capable of blocking something that Beth wanted to do.

'But they've only been goin' out for a year. Seems a bit radical.'

'They've got a history. Her brother was at university with James, and they now work together.'

'You think she always wanted to be with him?'

'I don't think so.'

Harvey pointed his empty glass at Matt. 'Don't give up, bruv. Don't give up on gettin' your family back.'

Matt could feel himself cracking under the strain. He shook his head. 'I think it's too late. I need to let Beth go.' He got to his feet. 'Speaking of which, I think I'd better leave. If the streets are too mean, maybe you can call me a cab.'

Harvey nodded, although he looked disappointed that the discussion was being curtailed. 'Sure thing. A friend of the family has a taxi company, just around the corner from here.'

Matt stood up, feeling disconcertingly unsteady on his feet from too much whisky. 'Thank you for the chat.'

'No, thank *you*, bruv.'

'For what?'

'For not tellin' the college about my knife collection. I saw you open the bag, when I was on the phone.'

'But you didn't say anything.'

'I wanted to see what you did.' Harvey waited several beats. 'Why didn't you tell someone?'

'I'm not sure. I guess I just wanted to give you a chance.'

'A chance to explain myself?'

'No, a chance to succeed.'

'And what about tonight? Are you gonna tell anyone at the college about what happened?'

Matt shook his head.

'Thanks, man. I really appreciate it.'

'Don't mention it.' Then Matt remembered, and pulled out the bag of cocaine from his pocket. 'You'd better have this back.'

CHAPTER THIRTY

Harvey watched as Matt pulled away in the taxi. 'Stay safe, bruv.'

He made to turn, but walked straight into the man who had come up behind him.

'Harvey, we need to talk.'

Harvey pushed down hard on his fear. 'No, man, we don't.' He tried to get past, but there was no way through.

'We need to talk,' the man repeated. 'About how you can help us.'

CHAPTER
THIRTY-ONE

'Matt, I didn't expect to see you. C'mon in.'

Matt followed Beth through into the living room. It had just gone ten in the morning. He had chosen this time because Charlie would be at school, and he didn't want the little guy around while he said what he was planning to say.

It would have just made it harder.

'Sorry for the mess,' Beth said, directing her comment at the stacks of clothes that were draped over the sofa. 'I'm in the middle of ironing. Trying to get it done before I go and pick Charlie up this afternoon.'

'It's okay, I won't keep you long.' Matt stifled a yawn, quite exhausted from the events of the previous evening.

'Oh no, I wasn't hinting or anything like that.' Beth blushed. 'You can stay as long as you like. Maybe you could even help?'

Matt appreciated the smile between them.

'Would you like a drink? Tea?'

Matt nodded, and Beth went to fill the kettle. He followed her into the kitchen. 'I've been thinking. About Australia.'

Beth paused, teabag in hand.

Matt swallowed down his reticence to release the words. 'I've been selfish, Beth. I don't want to be the one who stops you from doing what you really want to do. So I won't stand in your way.'

Beth still had the teabag dangling over the pot. She seemed troubled – or maybe sad.

'Well, that's . . . really good of you, Matt.' Finally, she mustered a smile. 'Thank you, Matt.' She walked over, brushed her cheek against his, and kissed him gently. When they parted, their faces were close, her eyes searching his. 'Are you sure?'

'I'm sure.' Matt tried to smile, but it faded fast. 'I can make sure I FaceTime with Charlie every week.' He bit into the inside of his cheek in an effort to stop his emotions getting the better of him.

Beth could sense his pain. 'You can visit. Whenever you like. We'll have a spare room, so you'll be right there, with Charlie.'

'That would be good.'

'I know how hard this is for you, Matt. I'm sorry.'

Matt shrugged. 'I know it's what you want to do. James told me you persuaded him to go for the move.'

'James told you that?'

'When I visited the office.'

She looked embarrassed. 'Well, that's not—'

'It's okay,' he said.

She was thinking out loud. 'Maybe UGT will grant you some extra leave to come over to visit for a few weeks – particularly as it's because of them that you'll be away from Charlie?'

'I don't work for them anymore,' Matt said. 'I quit – yesterday, during dinner with Gabriel. I'm not going back there.'

Beth seemed thrown. 'So what are you going to do?'

'Teach. I've decided I'm going to retrain. Probably start a course this coming September. In the meantime, I'll continue working at the college, on the financial management course.'

There was a pause as Beth reflected on the news. 'Well, that's great, if that's what you want to do. I'm proud of you, Matt, I really am.'

Beth was still smiling as she went back to making the tea.

'Look,' Matt said, 'there's something else. Something I should have told you when it first happened. Something happened at the swimming pool on Sunday. I lost Charlie.'

The smile was gone. 'You lost Charlie . . . ?'

'Just for a few minutes. He was using the slide, and I let him go back around there on his own. But he needed the toilet and just went off to find it without telling me. I alerted the staff, and someone found him in the ladies' loos and took him to one of the lifeguards.'

Beth looked sick. 'You should've told me at the time.' She shook her head. 'Anything could have happened.'

'But it didn't. That's the most important thing.'

She nodded at that, holding her tongue, but she still looked angry.

'I thought Charlie might have mentioned something to you already.'

'No. Nothing.' She thought for a second. 'Why tell me now?'

He was about to tell her about Catherine. About the man who had claimed she wasn't who she said she was. About the fact that she had moved out of her flat in haste after being challenged. About the fact that she had been the one to find Charlie, and how her presence at the leisure centre was troubling.

And then the cryptic response as she walked away.

Everything I've done, it's for your own protection.

But he didn't say any of it. Because he still couldn't make sense of it himself. And if he couldn't, then how could he possibly explain it to Beth?

'I told you now because you deserve to know.'

Surprisingly that brought back a smile, albeit one tinged with a lingering sense of anxiety. She reached for his arm and held him for a few seconds. 'Thanks, Matt. I really appreciate your honesty.'

◆　◆　◆

Matt sat at the kitchen table, his hands curled around a cup of tea. He'd returned from another successful teaching session – the best part of which was Harvey's presence. Both Harvey and he had kept their word and returned to the course.

Amy had been delighted. And it had felt good to be in the classroom. Good to know that this was his future – not a stopgap, but something he wanted to pursue.

But could there be a bright future, if the two people he cared about the most weren't going to be a part of it?

Matt pondered on Harvey's words of the previous day, about not giving up on his family.

And yet he had given Beth the green light for Australia.

He pulled out his mobile phone, but just as his fingers hovered over Beth's number, he looked at the wall clock. It was half past midnight. Calling at that time wouldn't go down well. It would make him look deranged, for a start. And it would only serve to push his family further away.

Instead, he checked his email. There was a message from Gabriel. It was brief but to the point:

> *Dear Matt. Call me if you change your mind. It's a*
> *lot to throw away. Think carefully. Best. Gabriel.*

Matt was so deep in thought about Gabriel's message that he almost missed the most important email.

It was from Catherine.

CHAPTER THIRTY-TWO

Matt approached the Serpentine, the lake in Hyde Park where Catherine had said she'd meet him. He couldn't see her and thought of reaching for his phone. But she'd warned him not to contact her. So instead he found a spare bench and sat down, watching the crowds stroll and roll past.

'Hi, Matt.'

She'd approached without him realising.

'Hi,' he said, shielding his eyes against the strengthening sun.

She joined him on the bench, but didn't look too comfortable. 'How are you?'

'Not bad. And you?'

'I really don't know.' She looked washed out, devoid of her usual energy, and the bright smile was missing.

'You said you were going to tell me everything.'

She nodded. 'My real name is Natalie – Natalie Austin.'

So Eddie was right in that respect.

'I've got a quite unusual job,' she continued. 'I'm . . . well . . .'

'You entrap men.' It sounded like an accusation, and Natalie took it as such, reddening ever so slightly.

'I find out the truth for my clients,' she corrected. 'I expose liars and cheats.'

Matt wanted to ask a thousand questions, but let her continue.

'I didn't plan for it. I was at university in Sheffield, studying psychology, when one of my classmates asked me to do them a favour. They'd been seeing a guy since first year, captain of the rugby team. But there were these rumours that he was sleeping with other girls. We got chatting over coffee one afternoon, and she asked me if I'd test out his resolve. I said no at first, but then I decided to help her out. I thought it might be fun, and it was, to be honest.'

'So you proved he was being unfaithful?'

'Yes. It was pretty easy. I seduced him on the dance floor during one of the athletics union club nights. The girlfriend dumped him the next day.'

'So he knew he'd been set up?'

'No. She never told him why. He begged her not to leave him. But she told him he'd started to bore her. She really knew how to hit him where it hurt – right in his ego.' Natalie smiled at the thought. 'That's when I realised how satisfying it was, helping people in that way. So I started to investigate, and I found out there were agencies who employed people to do what I'd done. It got me some extra money for that last year at university.'

'Seems like a strange way for a student to earn extra money.'

'You think? Haven't you heard what some students get up to these days to pay the bills? The escort business, and worse,' she said. 'There's a big market out there for pretty university girls. I see my job as a way for women to take back control. After university, I moved to London and it became my full-time occupation.'

Matt wondered what Natalie really thought of him, a man who had cheated on his long-term partner. 'So the man in the pub . . .'

Her jaw tightened. 'Two years ago, his wife got in contact with the agency I was working for, said she suspected he'd been having affairs for years. He was a salesman, travelled a lot. Turns out his wife was right. They almost invariably are – most women know when their man's being unfaithful. They come to people like me partly in the hope that I might prove them wrong, but it never really works like that.'

'That guy, he was pretty bitter. He found out about you, didn't he?'

'Yes. His wife told him everything. And unfortunately, he tracked me down.'

'He told me.'

She grimaced at the thought. 'I mentioned during one of our meetings about shopping at the local Waitrose. It was a slip, really. He found me and accosted me in one of the aisles. Bawled at me. Thankfully that was the last I saw of him. I changed where I shopped, and I was more careful from then on. I'd learnt a hard lesson.'

'Does it not worry you that you're putting yourself in danger?'

'I never saw it like that. Well, not until recently,' she added cryptically.

'His wife left him with nothing.'

She shrugged. 'He deserved it. Brought it on himself.'

'Everyone can make a mistake.'

She turned to him. 'Multiple affairs over years isn't a mistake, it's a conscious choice – an intentional decision to deceive the one who loves and trusts you. I do my job to help those who are being deceived.'

'And what about with me? You said what you've been doing, it's for my own protection. What did you mean?'

Natalie glanced around, eyeing those passing by. 'Normally I stick to the same type of job. From the very beginning, I've always been commissioned by a woman through an agency, and the task has pretty much been standard. I've been very careful not to stray from what I know, what I'm comfortable with. With you it's different.'

'In what way?'

'First of all, the job isn't through an agency. It's for a friend of a friend. And secondly, it wasn't about you being faithful or not.'

'Go on . . .'

Another glance around. 'I was told to get close to you, and stay close to you. But my job is – was – to look out for you, to make sure if I saw anything unusual, to report it back.'

'Anything unusual?'

'People following you, any suspicious activity, things like that.'

'People following me?'

'Yes.'

'But why would people be following me?'

'I don't know.'

Matt shook his head. 'Who asked you to do this?'

'I'm sorry, I can't say.'

'Can't or won't?'

'I never reveal the identities of my clients. These people trust me.'

'I thought you might be a stalker.'

'I'm afraid I wasn't as good at staying out of sight as I'd have liked. Like I said, this isn't my usual line of work.'

Matt thought some more. 'The person who asked you to do this, they didn't give you any indication of why I might need protecting?'

'No. I was told as much as I needed to know,' she explained. 'To be honest, I don't know the identity of the person who paid for me to do this. They went through my friend as an intermediary. But as I said, even if I did know, I couldn't tell you.'

'Then why are you even telling me this? Why not just walk away?'

'That was the plan. As soon as the guy blew my cover in the pub, I decided that was it. I called things off.'

'And you cleared out of your flat. Very quickly.'

'Yes. I made a big mistake with you a few weeks ago.'

'You took me back to the flat.'

She nodded. 'It was just after that lovely night out, in town, and we were both a bit tipsy. I kind of forgot what this was all about. We'd been spending so much time together, it surprised me how much I'd started to care for you and Charlie. I really didn't plan for it to happen like that, believe me.'

Matt was still processing the earlier revelations. 'So, you decided to clear out of the flat, because you knew I'd probably come looking and asking questions.'

'Partly.' She hesitated. 'I really regretted accepting this job. Even before what happened in the pub, I was torn about whether to just back out. I'm not used to dealing with this kind of thing.'

'What kind of thing?'

She shrugged. 'I don't know. Danger. I started freaking out about what I'd got myself into. I thought there might be people hanging around outside the flat. One night there was a guy sitting across the road, looking up at my window. Or at least it looked like he was. It really spooked me.'

'So you moved out because of that?'

'That was a large part of the reason. I wanted to make a fresh start.'

'But you didn't.'

'No. I tried, but I couldn't. I just couldn't walk away. I was genuinely worried about you.'

'So you kept following me.'

'Yes. It's obviously become more difficult, now we aren't seeing one another.'

'Are you still being paid to do this?'

'No. They cancelled the job.'

'So you're still involved because you're worried about me. And yet you won't tell me who asked you to do this.'

'I told you, I don't know who was paying me.'

'You know what I mean. Your friend, the go-between – you won't reveal their identity, even if it might help me to work out what the hell is going on.'

'I'm sorry, Matt.'

Matt felt like smacking the arm of the bench in frustration. 'What happened at the swimming pool?'

'I'd been following you since early morning – tailed you to Beth's. And then on to the leisure centre.'

'You were in the pool when Charlie went missing? Where exactly were you?'

'On the far side of the pool. I'd been watching you at the slide.'

'How did you come to find Charlie?'

'I was watching when he went around to the slide and then got out of the pool.'

'And you followed him?'

She was already reddening. 'Yes. I wanted to make sure he was okay.'

'But you could have come and told me.'

'Yes, I could have.'

Matt blinked as the anger bubbled within. 'Those few minutes, when I'd lost Charlie, they were the most frightening minutes of my whole life.'

Natalie looked away. 'I can imagine.'

Matt shook his head. 'You don't know what it's like to be in that situation, do you?'

'Look, Matt, I can totally understand how angry you must be feeling. Anger at me. I can totally see that. But I didn't want to let Charlie out of my sight. If I'd gone to tell you, then we'd both have lost him. I couldn't risk that.'

'What happened then?'

'I got out of the pool as quickly as I could, just in time to see Charlie turn towards the toilets. I didn't want to scare him, so I didn't call out or anything. When I saw him push open the door to the ladies, I followed him inside. He'd entered one of the cubicles and was trying to lock the door. There was no one else in there at the time, so I waited until he came back out. He recognised me straight away, so I helped him to wash his hands and then took him outside to the first member of staff I could find.'

'That's what the woman at the playground told me. She said she saw you walking out of the toilets with him and taking him to the lifeguard.'

'I only wanted to make sure he was safe. After I'd got him to the lifeguard, I changed quickly and left.'

'You told Charlie not to tell me about you being there?'

'Yes. Did Charlie tell you that?' She closed her eyes briefly. 'I didn't want to jeopardise my being able to keep following you.'

Matt looked off towards the lake. The sun was blazing down on its surface as a couple of swans glided past. 'So what's changed? What's changed between now and then?'

'I don't understand what you mean.'

'At the swimming pool, you didn't want me to know you were still following. And just after that, at the playground, you chose to walk away rather than tell me what was going on. But now you contact me and want to explain things. What's changed?'

'This has changed.' She handed her phone to Matt.

Matt stared at the image on the screen. It was of a well-built man, white, with short hair. Muscles rippled underneath his dark T-shirt. He was moving, not looking at the camera. The image was pretty good, but not perfect. There was a slight graininess about it. It seemed like a still from . . .

'CCTV,' Natalie stated. 'At King's Cross Tube station. Two days ago. Just after the incident on the tracks.'

'Incident?'

'Did you not hear about what happened?'

'I haven't really been keeping up with the news.'

She pushed back some strands of hair. 'A woman fell in front of a Tube train at King's Cross on Tuesday evening. Some of the witnesses claim she was pushed.'

'By this man?'

'That's the person of most interest to the police.'

'Is the woman okay?'

'She's alive, but was badly injured in the fall. There aren't many details in the articles – the police obviously don't want to say too much.'

Matt shook his head.

Why the hell would someone do such a horrific thing?

'That guy was seen running away from the scene,' Natalie continued. 'There are four images in all. I've got them all there – you can swipe through the other three.'

Matt did so. The images showed the guy at various points within the station, and they were of varying quality. In two wider images of the ticket-barrier area, the man was in the background. But the fourth image was better. It was at closer range than the first one Matt had been shown.

'They've not found him then?'

'No, not yet. He got out of the station before anyone really realised what had happened, and the last camera caught him getting into a car with another man, just around the corner. The plates were cloned.'

'I don't understand how this connects with me.'

'You don't recognise him then?'

Matt looked again at the images, swiping through all four. The man wasn't familiar in the slightest. He reminded Matt of the thugs who turned out at far-right rallies. 'Why, should I recognise him?'

Natalie hesitated, as if doing one final internal test of her instincts, of her theory, before voicing it out loud. 'I'm pretty sure – very sure – I've seen this guy before.'

'Where?'

She did a quick glance around, and didn't seem happy. 'Come on, let's talk and walk.'

Matt didn't argue, and they set off, not speaking, first of all along one of the designated paths that criss-crossed Hyde Park, and then off-piste on to the grass until they were some way from the nearest person.

'I've seen him a couple of times, I think,' Natalie said. 'Watching you. A couple of weeks ago, the day we all went to Greenwich, he was on the boat coming back.'

'He was on the boat?' As a treat, they'd taken a boat back from Greenwich along the River Thames to Westminster. Charlie had squealed with delight as they'd passed under bridges and passers-by had waved.

'I didn't really think anything of it at the time. I was looking out for any suspicious people, of course, all day. But I didn't see anything until we got back on the boat. Then I noticed this guy. I thought I caught him looking over at us once or twice, but I decided in the end I was letting my mind run away with itself. And then I saw this story, and I recognised him.'

'It's definitely the same guy?'

'Yes. Well, I'm as sure as I can be.'

Matt was about to propose the theory that this man being on the boat, even if he was the same man who had been involved in the terrible event at King's Cross, might be just a coincidence. And that she might be just jumping to the wrong conclusion. 'You said you think you saw him another time.'

'Yes. At the leisure centre.'

'My God. What the hell is this all about?'

'I don't know, Matt, I really don't.'

'Where was he?'

'Up in the spectators' gallery. To be honest, I can't be one hundred per cent sure it was him. I saw just a glimpse.'

'But you're sure enough to tell me.'

'Yes.' Then Natalie turned questioner. 'Are you sure you don't know what this might be about?'

'What? Why this guy might be following me? I haven't got a clue.'

Natalie had a strange look on her face.

'What?' Matt said. 'There's something you haven't told me?'

'Yes, there is. This is going to freak you out. And I should have told you sooner, I know. But before I saw the image of the man – I don't know, part of me was still thinking this might all be an overreaction. I wasn't really convinced he was in danger . . .'

'He?'

Natalie placed her hands on her hips and gazed down at the ground.

'Natalie, you said *he* was in danger.'

She slowly brought her head up until she was looking straight at him. He thought he could see tears glistening in the corners of her eyes. 'It's not you who I was asked to protect. It's Charlie.'

PART THREE

CHAPTER
THIRTY-THREE

Sean put up a hand as Matt entered the pub for their lunchtime drink. The Railway Tavern was set within Liverpool Street station and was a comfortable distance away from the UGT offices.

'I wasn't sure you'd want to speak to me again,' Sean said, as Matt took the seat opposite. The table looked out across the station concourse, and Sean's eyes tracked an attractive woman wheeling a roller suitcase past the window. He turned his attention back to Matt. 'You know, you looked pretty pissed off when you left the other day.' He passed across the pint of lager he'd already bought for Matt. 'That's why I thought I'd just leave you be for a while. But I've been thinking about you, bud – particularly since Gabriel let me know you two were meeting.'

Matt took a sip. 'He didn't tell you what happened?'

'No, he didn't. I thought maybe that's why you wanted to see me.'

It seemed inconceivable that Gabriel wouldn't have reported back, as they worked so closely together, but Sean genuinely didn't seem to know. In a way that was a pity, as Matt didn't particularly want the revelation to dominate their conversation.

'I told Gabriel I wanted to leave the company.'

'What?' And now there was no doubt. Sean's stunned reaction was not playacting. Mouth open, it actually looked as though the colour had drained from his face. He took a couple of seconds to gather his thoughts, and even then all he could manage was a disbelieving shake of the head. He gulped back some of his beer.

Matt felt the need to explain. 'I didn't really plan what I said, it just came out. And when it did, I realised it was what I wanted to do. I want to be a teacher. I don't want to work for UGT anymore – I don't want to work in banking anymore.'

Sean still seemed lost for words. 'I can't believe it,' he said finally. 'I *really* can't believe it.'

Matt shrugged. 'It's fine. I feel totally fine about my decision.'

'What did Gabriel say?'

'Not very much. To be honest, I can't remember much. It took the shine off the meal though.'

'Shit,' Sean said, as if to himself. 'You do realise you're not a Carla Conway, don't you?'

'How d'you mean?'

'I mean, she left the industry, moved across to do something deemed more morally commendable. But she was a big beast, Matt. She can walk back into the boardroom of any number of big City companies, or anywhere around the world. If she gets bored or frustrated in the health service, which she probably will do, then there'll be more than a welcome-back handshake for her. But for you, there's no going back. Do you really understand that?'

'I can't see myself wanting to go back.'

'Yes, but what I'm saying is, you go through with this and you won't have a choice. You *won't* be able to come back into the industry, *anywhere*. Sure, you could set yourself up as an accountant, do some tax returns for little people, but you'll never get back to where you are now. He won't allow it.'

'You mean Gabriel?'

'Yes, I mean Gabriel. He likes you, Matt, a lot. He really had your back during all your problems. If it wasn't for him, you probably wouldn't now have the chance to throw the opportunity back in his face.'

'Now hang on—'

'Can you imagine just how angry Gabriel must be? He put his neck on the line for you, backed you, and for nothing.'

'To be honest, he seemed to take it a lot better than you are,' Matt shot back. He was taken aback by the strength of Sean's reaction. Couldn't his friend just be happy for him and wish him luck?

Obviously not.

'Gabriel wouldn't have wanted to give you the satisfaction of knowing how annoyed he was,' Sean said. 'But I know how he'll be feeling. And he'll make sure you never work at the top of this business again. You know his contacts. Even our competitors will toe the line if he sends out a message not to employ you.'

'I think you're overestimating his influence.'

'You think? I've seen it before. Everyone who's ever crossed him is now out on their arse.'

Matt shrugged. 'As I said, I won't want to come back. Can't you just be happy for me, Sean? I'm finally doing something I really want to do. After all the problems over the past couple of years, I'm starting to feel good about myself again.'

Sean looked at him. 'Yes, I can tell,' he said, softening. 'Look, Matt, I don't mean to come across as a UGT fanboy, wanting to rain on your parade. I just want to make sure you don't do something you might regret, because I care about you. I'm just doing the big brother thing.'

'I know. And I'm sorry about walking out the way I did the other day. The business with Beth and Charlie and Australia, it's just very, very difficult for me.'

'I know, mate, I know. To be honest, the thought of my sister and Charlie being on the other side of world hurts like hell, so I can't imagine how you must be feeling.'

'I have this feeling of dread,' Matt explained. 'Every time I think about it, it just makes me sick in the base of my stomach.'

'I'm sorry, Matt. If there was anything I could do, I would. But I can't interfere, I really can't. It's just not my place.'

Matt considered what he was about to reveal, and whether that might change things. 'I understand. As much as I'd like you to beg Beth not to go, I know you can't do that.'

There was a pause as the understanding between them sank in.

Matt took a metaphorical deep breath. 'The main reason I wanted to meet you, it's about Catherine. You remember I told you about the man in the pub?'

'What, the guy who said she wasn't who she said she was?'

'Yes. I went back to the place and found him. He told me she worked for an agency that caught out men who were cheating on their partners. Two years ago, he was caught out by her – she was paid by the man's wife, who'd suspected he'd been cheating on her with other women for a while.'

Now he'd got Sean's interest.

'So I thought, well, maybe that's what was happening with me. She was being paid to entrap me.'

'Did you ask her about it?'

'I tried. But she wasn't answering her mobile. And I went around to her flat, but she'd cleared out. And I mean, totally. Her next-door neighbour said she hadn't given any warning about leaving.'

'You think she cleared out because of you? But who did you think had paid her to entrap you? Beth?' Sean looked unconvinced.

Matt shrugged. 'She was the only person I could think of.'

'But why would she do that? I mean, it wouldn't make sense, would it? After all, she's with . . . Well, you know what I mean.'

'I went through the same thought process myself,' Matt replied. 'But like I said, she seemed like the only person who would have done it.'

'Have you asked her about it?'

'No. Because there's more. On Sunday, I took Charlie swimming, and he went missing.'

'Missing?'

'Yes. For a few minutes. I was going mad, looking everywhere. And then someone found him – handed him in to one of the staff. From the description, I suspected it might be Catherine, but I didn't know for sure. Until a bit later, when a woman approached me in the playground across the road from the leisure centre. She'd seen the woman who found Charlie, and had just spoken to her. And that's when I saw her, walking away. I called and she answered the phone, but she didn't come back to explain. She just said what she was doing was for my own protection.'

Sean leaned forward. 'I don't understand. To protect you from what?'

'Last night she contacted me, and I met her this morning. Her real name is Natalie. The guy in the pub, he'd been telling the truth. But she said with me it wasn't about entrapment, it was different – it was about protection. Except it wasn't me who she'd been asked to protect. It was Charlie.'

Sean's face knotted in confusion. 'Protect Charlie. But why? What from?'

'She didn't know. But she said that's what she'd been asked to do.'

'By whom?'

'She wouldn't say. Said she had to maintain confidentiality for the client.'

Sean ran his fingers through his hair as he struggled to take in the information. 'I can't believe it,' he said at last. 'Why would someone, anyone, want to hurt Charlie?'

'I was hoping you might be able to help with that.'

'Me?' Sean said, shocked. 'But why would I be able to help?'

Matt had spent the past hour and a half after his meeting with Natalie walking around London, thinking about who could have employed her to protect Charlie. It wasn't difficult to zero in on his chief suspect, although he recognised his prejudices may well be clouding his judgement. 'Is there any reason you think James might pay someone to look out for Charlie? Any reason why he might be in danger?'

'James?' Sean thought. 'No, I really don't. I'm sorry, Matt, I have no idea. This doesn't make any sense to me. Do you believe this woman? She might be lying.'

Matt hadn't actually considered that option. It was certainly possible. But his gut instinct was that she was telling the truth. 'I don't think so.'

'What makes you so sure? I mean, you don't know her. You *thought* you knew her, but she was lying to you. She could be lying again.'

'There was something else,' Matt said. 'Something that happened the other day. A woman fell in front of a Tube train at King's Cross. The police think she may have been pushed.'

'I heard about that.'

'You saw the man the police are looking for?'

Sean shook his head. 'I caught the story on the radio. But it did say they were looking for someone.'

'Natalie thought – thinks – that the same man may have been following me and Charlie. She's pretty sure she saw the guy on the same boat as us, two weeks ago. And yes, she could be making it up, I know that, but it didn't seem that way. She seemed genuine.'

'But if it's true, what does it mean? Why on earth would the man who may have pushed a girl under a train be a threat to Charlie? And why would this have anything to do with James?'

'I don't know,' Matt admitted.

Sean rubbed at his left eye with the ball of his hand. 'It just seems fanciful, that's all. Maybe she doesn't want you to know the real reason.

Why do you suspect James? Apart from the fact that you dislike him intensely.'

That Matt couldn't argue with. But he had good reasons. 'Because I know it wouldn't be Beth.'

Sean's reaction was a tell.

'What? What is it?'

'Nothing.'

'I can tell there's something, Sean,' Matt pressed, as Sean hid his face with a long drink of his pint. 'The way you just reacted then, when I said it wouldn't be Beth, you know something.'

'I don't know anything,' Sean said, glancing at his watch. 'Look, Matt, I'd better shoot off. They let me out for a quick break—'

'Don't run off without explaining what you know.'

'If I don't return to the office soon, they'll be phoning me up, and you know that's never a good thing.'

'Then just tell me. And you can leave.'

Sean looked at the exit, and then back at Matt. 'Okay,' he surrendered. 'I'll tell you. But you've got to promise me one thing: you won't tell Beth about what I'm about to say.'

'I promise.'

Sean ran a hand across his face. He looked like he was about to start, before stopping himself and thinking something through. 'Now, Matt, please don't take this the wrong way. I want you to try to see things in the context of what was happening at the time.'

Sean took another moment to think.

'When you were going through your really bad patch – you know, just after you took a break from the company. You weren't yourself, and Beth was really worried, you know that.'

'I was feeling a little better by then.'

'I know. But Beth was worried about you still. We all were. You know the way you reacted when she got together with James. That day you came round to the house to get some things, and you were so upset.

She was worried you might do something stupid. It was real concern. She spoke to me about it a few times, saying how worried she was about your mental state.'

'Do something stupid – you mean, kill myself?'

Sean didn't have to reply; his expression told its own story. Suddenly an awful, sickening thought rose up from the depths. 'She was worried I might do something stupid with Charlie?'

Sean didn't look like he wanted to confirm it out loud. 'Well . . . not really . . . but yes, there was a concern there that you might not be thinking straight. Obviously, she never thought in your right mind you'd do anything to hurt Charlie, but the way you were acting, you've got to admit you were erratic, so she was worried.'

Matt shook his head in disbelief.

Have I got this all wrong?

He shuddered at the thought.

Was Charlie being protected from him, the boy's own father?

CHAPTER
THIRTY-FOUR

James Farrah exited the cubicle. He was shocked to see her waiting there, leaning provocatively against the bank of sinks, her pencil skirt flirting with the tops of her calves.

'Jessica, what the hell are you doing in here?'

She smiled seductively, moving towards him and looping her arms around his neck. 'I just wanted to catch up, that's all. You've been a bit distant lately.'

James ducked out of the embrace, conscious that a colleague could come walking in at any moment. 'What the hell, Jess – you followed me into the toilets?'

Again she wrapped her arms around him, but this time he didn't fight it. 'You didn't seem to have a problem with it last time. I'm sure you haven't forgotten our little timeout last month, in the middle of the executive board meeting.' She kissed his neck and he closed his eyes, chin tipping towards the ceiling.

She rested her hand between his legs.

'Jessica, no,' he said, pushing her hand away as he fought the urge to surrender. 'Someone might come in.'

'Come on,' she pressed. 'Into the cubicle. Now. I'm hungry.'

'No.'

This time she got the message, and her face twisted in displeasure. 'What is this, James? Is it all just a game for you?'

'Just go,' he said.

'What the hell is the matter?'

'Nothing.'

'You think I can't tell that you've gone cold? You've hardly spoken to me the past week or so. What's going on?'

He almost laughed. She didn't have a clue. 'Jessica, please, leave me alone.'

'You've changed your mind, haven't you? You're not going to tell her about us.'

James didn't deny it.

She shook her head in disbelief, laughing ruefully at the realisation. 'You *are* going to Australia with her, after all. That's what this is all about, isn't it?'

'Yes.'

'Two weeks ago, you said—'

'I know what I said,' he interrupted, 'but that was then.'

'That was then?'

'Things change,' he said dismissively.

'Screw you,' she said, slapping him across the face.

He swallowed down his anger. 'This conversation's over.'

But she blocked his path. 'You move to Australia with her and that will be it. The past two years, all those good times, over. Do you understand?'

'Oh, I understand.'

'You won't have me ever again.'

James shrugged it off.

'I mean it.'

'Look, Jess. I know you think you're something special, a real catch, but you're not. You're easy.'

'Unlike Beth? I mean, well, she's—'

He lifted a finger. 'Don't say it.'

'It's not you, James,' she tried. 'It's not who you are – the family man with a snotty kid in tow. She wants to mould you into the perfect family man, the perfect father. But that's not you, is it? I know the *real* you. Don't I?'

'Maybe you do.'

He let her kiss him deeply, enjoying her efforts at persuasion. She was trying to force him to submit.

They banged back against the cubicle door and slipped inside, hands fumbling in the tight space, hungry for one another.

◆ ◆ ◆

Minutes later, they both exited. James splashed his face in the sink, as Jessica watched on from behind. She looked smug.

But here was the twist.

'It's over,' James stated.

Her face collapsed in disbelief. 'What?'

He smiled. 'It's over. I thought you deserved a last time.'

She came at him with a raised arm, but he turned around and held her firm, so she spat in his face. 'Bastard!'

'Classy.'

'After what I did for you.' Jessica smiled as a plan formed in her mind. 'I'm sure once your darling Beth knows the truth about what you did, she'll see you for the arsehole you really are.'

Rage surged through him. He thrust his free hand around her swan neck and moved forward, pinning her back against the wall. He squeezed harder and delighted in her horror, her eyes bulging, choking noises gurgling from her throat. 'You utter a word to anyone,' he hissed into her face, 'and I swear I'll snap your neck in two.'

He let her drop to the floor and calmly straightened his tie in the mirror, brushing down his lapels.

'You know,' she gasped, clutching at her throat and looking up at him, 'you're a monster.'

CHAPTER THIRTY-FIVE

Matt retreated to his flat to mull over what Sean had said regarding Beth's concern over his state of mind, and how she'd worried about him being with Charlie.

It pained him to think that she could ever believe he'd pose a risk to his own son.

The thought that Natalie might have been hired by Beth to protect Charlie from him weighed heavily on his mind. Feeling helpless, he grasped for a way forward – something that could help to explain what was going on.

And then the thought came to him.

It didn't take long for Matt to find out where Rachel Martin was being treated. A quick search on the Internet revealed she'd been rushed to UCLH – University College Hospital – in central London.

He left the flat and headed for the Underground station.

If Natalie was right, and the man she'd seen on the boat was the same man wanted for the Tube incident, then this at least seemed a step in the right direction towards getting some answers.

◆　◆　◆

'Hi,' Matt said to the lady at the hospital's reception desk. 'I'm looking for Rachel Martin. I'm a work colleague of hers, and I know she's being treated here.'

'One moment,' the lady said. She tapped away on a keyboard, then frowned as she stared at the screen. 'I'm sorry, we're not currently allowing visitors outside of normal visiting times. Only very close family. It's because it's such a . . . sensitive situation. There are added measures.'

Security measures, Matt thought. They'd be worried that if someone had indeed tried to murder her, they might try and finish off the job. He tried to think. 'Are any of Rachel's family here?' he asked. 'It would just be good to speak to someone, to see how she is. I have to dash back to work in a few minutes, and this was the only time I could make it.'

The receptionist thought, then nodded. 'Okay, I'll call the ward, see if anyone is up there and willing to speak to you.'

Matt waited nervously as she called through.

'One of the family members will see you,' she said, as she replaced the handset. 'Do you know where you're going? It's ward 7B. Eighth floor. Straight through the double doors opposite the lift.'

'Thank you.'

Matt headed for the lift. As it ascended, he began to regret doing this. To speak with a family member, pretend he knew Rachel, it didn't seem right. Maybe there was another way he could phrase things.

He stepped out and, after pressing the buzzer at the double doors, was let in.

'You're here to speak with one of Rachel's family?' the ward clerk asked.

'Yes.'

'In the room across the corridor,' she directed.

As Matt entered the room, the woman who was inside turned and smiled softly. She'd been standing at the window, arms folded tightly across her chest, as if giving herself a comforting hug.

'Hi,' Matt said, wanting to leave and end the conversation before it began. But then he reminded himself why he was doing this. 'My name's Matt Roberts. I'm a friend of Rachel's. I was hoping to find out how she is.'

'Hilary McKenzie,' the woman said, extending a hand.

Matt clasped her hand. 'You're Rachel's . . . mum?'

'Oh, no,' she said, ending the handshake. 'Her parents have just flown in from the States. I'm not strictly family, but Rachel was my son's long-term girlfriend, so as far as I'm concerned, she is and always will be one of the family.'

Was my son's long-term girlfriend.

'How is she?'

'They're keeping her in a medically induced coma, until the swelling goes down.'

My God, it was serious.

'Her condition's stable,' the woman continued, 'so that's something to be thankful for.' She sighed and shook her head. 'I just can't believe this. After what happened to Alex. It's a nightmare within a nightmare.'

'Alex?'

She frowned. 'You don't know about Alex? About what happened to my son?'

Matt knew he was on dangerous territory here. 'Sorry, no. I'm afraid I only know Rachel from work. We used to work together,' he added. 'I haven't seen her for a while, but I spotted the news article detailing what had happened, so I wanted to see how she was.'

The lies were coming easily now.

Hilary seemed not to have even heard Matt's explanation. 'My son, Alex, Rachel's partner – he was killed just over two weeks ago. Hit and run.'

Matt blinked in disbelief.

Alex McKenzie.

He knew that name. Alex McKenzie was a trader at UGT. In a different department to Matt, but he knew of him.

Could it be the same person?

'I'm very sorry to hear that,' Matt said.

How could he find out for sure?

'Yes, it's been such a difficult time. The worst two weeks of my life. And now with this – well . . .' She threw her hands up in frustration. 'You begin to wonder what will be next.'

'Thinking about it, Rachel did mention her boyfriend. He was a City trader, wasn't he?'

Hilary nodded. 'A very good one. He was tipped for higher things. He was with UGT. You know it? The big City bank.'

'Yes, I know it.'

Again she wrapped her arms around herself. 'All that potential, all that life, those possibilities – marriage, children, a career – just snuffed out.' She grimaced. 'It's just not fair.'

'No, it's not fair.'

She looked off into an imagined distance. 'I'd better get back to Rachel. Would you like to see if you can go in the room? I can ask one of the staff.'

'It's okay,' Matt replied. 'Like I said, I just wanted to speak to someone.'

By the time Matt had left the hospital, he'd already found the online stories about Alex McKenzie. There were a couple of small pieces in the local newspapers, but it hadn't hit the headlines to such an extent that it would have come up on Matt's radar. If Matt had still been at UGT, then yes, he would know. But, distanced from the company, all his news about UGT came via Sean, who had obviously neglected to tell him.

After all, it wasn't as if either of them really knew Alex.

But now, under these circumstances, it had new importance.

Natalie had connected the attempted murder of Rachel Martin to Charlie through the presence of the mystery man.

And Matt now knew Rachel was connected to Alex McKenzie. A UGT worker. Now dead.

Was something or someone connected to UGT putting Charlie in harm's way?

He paced outside the hospital entrance as the traffic passed by, grasping for answers.

What the hell had he been caught up in? Attempted murder. A suspicious death. Charlie needing protection . . . What could be the link to UGT?

Then a name rose to the surface.

James Farrah.

He was a link between UGT and Charlie.

But he could also say the same of himself, and Sean . . . Could this all be connected to Matt?

But he hadn't even worked at the company in months. And he hadn't known Alex McKenzie.

Had Sean or James? There was only one way to find out.

Matt tried to call Sean. There was no answer, so he left a hurried message, asking him to call back as soon as he could.

Frustrated at the closure of that avenue for the moment, his thoughts turned to James.

Tonight he'd confront him.

It was worth a try.

CHAPTER
THIRTY-SIX

Beth had just lifted Charlie into the bath when there was a knock on the door. She exchanged glances with James, who was leaning against the bathroom doorframe.

'Let's just ignore it,' James suggested. 'It'll be someone selling something or collecting for charity – always is, this time of night.'

Beth wasn't so sure. 'Sarah mentioned she might pop round sometime this week after work – she's got those clothes for Charlie that Ewan has grown out of.'

James nodded. 'I'll go and answer it. But if it's a tin-rattler . . .'

'No, I'll go,' Beth said. 'If it is Sarah, then I'll have to come down anyway – and besides, you don't often get to give Charlie his bath. I won't be long, sweetie,' she said, kissing Charlie on the forehead. She got to her feet. 'You be good for James.'

'I will,' he replied. 'Can I have my submarine?'

'Sure,' she said, reaching for the plastic bath toy and slipping it into the water. 'I won't be long.' She touched James's arm on her way out of the room. 'Have fun.'

'We will,' James said. 'So,' he said, kneeling down at the side of the bath, 'it's just you and me. The men together.'

Charlie was splashing around with the submarine in the water, adding his own sound effects. 'I love my submarine.'

'I know you do, mate.'

'Daddy got me my submarine. Do you know that?' Charlie searched James's face for a reaction.

'I didn't, no. But I do now.'

'Yes, he bought it for me for my birthday. Before you lived here.'

James could hear Beth chatting to Sarah in the downstairs hall. 'C'mon, we'd better get you washed before Mummy comes back.' He did some quick wipes of Charlie's eyes and across his face with the flannel. It certainly wasn't as systematic as Beth's face-cleaning regime, but it got rid of the obvious grime.

'Daddy said he couldn't come to Australia,' Charlie stated. 'I asked him, and he said he couldn't come with us.'

'He can come to visit. Mummy and I, we've told you that, haven't we? Your daddy can come to visit whenever he likes.'

Charlie brightened. 'Whenever he likes? Every week?'

'Not every week, no.'

Charlie's brow knotted. 'But I see Daddy every week.'

James didn't really want to go there, but maybe this was a conversation that just had to happen, and maybe it was better without Beth being around. 'Do you remember, Charlie, I explained that Australia is far away? Well, that means that your daddy won't have time to see you every week.'

'Oh.' The disappointment was palpable. And worrying.

'But he will see you as much as he can. I promise that whenever he wants to come and visit you, he can stay in our house.'

Charlie's brow remained furrowed. Maybe this was realisation dawning. 'I don't want to go to Australia without Daddy. I want to stay here.'

James resisted the temptation to say what he really wanted to say.

If I had my way, little guy, you wouldn't be coming to Australia. You could stay here, with your good-for-nothing father, and let me get on with the rest of my life in peace, away from your whining.

Instead he dunked the flannel into the water again, squirted on the bath gel, and began lathering Charlie's back. 'You'll be able to see Daddy every week on FaceTime. On the iPad. Every week.'

'I don't want to go to Australia without Daddy,' the little boy repeated.

'Australia will be fun, Charlie.' James kept his voice even and the tone light. 'Remember all the amazing animals you'll see in Australia? Koalas, kangaroos . . . And the beaches – you were really excited about the beaches, and swimming in the sea.'

'Don't want beaches! I want to swim with Daddy. I *only* swim with Daddy.' Charlie smacked the water, droplets speckling James's shirt.

'Little shit,' James muttered under his breath, brushing himself down.

Charlie's eyes widened, a bubble-coated hand over his mouth. 'You said a naughty word!'

Instinctively, James glanced behind in the fear that Beth was standing there. But he could still hear her downstairs. 'I didn't, Charlie.'

'You did! You did!'

James placed a hand on each of Charlie's shoulders, and the little boy quietened, as if he could sense something was wrong. For a second or two, James imagined pushing Charlie under the water, pressing him firmly on to the bottom of the bath, watching the life drain out of him until it was over.

He shuddered at the dark thought.

Charlie was staring at him in fascination with those big brown eyes.

'Listen, Charlie. Your mummy,' James said, the embers of the fantasy still smouldering, 'she's really excited about Australia. *Really* excited. If you say you don't want to go, then she'll be very sad. Do you want to make Mummy sad? You don't want to see her cry, do you? Because of you?'

Charlie peered down into the water. 'No.'

'I know you don't – because you're a good boy, a very good boy. You want your mummy to be happy. Isn't that right?'

Still Charlie stared into the water. 'Yes.'

'Then that's why we need to go to Australia, so Mummy will be happy.'

Charlie's bottom lip was quivering. 'But Daddy . . .'

James watched tears form in Charlie's eyes. He had to lighten the mood and shut this down now, before Beth returned. Then he had an idea. 'I'll tell you what. Your daddy can visit whenever he wants. If he wants to visit every week, then he can visit every week.'

'Really? *Every* week?'

James smiled. 'Of course, if he wants to.'

'That would be *amazing*!' Charlie splashed the water again, and this time he really soaked James's shirt.

James stood up, the satisfaction with the outcome tempering his anger at the wet shirt. 'Time to get you out and dry,' he said. 'I've got lots to do tonight.'

He helped Charlie clamber out of the bath and then wrapped him in the towel, rubbing him dry.

'I'm so excited,' Charlie announced, wearing the towel like a Roman toga. He punched at the air. 'Australia with Daddy is going to be *great*!'

James watched the delighted little boy.

The boy that meant the world to Beth.

Maybe he'd have to change his plans.

CHAPTER
THIRTY-SEVEN

It was half past eight. Matt had waited until he knew James would be home, and Charlie bathed and tucked up in bed. Bath time was religiously set at seven o'clock, he'd be in bed just before seven thirty, then there were stories, and lights out at about a quarter to eight. Arriving at half past eight ensured Charlie would be properly asleep.

'Matt,' Beth said, shocked at his appearance at this late hour as she stood in the doorway. She was wearing her comfy joggers and a white T-shirt that reminded Matt of a holiday they had taken in Cyprus in the early years of their relationship. 'What are you doing here?'

'I need to talk,' he said. 'Is it okay if I come in?'

She looked back into the house, as if she was thinking about how James might respond to Matt walking in and spoiling their evening. She frowned, thinking, then said, 'C'mon in. We're just in the middle of dinner, but we can pop it under the grill.'

'Sorry,' Matt said, as he followed her inside. 'I wouldn't have come if it wasn't really important.'

'Matt,' James said flatly as he came into the living room. He'd obviously heard him at the front door. 'I've already put the food in to keep warm,' he said to Beth.

'Thanks.' Beth stood at James's side as they both waited for an explanation. Their positioning served to make this situation all the more uncomfortable.

'Maybe we'd better sit down,' Matt suggested.

'What's this about?' James said, not moving. Matt noticed his hand linking with Beth's.

Matt decided to get straight to the point. 'It's about Charlie. About his safety. I'm worried about him.'

'His safety?' Beth said, her face flashing concern. 'Why, what's wrong? What's happened?'

Matt tried again. 'Can we sit down?'

Beth nodded, encouraging James down on to the sofa, even though he looked less than happy about it.

Matt sat in the chair opposite and took a moment to gather his thoughts. 'This might sound crazy, but over the past few weeks I've had this feeling that I was being followed. By the girl I was dating, Catherine. I tried to dismiss it, that I was imagining it. But it turns out it was true. She *was* following me. Her real name is Natalie, not Catherine. And her usual job is to work for women, to determine whether their husbands are cheating on them.'

Beth was transfixed, while James just looked bored.

Matt continued. 'I challenged her about what she was doing. At first, she wouldn't tell me, and I assumed that maybe it could be something to do with you.'

'Me?' Beth said, perturbed. 'I promise, it isn't anything—'

'It's okay,' Matt interrupted. 'I know that now. Later she told me what she was doing was for my own protection.'

'Your own protection? She was protecting you? Like a bodyguard?'

'She was being paid to look out for anything suspicious, and to report back to the person who was paying her. But it wasn't me she was asked to protect. It was Charlie.'

'Charlie?' Beth said, aghast. 'But, why – why would Charlie need protecting?'

Matt looked across to James, eyeing him for any signs as he spoke. 'I had no idea at first. But now I have a theory. It's something to do with UGT.'

James just looked back at him impassively.

Beth turned to James, then back to Matt. 'In what way?'

'I don't know,' Matt admitted, eyes still trained on James. 'But I'm telling you all this now because I wonder if you, James, can help, or know anything?'

He laughed. 'Me?'

'Alex McKenzie, an employee at UGT, was killed in a hit-and-run two weeks ago. His girlfriend Rachel Martin was pushed under a Tube train two days ago. I think there's a connection between what happened to them and the bank. Do you know anything?'

'My God, you're actually serious, aren't you?' James shook his head. 'You're losing it, mate.'

Matt's eyes slid back to Beth. 'Charlie is in danger, Beth.'

Beth looked across at James. 'Do you know anything about this?'

James looked affronted. 'No, of course not! Yes, I heard the dreadful news about Alex, but I didn't know about his girlfriend's accident.'

'The police don't think it was an accident,' Matt carried on. 'And Natalie believes the chief suspect is the same man who has been following me and Charlie.'

'I don't know anything about this,' James said, directing his protest at Beth and studiously ignoring Matt. 'He comes here, making wild accusations—'

'I'm not accusing anyone. I just want to protect my son,' Matt stated.

'No,' James said, now turning to him. 'You want to try and drive a wedge between Beth and me. You'll try anything to stop us going to

Australia, won't you? Isn't that what this is really about? It's about you wanting to ruin everything for us.'

Now, under the gaze of them both, Matt felt defensive. 'It's true that the last thing I want is for you to move to Australia. For Charlie to be thousands of miles away. The prospect terrifies me. It keeps me awake at night. But that's not what this is about.'

'I don't believe you,' James said. 'You're a desperate man, and desperate people do desperate things. But the truth is, Matt, you threw away your great life, not anyone else. And it's too late to . . .'

'James!' Beth chastised. 'That's enough.'

All three of them eyed one another.

'Please, Beth,' Matt said. 'Please believe me. *Something* is going on. Something that has put Charlie under threat. And it *is* linked to UGT, I just know it.'

James got to his feet. 'I've heard enough of this. Beth, I'll be upstairs. Let me know once he's gone, and we can finish our meal that was so rudely interrupted.'

He left the room without a goodbye and tramped up the stairs.

'Beth,' Matt tried again, 'you have to listen to me.'

Beth pinched the bridge of her nose. She looked tormented. 'I'm sorry, Matt, I think you'd better go.'

CHAPTER THIRTY-EIGHT

'You really have no idea what Matt was talking about?'

Beth had suppressed her suspicions until the morning, satisfied to let things settle before raising the subject with James. But the moment he returned from the shower, she could resist no longer.

There was something about the way he had reacted to what Matt was saying. Some kind of tell, although she couldn't quite put her finger on it.

James stopped towel-drying his hair, his expression one of exasperation. 'Beth, please don't tell me you believe anything he said.'

'I . . . Of course not. But why would that woman say those things to him?'

'I don't know.' He began rubbing his head hard with the towel again, and Beth just watched, still troubled that her gut instincts were telling her something wasn't quite right here.

She heard Charlie giggle from downstairs as he watched *Peppa Pig* and her concerns crystallised. 'Nothing means more to me than Charlie's safety.'

And there it is again. Something in his face.

The phone saved him from further questioning. 'I'd better get this. Might be the office.' Before Beth could argue, he swiped up his mobile and retreated into the back room. Beth moved to the door, straining to listen as James spoke in hushed tones. She couldn't make out what he was saying.

'I need to leave now,' he said, passing her on the landing, heading for the stairs.

'What is it?'

'Trouble at work.'

She pursued him downstairs as he grabbed his jacket and bag en route.

'Aren't you going to say goodbye to Charlie?' she asked, watching him fumble to unlock the front door.

He seemed oddly distracted. 'Oh, yes. Bye, Charlie. See you later!' he shouted down the corridor. Beth doubted Charlie had heard. 'See you, Beth.' James went to kiss her, but she pulled away.

'What's going on, James?'

'Work trouble,' he said, not looking at her. 'I just need to nip things in the bud, before the situation gets out of hand.'

Before she could reply he was off and heading down the street with purpose.

He didn't look back.

Beth unbuckled Charlie from his booster seat and gazed up at the house. James had been out of contact all day, with calls to his mobile ringing through to voicemail. She'd wondered on the way home from school whether he'd left his phone at home by mistake, such was his rush to leave this morning. She could have called his desk number, but UGT management had recently sent around a memo to staff warning about taking personal calls on work phones.

'Mummy, can I watch *Fireman Sam*?'

Charlie ran off towards the living room, and Beth turned on the television and settled him down with some orange squash and a banana.

'Mummy's just going to do some housework.'

'Boring!'

Beth searched around the ground floor for signs of James's mobile. It wasn't anywhere obvious.

'Charlie,' Beth called out from the base of the stairs. 'Mummy will just be upstairs for a few minutes. Are you okay?'

'Yes, Mummy!' he shouted back. 'Fireman Sam has just rescued a pelican.'

She knew something was wrong even before she entered the master bedroom.

The wardrobe was open, and half of James's clothes were gone.

She crossed the landing and went into the back bedroom, driven on by a sudden, irrepressible thought.

He's gone to Australia without me.

Heading straight for the drawer where they kept the various bits and pieces relating to their move, her suspicions appeared to be confirmed.

James's passport was gone.

◆　◆　◆

Beth busied herself in the kitchen, preparing tea. It seemed crazy, but she made it for three.

Maybe there's another explanation for all this.

And yet she didn't really believe that.

Had Matt had been right? And if he was, what did that mean for Charlie's safety?

Suddenly Charlie burst into the room. 'Mummy, I need the toilet!'

Beth caught her breath, shocked by his entrance in the midst of her thoughts. 'Can't you go yourself, darling?'

Charlie danced on the spot. 'No, you come! I'm frightened of the naughty man.'

'What naughty man? On television?'

'No. The naughty man at the top of the stairs.'

CHAPTER THIRTY-NINE

'Matt.'

It was Beth. She didn't sound right. Even just with that one word, Matt could sense the difference in her voice. 'Beth. Are you okay?'

'I think you were right. It's James. He's gone. Taken his stuff and disappeared. And there's something else. Someone has been in the house. They've been up to the top floor, turned everything upside down.'

'What? Are you there now? Have they definitely gone?'

'There's no one here now.'

'Good. I'll be right there,' Matt said, already grabbing his keys from the kitchen table. He paused. 'As long as you want me to come over.'

There was a painful silence, and for a moment Matt thought there might still be some resistance.

'Yes, please come over, Matt.'

She left the door open for Matt to close as they both made their way into the living room. Charlie was now sitting on the sofa, watching the *Cars* movie.

'Hey, Charlie,' Matt said. Charlie didn't so much as move a muscle. 'Lightning McQueen, eh?'

'Quiet, Daddy, I'm trying to watch the movie,' he replied, putting a hushing finger to his lips.

'Okay, I'll be quiet,' Matt smiled.

'Daddy and me, we're just going to have a chat in the kitchen,' Beth explained to him. Charlie didn't seem bothered, his face not even flickering. 'If you need anything, just let us know. We'll keep the door open, okay?'

'So, what happened?' Matt said, as he and Beth settled down around the kitchen table.

'Charlie went to go to the toilet while I was preparing tea, and he said he saw a man upstairs. I thought it was just Charlie's overactive imagination, but when I went to look, the top-floor room was turned upside down, as if someone had been looking for something.'

'And James has gone?'

'James rushed out of the house this morning, after getting a phone call. Said it was about work. I tried to call him today but couldn't get an answer. And when I got back from picking Charlie up from school, James had been back to the house and taken clothes and his passport.'

'I'm sorry, Beth.'

Beth shook her head. 'What the hell's going on, Matt?'

'I don't know.'

'Could James be in danger?'

'Maybe. I just don't know.'

'And Charlie?'

He saw a single tear trickle down her cheek. All he wanted to do was embrace her and tell her everything was going to be alright.

But he had to keep his distance.

They both looked towards the living room, where they could see Charlie still sitting on the sofa.

'If anything ever happened to him, I don't know what I'd do,' Beth said.

'Me neither.'

Beth closed her eyes briefly. 'I can't believe this. Shouldn't we call the police about the intruder?'

Matt looked over at Charlie again. 'Yes, let's do it now.'

◆　◆　◆

Matt waited in the living room with Charlie, as Beth said goodbye to the officers.

'Well, I'm not sure what good that did us,' Beth admitted as she sat down on the sofa next to Matt.

'I guess they can't do much,' Matt said, 'when Charlie couldn't describe the person he saw.'

Charlie, who was pushing his toy train around the carpet, didn't look up.

'The way they kept coming back to James,' Beth said, 'they probably thought it was him, didn't they?'

'It seemed so.'

'Do you?'

'Charlie,' Matt called, 'are you sure it wasn't Uncle James you saw?'

Charlie turned around. 'It was a naughty man.' He went back to playing.

'This is such a strange situation, Matt,' Beth said, shaking her head. 'I *really* don't like it.'

'I know. Neither do I.'

CHAPTER FORTY

An hour after the police had left, Matt approached Charlie, taking a seat next to him on the sofa. Maybe with the passing of a bit of time, Charlie might be prepared to open up a little. 'Charlie,' he said, 'the naughty man you saw at the top of the stairs, what did he look like? Have you seen him before?'

Charlie's attention was back on the movie.

Matt tried again. 'Charlie, it's really important that you answer my question. The man at the top of the stairs, have you seen him before?'

'Yes,' he said flatly, 'I've seen him before.'

Matt shot Beth a glance. 'Where, Charlie? Where have you seen him?'

He didn't turn his attention away from the screen. 'I can't remember.'

Matt wanted to shout at his son, wanted to turn off the TV and force him to pay attention. But he knew that would be completely counterproductive. 'Charlie, you've got a really good memory. You remember lots of things, from a *long* time ago. Don't you?'

'I remember lots of things,' Charlie agreed, eyes straight ahead.

'So I think you might be able to remember where you saw the naughty man before. Can you have a good think about it, Charlie?'

Matt looked up at Beth, who signalled for him to cut the conversation. He nodded, but had one last question for now. 'Why did you call him a naughty man, Charlie?'

Charlie slid his eyes across to meet Matt's. 'I'm sorry, I'm not allowed to tell you that. I promised.'

'Promised who? Was it Uncle James who you saw? Is he the naughty man?'

Charlie's face darkened. 'Too many questions, Daddy.'

'Matt,' Beth tried again. 'Let's talk. Next door.'

As they re-entered the kitchen, Beth said, 'I still don't think it could have been James.' She saw Matt's doubtful look. 'What, you now think it could be?'

'I don't know,' Matt admitted. 'Probably not.'

'But if not James, then it must be connected to James?'

'Maybe.'

'And be someone who might have a key to our home?'

'I don't know, Beth.'

'I don't feel safe here,' she said.

'Well, you can't stay here. You need to get some things together, for you and Charlie, and we need to leave as soon as possible in case whoever was just in here comes back. We need to get to a safer place. I was thinking you could both stay with Sean.'

Sean's place, an apartment in an exclusive development overlooking the River Thames and Tower Bridge, was guarded by security on the reception desk.

'And you too? Sean has the space,' Beth said. 'There's the pull-out sofa bed. I think it's best if we stick together.'

Matt nodded.

'I want you to be with us, Matt.' Beth's anxiety was still all too visible. 'I'll go and get packing. I don't want to stay here a moment longer than we have to.'

'Wait,' Matt said. 'Before we do that, I want to talk some more about James. And I want to take a look in the office.'

'Why?'

He shrugged. 'Just in case there's something that might help to explain all this.'

'Okay,' Beth conceded. 'But can you be quick? I really don't want to be around here much longer.'

'I understand,' Matt said, already heading out of the door and towards the stairs. 'If you want to wait in there with Charlie, I'll be as quick as I can.'

Matt entered the top-floor office. He didn't know where to start, such was the mess. He stepped over the piles of papers, some of which crunched like snow beneath his feet, and began to sift through the items on the desk.

In the not too distant past, this room had been Matt's bolthole, the place where he'd come to shut out the world, even for a few minutes. Well, that had been the plan. The reality was that, in the latter months of his relationship with Beth, it became an extension of his workplace, and he'd lock himself away until the early-morning hours, working on reports that should have been done during the day. Beth used to drift up from the floor below, knock on the door and ask, with some frustration and sadness, when he was coming downstairs to bed. But after a while, the visits stopped, and Matt was left to work all the way through the night on more than one occasion.

It might have got him ahead at work, but it killed his home life.

And what was the point of succeeding at work when you were failing at life?

Matt hunted through the many papers that lay scattered around the room. A thought then occurred to him: whoever had just been in the house knew which room to target. They had left the rooms on the first floor untouched. Yet this one they had ransacked. So the person had known the layout of the house well, and had zoned in on the room where James was most likely to keep his personal documents. Again, the thought turned to whether it had been James himself. Maybe he had left in a hurry, before realising he had forgotten something. He might have known it was in this room, but had been unable to find it.

Matt didn't really know what he was searching for. Yes, he was looking for a smoking gun that would explain everything – but what, exactly? All he could find was bank statements, paid credit card bills. He started looking in more detail at the bills, examining the transactions. There were various recognisable and unsurprising outgoings – he knew James and Beth ate out a lot, and there were numerous restaurant names on there, along with petrol charges and drinks bills. Nothing that screamed suspicious.

He pulled out the desk drawers, but whoever had been up here had already emptied them. Then he remembered the storage area behind the wall. It was a small space running along the outer edge of the room, behind the structural beam and the wall facade. Matt and Beth had used it for storing some of Charlie's baby clothes and toys, getting them out of the way but close at hand, in case a second child came along. He wondered whether Charlie's stuff was still there, undisturbed, or whether James had found a new use for the space.

Matt walked over to the storage unit, positioned against the lowest point of the wall as it sloped down at the room's edge. The small door that led into the space was hidden behind the unit. Unless an individual knew about it or happened to move the unit, the door and space behind it would remain undetected.

Matt lifted the unit aside and was pleased to find the door closed and to all appearances undisturbed. He pulled at the door but was surprised when it failed to open. Only then did he spot the padlock that had been fitted down at the bottom.

'Damn it.' James must have added the lock.

The padlock required a small key, and Matt spent the next five minutes searching the room for it. When that search proved fruitless, he retreated downstairs.

'Are you okay?' Beth looked up from the sofa, her arm around Charlie.

Matt realised he probably looked hot and flustered. 'The storage area in the top room. Did James fit a lock to the door?'

Beth frowned. 'Not that I know of. But I don't really go up there. It's James's space.'

'There's a new padlock on there. But I can't find the key. Have you any idea where it might be?'

Beth kissed Charlie on the forehead and got up. 'We still keep all the keys in the kitchen cupboard, where we used to have them.' She moved into the kitchen and opened the cupboard unit, which was filled with bunches of keys dangling from hooks. None of them looked small enough to fit the padlock upstairs.

'How about that one?' Beth suggested. She picked out a small key.

'Too big,' Matt said, scanning the others. He stopped and looked at Beth. 'Do you have any idea what is up there now, in the storage area?'

'No. I can't remember the last time I looked in there. When James moved in, well, he adopted the room for his office, and I was glad to give it to him. As far as I know, it still has Charlie's baby toys and clothes.'

'But he wouldn't fit a padlock on it if that was all that was up there.'

'No, he wouldn't.'

'Maybe he's kept it secret from you.'

Beth seemed to find that thought disturbing. 'Maybe.'

Matt wanted to reach out and comfort her, but he resisted the temptation. 'I'm really sorry, Beth, for making you question James like this. Whatever you might think, it doesn't give me any satisfaction. Not in these circumstances.'

Beth placed her hand on his arm. 'I don't think that, Matt, at all. I know you're doing this to try to protect Charlie.'

'And you too.'

Only then did Beth seem to realise that she was still touching Matt's arm, and she withdrew her hand self-consciously. She looked away, embarrassed.

A thought came to him. 'How about the floor safe?' Matt and Beth had had the fire-resistant floor safe concreted into the floor of their utility room a year after they moved in, to hold their passports and most precious jewellery.

'I lost the key to the safe a few weeks ago,' Beth admitted, reddening. 'I needed my passport for, you know, the Australia plans.' She looked sheepish. 'I don't know where the key went. I remember unlocking the safe, then locking it back up, but I just couldn't remember what I did with it after that. We looked everywhere.'

'I know where there's a spare.'

'You do?'

'Unless it's been moved,' he said, moving back into the living room. Charlie was building something with Lego. He'd switched off the TV. 'Look, Daddy, I've built a spaceship! Whoosh!'

Matt crouched down and Charlie handed him his creation. 'Wow, that's brilliant!'

Charlie beamed. 'I love building. I build lots of things in school.'

'I know you do,' Matt said, kissing the top of his head.

Charlie returned to his play as Matt went over to the bookcase. He pulled out the hardback copy of the *Oxford English Dictionary*, and there it was, still taped to the inside of the back cover. A smile broadened his lips. 'You beauty.'

Beth had entered the room. 'You got it?'

'Yes,' Matt said, heading for the utility room. A quick half-turn of the key in the lock, and the safe revealed its contents.

Two rings. And one small padlock key.

'It's in there?' Beth said.

'Looks like it could be.'

They all made their way upstairs, wanting to stay together. 'You know,' Matt said, as he paused at the bottom of the final flight leading to the top-floor office, 'this key might not be the right one after all.'

'It is,' Beth said. 'I can feel it.'

'I hope so. You wait here with Charlie.'

Beth nodded. A ransacked room wasn't the place for a child.

The key fitted the lock perfectly, and a quarter-turn saw the bolt flick out of its clasp. 'It's the right key,' Matt shouted downstairs to where Beth and Charlie were still waiting.

He pulled back the door and flicked on the light switch that he remembered was on the right, just inside the crawl space. The storage area lit up, and Matt was left staring at the familiar bags of Charlie's toys and clothes. For a second he thought that was it, but beyond those bags was one he didn't recognise – a cream-and-brown rucksack. He wriggled further forward and hauled the toys and clothes out of the way in order to reach the bag. Heaving it out of the storage area and into the office, it hit the ground with quite a thud.

'Is everything okay?' Beth shouted.

'Yes,' Matt said, kneeling over the bag.

He grabbed the zip and pulled.

CHAPTER FORTY-ONE

'So, you wanted to see me?'

Harvey watched Tyrone as his sister's boyfriend put on a show of bravado, puffing out his chest and approaching with a swagger. 'Yeah, bruv, I did.' Tyrone smiled.

'How are the injuries?' Harvey quipped. A bruise blossomed along the left side of the man's face, where Harvey had caught him beautifully with a left hook.

Tyrone smiled again. 'I don't feel no pain, man.'

Harvey laughed off the bluster. 'Whatever. Look, did you get me here to tell me somethin' important, or are you wastin' my time?'

Tyrone smiled again. 'Oh, I'm not wastin' your time, I promise.'

Harvey wanted to push his fist through that grin. 'Then spill it, man, before you're spillin' out your teeth. You get me?'

'Hey, cool it, Harvey,' Tyrone soothed. 'Calm it, man. Don't get in no aggro like your brother.'

Harvey's fists balled up. He took a step forward, his head cocked. 'What you say?'

'Hey, bruv, I didn't come here lookin' for no fight,' Tyrone stated, holding up his hands. 'I came to help you.'

'Help me?' Harvey sneered. 'Why? We both know we don't like each other, man, and I'm happy with that.'

'I love Rochelle,' Tyrone said.

The honesty caught Harvey off guard, and he stood down from imminent attack. 'So?'

'So, I wanna marry her. I wanna have a family with her, have kids, like—'

Harvey put up a hand to stop Tyrone in his tracks. 'Stop, stop, man, you're makin' me sick. My lunch is on its way back.'

'I want a truce. Between me and you.'

'A truce?'

'Yeah. No more fightin', no more of that rubbish.'

'I still don't think you're good enough for her,' Harvey said.

'Maybe I'm not. But she thinks I am.'

Harvey thought on that. 'You're right about that, Tyrone. And I should know – she's told me enough times.'

'Thanks, man.' Tyrone's gratitude seemed genuine.

'You ever hurt her, and I'll hurt you. You understand?'

'One hundred per cent. It won't happen.'

'Glad to hear it. So now we're at peace,' Harvey said with some irony, 'what you wanna tell me?'

Tyrone was suddenly serious. Gone was the bravado. 'I'm here to give you answers to somethin' you've been wantin' to know for a long time. Somethin' you've probably given up ever findin' out.'

Harvey's legs felt weak and his skin prickled in anticipation.

Tyrone could only be talking about one thing.

'About Jason?'

Tyrone nodded. 'Now you understand.'

CHAPTER
FORTY-TWO

'Is everything okay?' Beth asked again.

Matt was staring down at the contents of the bag. 'Yeah, I'm fine,' he said, knowing that he probably sounded anything but.

The bag was stuffed with money – wads of banknotes, mostly in denominations of fifty.

Matt picked up one of the wads and thumbed through the individual notes. He clung on to it while thinking things through. Certainly, this amount of cash would attract anyone's attention. But the question was, what was James doing with it, and why would he disappear – if indeed he had disappeared – and leave it behind?

'Matt? Did you find anything?'

'I'll be down in a second.' He delved into the bag, checking if there was anything else apart from the money. The main compartment was stuffed full of banknotes, but that was it. The front compartment was empty.

Beth was looking up at him as he carried the bag down to the landing.

She frowned. 'What's that?'

Charlie appeared at her side, gazing up. 'Is that treasure?' he asked excitedly.

'Something like that,' Matt said. He joined the two of them on the first floor, feeling constrained by Charlie's presence. Matt held the bag down at his side, partially hidden from Charlie's view. But his son wouldn't give up that easily, so Matt deployed the diversion plan he had devised upstairs.

'Here you go, Charlie,' Matt said, handing him the wad of notes he had slid into his back pocket on the way down the stairs.

'Wow!' Charlie said, grasping it tightly. 'Real treasure!'

'Yes, real treasure.' Matt tried to give Beth a look of reassurance.

'Can I keep this?' Charlie asked.

'Let's see,' Matt said. 'Would you like to go and count it in your room, while Mummy and I have a chat?'

'Okay then,' Charlie said. 'You're always chatting these days,' he added, as he padded off to his bedroom.

Matt watched him go before turning to Beth. He lifted the bag up. 'It's full of notes. It was in the storage area, behind Charlie's old toys and clothes.'

'What?' Beth's mouth hung open in shock.

'Do you have any idea where all this money might have come from? Is there anything that might explain this?' Matt said.

Matt knew Beth was thinking about whether to say something. 'I might have an idea,' she said finally, 'about where it's from.'

'Go on.'

'James has been going out a lot recently – sometimes three, four times a week. It's been causing arguments between us for months. He was always cagey about what he was doing – said it was networking with business contacts. I didn't really believe that, but because we were focusing on Australia, I let it drop. But things came to a head about two weeks ago, when he only got back home the next morning. He said he'd decided to stay in a hotel so he wouldn't disturb us, but I was convinced he was having an affair. I confronted him and gave him an ultimatum. I said if he didn't give me a satisfactory explanation of where he kept going, then we were over. And that's when he told me what he'd really been doing.'

'Which was?'

'Gambling. He'd been going to that casino.'

'Samson's?'

'Yes.'

Samson's. The favourite gambling den of UGT traders.

Beth continued. 'He admitted he was a gambling addict and he said he needed help. He was spending a lot of money.'

Matt glanced down at the bag. 'But winning a lot, if this is anything to go by.'

'That's not what he told me. He said he was just about breaking even.'

'Right.'

'It looks like he was lying,' Beth said. She shook her head. 'I'm such a fool. He even told me he was attending a Gamblers Anonymous group, because he didn't want to risk losing me and Charlie.'

'He may have been telling the truth. Maybe he was getting help.'

'I don't know what to believe anymore. You know he lied to you, about Australia? He persuaded me the move was a good idea, not the other way around. I certainly didn't convince him to go for it. I used to think I was a good judge of character, but now I'm not so sure.'

Matt reddened.

'I'm sorry, Matt, that wasn't directed at you, I promise.' She looked down at the bag and promptly changed the subject. 'How much do you think is in there?'

'Ten, twenty thousand, I'm not sure.'

'Why would he leave that amount of money behind? It doesn't make sense.'

'Maybe he's planning to come back and retrieve it when you're out.'

'But why not take it now?'

'Who knows? Maybe he was in such a hurry he didn't have time.'

'Why would he be in such a rush to leave that he'd literally run away without tens of thousands of pounds in cash?'

'If getting away quickly was worth more.'

Beth nodded to herself. Realisation was dawning. 'This is connected with what's been happening to you. That's what you think, isn't it?'

'Yes.'

'That's why he was pushing to go to Australia,' she said. 'All that talk about wanting to start a new life, begin again somewhere different. He was just desperate to get away. And Australia is about the furthest place you can go.' She paced up and down the landing. 'James is in trouble for some reason. And Charlie is at risk because of it. I should have listened to you.'

Matt placed a hand on her arm. 'Let's just focus on now.'

'So what do we do?'

'Start packing. I'll call Sean to ask about staying over tonight. I think we should leave right now.'

CHAPTER
FORTY-THREE

Jessica was already waiting for him in the Waterloo wine bar, which was situated just down from the station of the same name, on the bank of the Thames.

'Matt, hi.' Jessica stood as he approached.

She had called him just after he'd got back to his flat, having dropped Beth and Charlie off at Sean's apartment. He'd planned to leave the rucksack of money, collect some clothes, then return to Sean's, but Jessica's call had been persuasive – she'd said she had something very important to tell him about James.

Matt felt extremely uncomfortable as they air-kissed a hello and he took in her expensive, familiar perfume – they hadn't exchanged a word since that fateful night at the UGT party, at this very venue. It hadn't been that hard to avoid her in those intervening months, given that they worked in separate departments, on different floors. He could count on one hand the number of times they had been in close proximity. There was that one time, when he'd got into the lift only to find her and James inside, on their way to a meeting with Gabriel on the top floor.

The thirty-second ascent, in stony silence, had felt like a lifetime.

'Would you like a drink?' Jessica smiled. She already had a glass of red.

'I'm okay, thanks.'

She nodded. 'You must be wondering why I asked to see you. And in this place.'

'I am, yes. Look, Jessica,' he added, 'before you say anything, I wanted to say my piece. About what happened between us.'

'Matt, you don't need to—'

'No, I do. I'm sorry about the way I acted with you after it happened. I shouldn't have ignored you the way I did. It was immature and insensitive.'

'Matt, it's okay, really.'

'No, it's not okay. At the time, I wasn't thinking straight, but now I know I should have handled things differently.'

'You lost a lot because of what happened, didn't you?'

'Yes, I did,' he replied, not wanting to share any more than that with her.

'Did you fight for Beth?'

That unexpected question really made him think. 'No, I suppose I didn't.'

'Wasn't your relationship worth it?'

'I don't want to talk about it.'

'It's not too late, you know.'

Matt gazed at Jessica. 'Why are you doing this, giving me this pep talk? Why do you care?'

She took a sip from her glass. 'Because there's something you don't know about what happened between us – about what happened that night.'

'I don't understand.'

A smile formed on her moist lips. 'You think us sleeping together was an accident, fuelled by alcohol and party spirit? Well, it wasn't. It was carefully planned.'

'Planned. By you?'

She laughed, patting Matt playfully on the arm. 'God, no. No, Matt, if I'd wanted you, I would have done things differently.'

'Jessica, I really don't get what you're saying.'

'Matt, I'm saying that I didn't conjure up the plan to seduce you and ruin your relationship with Beth. But someone else did.'

Suddenly it was so obvious. 'James Farrah.'

She nodded. 'He did it because he wanted Beth.'

Matt thought back to the speed with which James had moved in on Beth. It was just enough time after her split from Matt, but not much longer. 'Son of a . . .'

'He knew how Beth would react.'

Of course he knew.

'He persuaded me to approach you that night. I waited for the right time, then moved in, and things went from there.'

She had made it all seem so natural, so effortless. They'd bumped into one another at the bar, and had got chatting. He remembered being flattered by her flirting. What a fool he had been. 'Why did you do it?'

'Because I was stupid and naive.' She waited a beat. 'Because I wanted to please him. He had a hold on me – control, power over me, call it what you like. I guess I was willing to do almost anything to keep him.'

'You and him were in a relationship?'

'I thought so. But I've been kidding myself. It's Beth he really wants. I'm sorry, Matt.'

'He always gets what he wants,' Matt said, partly to himself.

'Maybe not this time,' she replied.

'Why tell me this now?'

Jessica played with the rim of her wine glass and flashed him a white smile. 'Because he thinks he can treat me like a piece of dirt he can scrape off his shoe. But I'm not going to let him get away with it.'

'So now you're looking to break up another relationship?'

She looked affronted that he hadn't embraced her aim. 'I would have thought you'd be delighted at the thought.'

He was thinking of Beth and how this new betrayal would affect her. 'I hurt Beth a lot by what I did.'

'By what *he* set you up to do.'

'No. By what *I* did. I might have been in a bad place, but no one dragged me to bed with you that night. James might have set things up, but it was my mistake. James Farrah didn't take Beth from me, as much as I've liked to think that over this past year or so. I lost her.'

'Does it matter?'

'Yes, it does. I won't win her back by telling her what a bad person James Farrah is. And I won't get my family back by taking revenge on the person I blamed for tearing it apart.'

'Well, I want revenge,' she said. 'And I'm not afraid to admit it. I want to see him suffer.'

Matt stood. 'I'd better go.'

'There's one more thing you should know,' she said, 'that might change things for you.'

He waited.

'James might be playing the happy family man, the stepdaddy extraordinaire. But he really isn't that person.'

'What do you mean?'

'He doesn't like children at all. Least of all your son. Charlie, isn't it? He can't stand him. Said he's a constant reminder of you, and he just cramps his style. Calls him the "snotty little brat", among other things.'

Matt struggled to suppress his anger. But he was determined not to let Jessica see her vengeful arrow had hit its target.

Not quite getting the reaction she had hoped for, Jessica pressed home her point. 'Do you really want your son to be thousands of miles away, controlled by a man who not only destroyed your relationship, but also hates the sight of him?'

'I think you know the answer to that.'

She nodded, satisfied. 'There's something else. Something you need to know.' She unbuttoned the top three buttons of her shirt and pulled back the fabric to reveal the full extent of her neck.

Matt could see blossoming bruises on each side of her throat.

'He did this,' she said, buttoning her shirt back up. 'We were having an argument. He wrapped his hands around me and squeezed tight. Then he threw me against a wall. I thought he was going to kill me.'

'You need to go to the police.'

'I'll be fine. I'm not planning on going near him again.'

'Has he been violent with you before?'

She nodded. 'Once or twice.'

'Tell the police.'

'Maybe. But it's more important you know what kind of man he is. That's why I wanted to speak to you – to warn you. I honestly think your little boy could be in danger. You need to get your son away from him.'

CHAPTER
FORTY-FOUR

Later that night, Matt found himself approaching Samson's casino with a sense of trepidation. He'd made the decision to go there shortly after the meeting with Jessica. The revelation about James's scheming, cheating, and violence had convinced him that whatever had placed Charlie at risk was linked to James Farrah. If the money had come from the casino, then perhaps he'd find some answers there as to where James was and what was going on.

Whatever James had been doing, he wasn't going to let him get away with it.

So he called Sean to make sure Beth and Charlie were well, warned him not to let James in the apartment should he reappear, and spun the line that Amy had just asked him over to her place for a late-night chat to discuss some teaching opportunities. Sean was already very concerned about what was going on, and hadn't even wanted Matt to leave his apartment to grab some clothes from his flat once he had explained everything. If Sean or Beth had known his real destination and purpose, they'd definitely have tried to talk him out of it.

Matt took a deep breath when he saw the casino ahead. It wasn't comfortable ground for him. Even though it was a popular haunt of UGT employees, Matt had only been there once before. Encouraged to try it out by Sean one night to celebrate a particularly successful trading day, the experience had left him largely cold. That was just over two years ago. He still had his membership card, though, tucked away inside his wallet, which he played around with nervously in his pocket as he came up to the entrance. He had to hope his membership was still active, as he seemed to remember that the casino as a rule didn't allow people to join and enter the club on the same night.

A burly security guard who looked like a professional boxer nodded at Matt as he passed through the entrance door and into the foyer. At least he was past the first hurdle. He waited at the desk, behind another customer, who was just being told he'd have to wait twenty-four hours until membership. The young guy wasn't happy, but his reaction was no doubt tempered by a second guard watching from just a few feet away. The guy merely shook his head and walked away.

'Hello, can I help you?'

Matt smiled and fished the card out from his wallet. He handed it over for the woman to scan. 'Matt Roberts,' she read from the screen. 'Welcome back to the club, Mr Roberts. It's been a while.'

'Yes,' Matt said, relieved that it had worked.

'Are you aware of the new funding arrangements?'

'No.'

'We've introduced contactless payment. Use your debit or credit card at the terminals near the tables. There are instructions on-screen, or just ask a member of staff if you get stuck. Have a good evening,' she said, handing him back the card.

He slipped it into his pocket. 'Thank you.'

Another customer stepped into his place as he moved off towards the archway that he remembered led through to the gaming area.

'One moment please, sir.' Matt tensed as the second security guard came up to him, imagining he was about to be challenged and removed. 'If you don't mind,' the man said, holding up a metal detector.

'Of course.' It was not like Matt had a choice in the matter. But at least he knew there was nothing to hide, and it didn't seem as though the guard was looking to eject him from the place.

'If you can just hold your arms out to the side.'

Matt did as requested, and the guard began sweeping up and down his body. The machine remained silent.

The security guard replaced the device in the holster on his belt. 'If you don't mind, just a quick pat-down.'

Matt stayed rooted to the spot as the guard completed what could only be described as a thorough frisk. As the man who had been queuing behind him at the front desk strode straight through without any glance from the guard whatsoever, Matt wondered why he had been singled out.

Had it just been random? Had the guard picked up on his nervous demeanour, like a dog sniffs out fear?

Or was it something else, something he should be more concerned about?

The guard stepped back. 'You're okay. Sorry for the delay, sir.'

'No problem,' Matt replied. The guard nodded and immediately looked past Matt, eyeing the next customer. Matt moved through the archway and into the semi-darkness of the main gaming area. He emerged on to a balcony overlooking about a dozen large round tables, all of which were staffed and had games in progress. Around the perimeter of the room, banks of slot machines flashed and blinked. He glanced at his watch. It was half past ten. For the club, the night was only just beginning, and would go through until five in the morning. But in here, apart from for the staff counting down their hours until they could go home, day or night was almost an irrelevance. There were no clocks on the walls, and no windows. It was an intentional design feature, to suck customers into an all-consuming world, where there was no time except time to gamble.

As he scanned the floor, Matt half expected to see one of his colleagues from UGT. Maybe even James himself. He strained to look across at the gamblers on the far side, but it was just that bit too dark to make out faces. He wondered whether this venture would turn out to be a waste of time.

A staff member, a youngish girl who was walking past, caught his eye. 'Are you okay, sir? Anything I can help you with?'

'I'm fine, thanks.' He'd have to move, as he was attracting attention.

Matt retreated to the bar and ordered a very expensive Coke. Sipping at the drink, he suddenly realised how unprepared he was for this task. He decided he'd head for the roulette table – the game he'd be most comfortable with – and see who was there. If there was an opportunity to ask a fellow player about James, then he'd do that before asking any of the staff.

There were three players at the table, and a croupier, a man in his fifties, who nodded a greeting. Matt waited for the next spin and then joined the game. His number didn't come up. He played again, with another loss.

Gambling really was a game for mugs.

'Hi,' Matt said to the suited man sitting next to him. He was in his mid to late thirties, sporting a dark, closely cropped beard. The guy smiled tightly, seemingly irritated at Matt's attempt at conversation. 'I was wondering, do you know James Farrah? He's a regular here.' The man just glowered at him before turning his attention back to the game, making his response crystal clear – the conversation was not going to happen.

Matt felt himself flush at the blunt rejection, and played again.

Another loss.

At this rate, his money wouldn't last long.

One of the other players left the table for the bar, and Matt looked at the other remaining person. An older man of Eastern European appearance – he could have been Polish or maybe Russian – he didn't meet Matt's smile and merely turned away. There would be no point in engaging him further. Matt looked again at the croupier, opened his mouth to speak, but then thought better of it.

This had been a stupid idea.

Matt headed back to the bar, but on the way an opportunity presented itself. He saw the receptionist. Surely if anyone would know a particular member of the club, it would be the person on reception. It looked as though she was heading for the toilets, so Matt upped his pace to intercept her.

'Excuse me?' he said, just as she was reaching for the door handle.

She stopped dead, confused by the interruption. 'Yes?'

'I'm looking for someone,' Matt began, instantly regretting his choice of words – he had meant to say something that came across as more casual, instead of sounding like he was leading a manhunt. She already looked like she was on edge. 'My friend, James Farrah. He's gone missing, and I'm just trying to piece together his last movements. I wondered whether you knew him.'

'Sorry,' she said, stony-faced. 'I'm not allowed to discuss other members.'

'But you do know him?'

'I'm sorry,' she repeated. 'I can't discuss the business of other members. The company prides itself on its approach to matters of confidentiality. I'm sorry.' She went to pull at the door, but Matt stopped it with his foot. He saw the look on her face and immediately withdrew it. 'Thank you,' she said, pointedly.

'Is there anyone who could talk to me?' Matt said, as she opened the door.

'I'm afraid not,' she replied, as the door shut behind her.

Despite feeling a deep sense of unease and a realisation that any other attempts at getting information would probably be fruitless, Matt resisted the temptation to quit, and instead got himself another drink. Maybe inspiration would strike.

He retreated to one of the sofas that ran along the edge of the balcony.

'Are you police?'

Matt turned his head. The croupier from the roulette table was peering over the railing at the gaming area below. 'Pardon?'

'Are you police?'

'No.'

'Didn't think so. Listen, I'd leave if I were you. Right now.'

'Leave? Why?'

But the croupier had already gone. Matt got to his feet, but there was no sign of him. He looked down at his quarter-drunk Coke before deciding to heed the man's warning. At the very least, his clumsy attempt to find out information had attracted the wrong kind of attention. He headed for the exit.

Just as he neared the archway that led back through to the reception area, he felt a hand grip his left arm from behind, and another hand take hold of his jacket collar. The force of the hold was vice-like. His assailant directed him to the right, and Matt stumbled as the person's weight bore down on him. For a split second, he considered fighting to break free, but then, in one of the mirrored walls, he caught a glimpse of the hulk of the person who had him in his grasp.

It was obvious that resisting would only make things worse.

CHAPTER
FORTY-FIVE

Matt submitted to the man's pushes and shoves as he was propelled down the corridor. The guy hadn't said a word – his attention appeared totally focused on the task at hand.

'I'll leave,' Matt said, trying to initiate conversation, his voice cracking with fear and anxiety. 'If that's what this is about, I'll go, right now.' And that was the truth. If he could have wished himself out of this place, he'd have done so in a heartbeat.

But the man said nothing. He was probably looking forward to launching him out of a back exit. Stomach churning, Matt's mind flashed back to the terrifying experience with Tyrone in the alleyway – how scared he had been. He felt just as fearful now. Except that this time, Harvey wasn't there to protect him.

They continued to the foot of a staircase.

'Up to the top,' the man instructed. 'I'll be right behind you. Don't try anything funny. It won't end well.' He released his grip. 'Up.'

Matt climbed the stairs, with the man right at his back. It wasn't clear how he could have tried anything, given the hopeless situation he was in.

'Knock,' the man said, when they reached the closed door at the top.

Matt did as instructed. His hand was shaking as he brought his fist up to the wood of the door. The knock was weak and nervous.

'Come in,' a deep voice said on the other side.

'Go on,' the man behind him prompted. 'Don't keep Mr Samson waiting.'

Nick Samson? The club owner?

He opened the door and was steered into the room by the man who had brought him there. The door closed behind them.

It was like they'd just walked into an industrial studio apartment. The large open-plan room was subdivided into zones, with a kitchen area, gym and living space. In the living space, a huge flat-screen television hung on the wall, showing a baseball game. The man who was sitting on a sofa in the corner stood up to greet him.

'Nick Samson,' he said, proffering a hand as he approached. His tight polo shirt showed off a toned physique. Matt could see he was a few years younger than himself. 'I own this club. And you are?'

'Matt Roberts,' he managed weakly.

Samson smiled professionally. His grip was firm. 'Drink, Matt?'

'I'm okay, thanks.'

'Fair enough. It's okay, Joseph, you can wait downstairs.'

The man who'd manhandled Matt all the way to the office looked perturbed by that order. He seemed to be about to question it, but thinking better of it, just nodded and left the room.

'I do hope Joseph treated you well,' Samson said. Matt realised he had a surprisingly well-spoken accent.

'He did,' Matt lied. He wasn't going to complain about the pain just now.

'That's good. He can be a bit overenthusiastic. Into mixed martial arts.' Samson gestured to the corner of the room. 'Please, do take a seat.'

Matt perched on the edge of a comfy chair, as Nick Samson seated himself on the sofa opposite.

Samson gazed up at the television. 'Three weeks ago, I was there in Boston, watching the Red Sox.' He smiled at the memory. 'Amazing game. And a great city.'

'I can imagine,' Matt managed to say, his nerves so fraught that his teeth were chattering and his body was buzzing. The gravity of the situation, that he'd just been frogmarched into the private office of Nick Samson, was only just hitting home.

'So,' Samson said, 'you're not a regular here, are you, Matt?'

Matt tried to slow his breathing, without making it obvious. 'No, just my second time.'

'Well, good to have you back. I'm sure you're wondering why I brought you up here.'

'Because I was asking questions about a friend of mine who's gone missing.'

There was no point in lying.

Samson nodded. 'James Farrah. He a good friend of yours?'

Matt was struggling to calm himself as Samson gazed at him with intense grey-blue eyes. 'A work colleague.'

'And he's gone missing?'

Matt nodded.

'What makes you think anyone in this club knows his whereabouts?'

'It was somewhere he visited. I thought someone here might be able to help.'

'Matt, I appreciate you're worried about your friend, but what you did down there wasn't very smart.' Samson smiled tightly.

Matt felt his heart skip a beat. 'I don't understand.'

The smile faded. 'Since I took over this club four years ago, I've worked hard to keep it clean and ensure it's a safe and secure place for my clients to come and enjoy a night out. In the main, I've succeeded, but that doesn't mean to say it's the kind of place where you can go around asking questions, bothering people.'

'I'm sorry . . .'

Samson held out a hand. 'I didn't bring you up here for an apology. I got you up here for your own safety. You were the talk of the gaming floor. In this kind of place, people don't ask questions. They hardly even look at one another. The guy you tried talking to at the roulette table, a very important client for us, he wasn't happy. And really, he's one person you don't want to annoy.'

Matt flushed as he thought back to his amateurish efforts at investigation.

'Why are you looking for Farrah? He's a grown man,' Samson said.

There was no way Matt was going to bring Charlie into this, so he'd not be explaining the full situation here. 'I'm concerned about him.'

'I'd like to help, Matt, but we don't reveal any details about members – only to the authorities, not to members of the public.'

Matt nodded. 'I understand.'

'So I'm afraid we can't help you. What I can tell you is that, yes, James Farrah is a member here. He's a regular visitor – or at least he was, up until recently. But that's as much as I can help you with.'

Matt stood. 'Am I free to leave?'

'Of course, of course. Joseph will show you out.'

Matt moved towards the door.

'Matt,' Samson said. 'I'm afraid I'm going to have to ask you to hand in your membership card on the way out. When our members cross the threshold to Samson's, they expect a certain sense of security. I hope you understand. We have to protect our clients.'

'Of course.'

'One more thing,' Samson called out, as Matt pulled open the door. Matt turned to face him. 'I admire you for searching for your friend. I really do. But sometimes when a man disappears, it's because he doesn't want to be found.'

CHAPTER
FORTY-SIX

On edge and fearful, adrenaline was pumping through Matt's body as he slowly walked away from the casino and back towards the Tube station. The night hadn't gone the way he had planned. He sensed that the opportunity to uncover James's secrets had been wasted.

Matt was still within sight of the casino when he sensed someone approaching him from behind. He tensed at the realisation that this person, whoever they were, was closing in. As they neared, they appeared to slow down. He wanted to turn around, but forced himself to carry on.

'Don't turn around. Keep walking,' the voice said from just behind his shoulder. 'We should talk, but not here. It's okay, I'm a friend.'

After everything that had just happened at the casino, Matt's instinct was to walk away. But curiosity got the better of him. 'Who are you?'

The man ignored his question. 'I know a place just down the road. An all-night cafe. We can go there.'

'Okay.'

'Let's go there separately. Just in case any of Samson's men are watching. I couldn't help but notice that you caught their attention this evening. So they may still be retaining an interest, if you know what I mean.'

Matt nodded.

The man now came up alongside Matt and met his eye for the briefest of seconds. It was the croupier who had tried to warn him off asking questions earlier, just before Samson's heavy had intercepted him. 'Just keep looking straight ahead,' he said. He continued speaking, but didn't look at Matt again. 'If you continue down the road, take the first turning on the right, and the cafe is about five shops along. It's called Daphne's. You can't miss it, as it'll be the only place open. I'll be along in a few minutes.' And with that, the croupier increased his pace and crossed the road, disappearing around a corner.

Matt continued walking, following the directions to the cafe, which was indeed brightly lit, in stark contrast to the surrounding shuttered shops. Through the window, Matt could see rows of white moulded tables and chairs, populated by just two people, both of whom had mugs in front of them. Pushing open the door, he attracted the attention of the customer on the far side, a man with a bushy seaman's beard, who glanced up from his book before returning to read. The other customer, a younger man in what looked like a haulage company's uniform, didn't even look up from the newspaper spread across his table.

At the counter, a lady was drying the surface with a tea towel. 'Take a seat,' she said. 'I'll be along in just a minute.'

Matt ordered a tea and pulled out his phone, wondering whether the croupier would indeed show up. After a few minutes, he'd begun to think it wasn't going to happen, but then the door opened and the man entered. He nodded at the woman behind the counter. 'The usual, please, Sharon,' he said, and sat down opposite Matt. He shook off his jacket, wrapping it carefully around the back of the chair.

'My name's Tony Casey,' he said, extending a hand, as Sharon returned with a cup of coffee. 'Thanks, Sharon.' He watched for a second as she walked away before continuing. 'I'm the union rep at Samson's. Any issues that arise in the casino among members – terms and conditions, health and well-being, and the like – I'm the first port of call.' He slurped some coffee. 'God, I needed that. Been on shift for twelve hours.'

'I don't know how you work in that place.'

Tony laughed at the thought. 'Neither do I. It's like survival of the fittest. Most people, they don't stick at casino work – the pressure, the aggravation of punters, the hours and hours without daylight, it gets too much very quickly. Old-timers like me, been working in the business for twenty-five years, we're survivors. But I'm not sure surviving in this industry is anything to celebrate.'

'You don't enjoy the work?'

He shrugged. 'I used to, but not for a long time now. I worked my way up through a few of the clubs around London. It was more fun back then, I guess. Or maybe I was just younger and more resilient. Now, well, it's not much fun.'

It reminded Matt of the way he felt about UGT. 'You haven't thought about getting out of the industry?'

'I've thought about it. But it's too late. I'm pushing sixty. This is all I know. It's what I'm good at. It's okay,' he said, noting Matt's expression. 'Don't feel sorry for me. Feel sorry for the new guys and girls who've got another thirty, forty years left in this business. It's one of the reasons why I stay. I get the satisfaction of helping them out when they're being mistreated by management. If I leave, they'll have no one to protect them or their interests.'

'There wouldn't be another union rep to replace you?'

Tony laughed at the suggestion. 'They've been trying to get rid of the union influence for years now.'

'But they can't do that, can they?'

'They can do whatever they want.'

Tony put down his coffee cup and took a breath, looking directly at Matt. It was as if he was trying to read him as he would a player, and it made Matt feel slightly uncomfortable.

'I don't recognise you,' Tony said. 'Was tonight your first night in the club?'

'I've been once before, but it was a few years ago.'

Tony smiled. 'Not much of a gambler then?'

'No. It really doesn't do anything for me. Sorry.'

'No need to apologise.'

'I know a few of your regulars though. From UGT Bank.'

'Ah,' he said. 'Including the one you were asking about?'

'Yes.'

'That's why I wanted to speak to you.' Tony looked over his shoulder. 'We do our union debriefs in here, and meet with members, because we know management wouldn't be seen dead in a place like this. But you can never be too careful.'

'You tried to help me in there,' Matt said. 'Thanks.'

'Don't mention it. I'm afraid you can't do what you did tonight and not get picked out. Samson's too sharp an operator to let that go unchecked.'

'Yes, I should have been more careful.'

'You were lucky,' Tony said. 'I don't know what you're after, but he obviously decided you weren't worth the trouble.'

'Meaning?'

'Meaning he let you walk out of there in one piece.'

'Is he really that dangerous?'

'He's a *very* dangerous man.'

Matt gulped down his fear with a slurp of tea. 'But he's just a businessman, isn't he?'

'He has his fingers in many pies,' Tony said.

'In what way?'

'Well, he makes most of his money from online gambling. Poker, mainly. You might have heard of his platform, Ace of Clubs?'

Matt nodded – Sean had the app.

'That's his main focus. The club is very much a sideline. He bought it mostly for the networking opportunities with clients. And then there's his latest venture, the gentleman's club in the West End, Delilah's. Again, he networks there a lot.'

'But why dangerous?'

Another glance around. 'Extortion, fraud, money-laundering, drug-running . . .'

'Really?'

'You remember that big robbery last year? The one where the thieves tunnelled into the vault of safe-deposit boxes, got away with millions?'

'Birch Grove?'

'Yes, that's the one. They still haven't found out who did it.'

Matt knew that case well. 'Some of my colleagues, they had boxes there. Lost hundreds of thousands of pounds between them.' Those colleagues included Sean and Gabriel. And while Gabriel's loss was a closely guarded secret, Sean had confided in Matt that his box, which had been emptied, had contained forty thousand pounds' worth of gold bullion.

'There are rumours, probably coming from himself, that Samson was involved. He likes people to know how clever he is – likes toying with the authorities. He knows he'll never be caught.'

'Why won't he be caught?'

'Friends in high places. And that includes the Metropolitan Police.'

Suddenly Matt's idea that night to walk into the club and start asking questions seemed not just reckless, but downright suicidal. And yet, Samson had let him leave unscathed, after only some minor, if uncomfortable questioning. But why? Maybe the croupier was right, and Samson had decided it wasn't worth the hassle to take things any further.

Or maybe there was another explanation.

Matt looked across at Tony, who was slurping at his coffee.

Could this all be a trap? Was this man actually acting under the orders of Samson – told to follow Matt and find out what he was really after?

'Why are you telling me all this?'

'Because I've seen too many people done over by Nick Samson. When I heard you asking about James Farrah, then saw you getting kicked out, I decided maybe I should help. Ten years ago, I would have shrugged it off, but what the hell. James was a good tipper. I've been wondering what happened to him myself.'

'So how can you help?'

Tony placed his mug on the table and began rubbing his hands, pushing the skin towards his knuckles. 'You and him, you're close work colleagues?'

'I wouldn't say that. We worked in the same department at UGT, but we don't really get on.'

'So why were you asking about him?'

'To protect my son.'

'I don't follow.'

'James Farrah is in a relationship with my ex-partner. I think he's involved with something that has put my son at risk, and I think it might be linked to the casino.'

'What makes you think that?'

'I found something. And I think it's related to Nick Samson. I think maybe he owes him money.'

Matt expected to see some sign of confirmation that his hypothesis was along the right lines, but Tony's reaction was the opposite. He laughed in disbelief at Matt's suggestion. 'James Farrah owes Samson money? I don't think so.'

'What makes you say that?'

'Because James is one of the most successful players at Samson's. He wins big, and often. He's been so successful, in fact, that a call went out some months ago to do enhanced monitoring to make sure he's not using a system. I know Samson's always wary of your lot, given you work with numbers, risk, and odds all day, but statistically the UGT crowd are usually no more likely to win than anyone else who comes to the club. Personally speaking, I think James is just on an extended lucky run. It happens. Eventually the odds equalise. The punters come out of it in the black if they quit while they're ahead. Or they start believing the luck will return, and run themselves into the red. But this has been going on for a long time. I've heard rumours they were thinking of banning him.'

'But they haven't done that yet?'

'They were close to doing so, about three or four months ago. He had a pretty massive win, even by his standards. I'm talking thirty thousand pounds. That really disturbed Samson, from what I hear. But all of a sudden, he stopped coming. I haven't seen him now in a couple of months. I did wonder if Samson had brought in the ban without an announcement, but that doesn't really happen, as the staff need to know in case the client tries to get back in. Then I wondered whether he'd just gone on an extended holiday with all his winnings. He could travel around the world several times with what he's taken out of the club. I would have asked one of his colleagues, but they've stopped coming too.'

'All the UGT employees, they've stopped coming to the club?'

'Yes.'

'That seems strange.'

'Yes, it is. The club has had a very close relationship with UGT for the past few years. Samson has cultivated it. He's provided private gaming rooms for UGT, with VIP service. Free drinks, food, service, you know. It's like a club within a club. Financially, it's well worth his while because of the money UGT staff spend. I don't really get to work in there very much, but because of my union role, I've been inside a number of times, checking the staff are okay.'

'But now all the UGT staff have suddenly stopped coming.'

'I wondered whether another club had poached them. It can happen. There's that new club in Mayfair, owned by the Arab prince. I wouldn't be surprised if they've targeted the City workers to get them through the doors.'

'You're not convinced?'

Tony shrugged. 'Who knows what goes on in the casino industry. I've been in the game a long time, and I still get surprised by the things that happen.'

'It's all still a mystery then.'

'Have you asked James outright?'

Matt still felt a slight hesitation in telling this guy everything. But he decided he'd reveal a little more. 'He's disappeared. This morning.'

'You think he's running from something?'

'Yes.'

'And you say your son might be at risk because of it?'

'I do, yes.'

'I can see why you did what you did tonight. Where is your son now, if you don't mind me asking?'

'With his mother, my ex-partner, staying with a relative.' Immediately he regretted giving an answer so readily.

What if this guy really was working for Nick Samson – as more than just a croupier – and Matt had now provided him with information that could be used against him and Charlie?

'So you've told her about your fears?'

'Yes. Although I'm not sure she really believes me.'

'She obviously believes you enough to not stay at home this evening.' Tony rubbed at his face. 'I wish I could help you more. But I've told you all I know.'

'I appreciate it.'

Tony checked the time. 'I'd better be going.'

Matt gazed down into his tea, thinking about Charlie and Beth staying the night at Sean's apartment. Charlie would be excited at the change of scenery. His innocence would ensure that for him this was all a bit of an adventure.

He snapped out of his thoughts and looked at Tony, who was zipping up his jacket. 'You've been really helpful. Thank you.' Matt handed him an old business card from his wallet. 'If there's anything else you think might be helpful, anything at all, then do get in touch. My work details aren't current anymore – I've left UGT – but my mobile number is still correct.'

Tony nodded, flipping the card between his fingers as if he was dealing on the blackjack table. 'Of course. Anything I can do.'

He went to walk away, then stopped.

'Look, I know this is probably stepping over the line, and feel free to tell me it's none of my business . . .' He hesitated.

'It's okay. What is it?' Matt said.

'It's just that, if I was in your position, and knowing what I know about Nick Samson, I wouldn't let my kid out of my sight for a second.'

Matt imagined Charlie sleeping peacefully in his bed, arm wrapped around his favourite Funky Monkey stuffed toy, as Samson's men closed in. Matt grabbed his jacket and headed for the door. In his panic, he forgot to even say goodbye to Tony as he headed back to Sean's apartment.

CHAPTER FORTY-SEVEN

Sean Carey lay back on the sofa, waiting for the doorbell. The pizza delivery would be here any minute.

And there it was.

He pushed himself up and jogged over to the door. The stress had made him ravenous.

'Thank goodness you're—'

Sean doubled over from the thunderous punch to his solar plexus, staggering backwards into the apartment. 'Please,' he pleaded, gasping for breath. 'Please don't kill me.'

CHAPTER
FORTY-EIGHT

Matt raced across London to Sean's place. He'd phoned Beth, then Sean, with both calls ringing through to their voicemail, which had really set him on edge.

He tried the door, before remembering what Sean had told him – the security on the reception desk left at ten thirty, and it was now half past twelve. On the left of the door was the digital buzzer system that Sean had instructed him to use. He typed in the apartment number, but there was no answer.

Is he asleep?

He typed it in again and pressed 'Enter'.

Again, there was no answer.

Matt pulled out his mobile and dialled Sean's number once more, willing him to pick up.

Someone answered.

'Sean, I buzzed up, but there was no answer. I'm waiting downstairs. Is that you? Where are you?'

'In the apartment,' Sean said groggily. 'Sorry. I'll buzz you through.'

'Are you okay?'

But the line had gone dead.

The light by the door flashed green and Matt entered. He headed for the lift and ascended to the third floor. Sean hadn't seemed himself. Maybe he'd just woken up.

Matt exited the lift and hurried towards Sean's front door. It was ajar. His anxiety levels rose.

Something felt wrong here.

'Sean, are you there?' He moved into the dark apartment and along the hallway. He could hear the television in the living room. 'Sean?'

Sean was sitting on the sofa, lit only by the TV. He was hugging his chest, and grimaced as Matt looked on. His nose was swollen and bloody, his cheek bruised.

'Oh my God.'

Matt dashed towards the bedrooms.

Sean called him back. 'It's okay. They're not here.'

Matt stepped back into the room, breathless. 'Where are they?'

Sean had risen from the sofa and was holding his side. 'At a hotel. The Excalibur.'

'A hotel? Why?'

'Because it wasn't safe,' he said, grimacing again. 'I didn't want to risk it, in case they came looking here.'

'Who came looking?'

Sean didn't answer.

Matt took him by the shoulders. 'Sean, talk to me. *Who* came looking? Who did this to you?'

'Samson.'

'You're involved in all this, aren't you?' Matt exclaimed.

Sean nodded.

'You should have told me!'

'I know, I know.' Sean shrugged off Matt's hold.

Matt resisted the temptation to grab him again. 'We need to go and get Beth and Charlie. I can't believe you've left them on their own.'

Another grimace. 'They're safe at the hotel. I took them there myself, made sure they were settled.'

'What did you tell Beth?'

'I made up a story. Said I'd been having some trouble with an ex, that she's been coming around to the apartment in the middle of the night and phoning me in the early hours.'

'We've got to go and get them,' Matt repeated.

'That might not be a good idea.'

'Why?'

'Because the man who did this,' he said, gesturing at his face, 'he might still be around. We don't want to risk leading him straight to them.'

'Who is he?'

'Joseph Deed. Nick Samson's associate.'

The man from the casino.

'Sean, what the hell is all this about?'

'They were looking for James.'

'Why?'

'Because he has something they want.'

'Which is?'

'Drugs. And fifty thousand pounds in cash. We never intended things to turn out like this,' Sean said. 'And if I'd thought for one minute that it would put any of you in danger, I'd never have gone for it. I've tried my best to protect you from all of this.'

Suddenly, Matt knew.

'It was you, wasn't it? You paid Natalie to protect Charlie.'

Sean moved over to the kitchen area, placing a steadying hand on the granite worktop. 'I need to explain from the beginning.'

'I'm listening.'

Sean looked to be struggling, bent over with the pain. 'Sorry, this is so difficult.'

'Just tell me, Sean.'

Sean took a breath. 'We're in big trouble, Matt. *Really* big trouble. You know I've been a regular at Samson's for years. We were treated like royalty. But a year or so ago things soured. James had a winning run on blackjack. And he kept on winning and winning – tens of thousands of pounds. The word was that Samson was pretty upset about it all. We had a tip-off that the club was thinking of banning James, on the pretext he'd been using some kind of system.'

'Was James using a system?'

'He said not.'

'So what happened?'

'They took away the perks – the food, drink, women. Tried to push us out. Relations really broke down. But to be honest, when you're winning so big, you don't really care about a lack of nibbles and nipples.' He grimaced at his own joke. Matt frowned. 'But then Samson found another way to get his money back.'

'How d'you mean?'

'Birch Grove.'

Matt made the connection immediately. 'Samson arranged the robbery at Birch Grove as revenge for James winning big in his casino?'

'Yes.'

'You know that for certain?'

'He told us straight. He was very open about the whole thing. He took delight in letting us know – firstly, that he'd done it, secondly, that there was no way he'd be caught, and thirdly, that we'd never get our money back.'

'But I don't understand. If Samson won, cleared you out, then why are they still looking for James?'

'This is where it started to go badly wrong. We tried to hit back at him. And we made a massive error of judgement. We should have walked away, but we thought we could take him on.'

'How d'you mean?'

Sean hesitated. 'Our relationship with Samson. It went deeper than the casino.'

'In what way?'

'He supplied us with food, drinks, women. He also supplied drugs.'

'In the club?'

'One of our guys was caught snorting coke in the toilets. Then Samson approached us, and offered to supply.'

'So he supplied you with cocaine?'

'Among other things, yes.'

'For when you were in the club.'

'It started off that way, but after a short time he made us an offer. Wanted to see whether there was a wider market for supplying within UGT. He asked if we'd be interested in being middlemen between him and the workforce there.'

'"We" being?'

'Me, James, a few of the other regulars.'

'Bloody hell, Sean.'

'I know, I know. It was a stupid thing to get involved with. But, hell, you know how rife drug use is within UGT. I thought, well, I might as well—'

'Be profiting from it?'

'Yes,' Sean said, unblinking. 'If it wasn't me, it would be someone else. Then, after the robbery, we tried to think about how we could get Samson back. We thought about going to the police, telling them he'd admitted his guilt, but we decided it would have been a waste of time.'

And you didn't want the police poking around, in case they discovered your drug sideline, Matt thought.

'So we thought of another way we could get some compensation.'

'You siphoned off the profits from the drugs.' Matt was beginning to understand now. It was all starting to make sense.

'We realised there was a more profitable technique we could employ. We made the drugs go that bit further.'

'You cut them?'

'Yes.'

'With what?'

'Various things. It worked like a dream. We were doubling the quantity and our profits were skyrocketing . . . What?' he said, seeing the look on Matt's face.

'You sound like a drug dealer,' Matt said. 'You might have started all this to get revenge on Nick Samson, but all the talk about profit – it became something different, didn't it?'

Sean frowned as he processed the words. And then he did something Matt hadn't expected – he smiled. 'Yes, I suppose it did.'

Matt shook his head. 'Sean, you *have* to stop this.'

The smile vanished. 'It is stopped. Samson found out what we were doing.'

'And then what?'

Sean was unblinking. 'Things got really bad.'

'Alex McKenzie?'

'Alex was one of our group.'

'So his death – it wasn't an accident?'

'I don't think so. Although I can't be sure.'

Matt couldn't quite believe what he was hearing. 'And what about his girlfriend, Rachel Martin?'

'I don't know. Maybe.'

'This is just crazy.'

'I never wanted to put any of you in harm's way, believe me.'

'But I don't understand. Why would you think Charlie was at risk? Why would Samson go after him?'

'Because of this,' Sean said, moving across to the bookcase. He pulled out a photograph from in between two books and handed it to Matt.

Matt gazed at the image.

'It was the day we all went to the farm park,' Sean said. 'I took Charlie on the castle climbing frame.'

Sean was holding Charlie high in the air, Charlie's mouth open in joy.

'Turn over the photo,' Sean directed.

'What the hell?'

The handwritten line read:

Don't let Charlie down, Uncle Sean.

Matt felt sick to the stomach.

'It came in the post,' Sean explained. 'Just over two months ago. I panicked. Didn't know what to do. I told James, but he said it just made it all the more important to deny everything. But then I remembered one of the girls from work talking about her friend who had paid to have this woman entrap their man. I got the contact details, wondered whether she could help. I asked her to follow Charlie wherever he went, including when he was with you. I couldn't go to the police.'

'You *could* have gone.'

'Yes, I could have gone, but . . .'

'You could have told me. If you thought Charlie was in danger, you *should* have told me.'

'I didn't want to drag you into this situation.'

Matt was enraged. 'Didn't want to drag me into the situation?'

'I know, I know, I should have told you.'

'Does Beth know?'

'God, no,' Sean said.

'What does Samson want from you?'

'His money back. The additional profits from the drugs we cut. And any drug supplies we have left.'

'So give it to him, and he'll go away.'

'I wish I could.'

'Why can't you?'

'Because I don't have access to the money or the drugs.'

'Who does?'

'James. The plan, to defraud Samson, it was his idea. He dealt with the finances for everything and controlled the supply of the drugs.'

'Then tell him to give everything to them.'

'I've tried,' he said. 'I tried to reason with him, to tell him to just hand it all over, and then maybe they'd leave us alone. But he said he'd sold the remainder of the drugs and spent all the money.'

'He did you over?'

'I wasn't convinced he'd spent all the money. And when you told me about finding that bag of cash hidden in Beth's house, well, it kind of changed things in my eyes.'

'You think Samson believes James has run off with the money and the drugs?'

'Yes.'

'So he sent Joseph Deed around here to get you to tell him where James was?'

'Yes.'

'I'm surprised he let you off with such a light beating.'

'He was in the middle of beating the crap out of me when he got a phone call. Said I was a very lucky man. Then he left.'

'What if he comes back to finish what he started?'

'Then we're in big trouble.'

Matt checked the time. It was gone 1 a.m. 'First thing in the morning, we go and get Beth and Charlie. Then we're going away, to lie low for a while.'

'You serious?'

'Of course. I'd do anything to protect my family from danger.'

CHAPTER
FORTY-NINE

Matt lay on his back, staring at the ceiling in Sean's spare room. The thin cream curtains let the city light flood in from outside, casting shadows across the room. In the distance, he heard a siren. He leaned over and checked the time on his phone – twenty minutes to two. This promised to be a long and painful night. He rolled over on to his side and closed his eyes, willing himself to drift off.

But sleep proved impossible.

He looked again at his phone. For a second, he considered calling Beth. But she'd be asleep, as would Charlie. A call now would probably wake both of them. It would serve no purpose except to put his mind at rest. He toyed with the phone, then sat up in bed and began typing a text message.

Hope you're both okay. I'm staying the night at Sean's. Will be around first thing in the morning. Matt xxx

He deleted the kisses, then pressed 'Send', before placing the phone back on the side table.

Less than a minute later, his phone buzzed.

Matt. What's going on? I'm really worried. Sean wouldn't tell me anything.

So Beth was awake, too – worrying. He typed back a reply:

> He told me everything earlier. Will tell you tomorrow morning.

Then, as he waited for the reply, he shot off another message:

> Is your door locked? Turned from the inside?

A few seconds later came the answer.

> Yes. Why?

His reply:

> Put a chair in front of it too. If anyone knocks in the night, DON'T answer it.

And another thought came to him:

> If there is a phone in your room, DON'T answer if it rings.

He waited for the reply.

> You're scaring me Matt. What the hell is going on? I wish you were here now.

He replied:

> I wish I was too. But we have to wait until the morning.

Her answer was one word:
Okay.

Matt tapped out his final message of the conversation:

See you in the morning.

And then he added:

I will always love you and Charlie. I was a fool to throw it all away. Matt xxx

He didn't expect a reply, and none came.

The text conversation with Beth must have soothed his mind, as he woke at 7 a.m., feeling more refreshed than he'd dared to hope. He showered quickly and wolfed down his breakfast, waking Sean up as he got himself ready. By eight o'clock, they were ready to leave the apartment.

'What if they're still around, waiting for us?' Matt said, as they stood in the hallway.

'Then we don't go to the hotel,' Sean replied. 'We try to lose them. Maybe call Beth and get them to go somewhere else, away from London. We could meet up with them there.'

'Sounds like you've given this some thought.'

'I was up quite a lot of last night,' Sean revealed. He smiled apologetically. 'Did quite a bit of thinking, to see how I could get you out of the mess I've helped to create.'

'Don't worry about whose fault it is or isn't,' Matt said. 'Let's just concentrate on getting through this in one piece, with everyone safe.'

Sean's hand had just touched the door handle when his phone shrilled. He shot Matt a worried look as he put it to his ear. Sean raised his other hand as he listened, his face ashen.

'Yes, I understand,' he said finally, bringing the phone back down by his side. He appeared crestfallen.

'No,' Matt said, 'they've not . . .'

Sean winced as his hand went to his swollen nose, eyes closed, his face a mass of bruises.

'Sean?' Matt demanded, taking him by both shoulders. 'What is it?'

'That was Nick Samson. They've taken them. They've got Beth and Charlie.'

PART FOUR

CHAPTER FIFTY

'He said he wants the drugs and the money back. Six hundred grams of coke and fifty thousand pounds. By twelve noon.'

Matt felt sick with helplessness. 'Or he'll do what?'

Sean's expression was ominous. He hesitated. 'He said we'd never see Beth and Charlie again.'

Oh my God.

Matt paced around. 'They must have followed you last night, to the hotel, saw you drop off Beth and Charlie.'

'I tried to be so careful.'

Not careful enough.

Matt had a thought. 'What about the money James left? What if we offer them that?'

'It's a lot of money, but it's not enough.'

'But we could offer it as a first instalment.'

'He wants the lot, Matt.'

Matt shook his head, frustrated and scared. He pulled out his mobile phone.

Sean's face flashed with panic. 'Who are you phoning?'

'The police.' Matt keyed in '999'.

'No,' Sean said, snatching the phone from Matt's hand. He cut the call. 'You can't do that.' He set off towards the living room, with Matt in pursuit.

'Sean, give me back the phone, now.'

They faced up to one another.

'Calling the police would be the worst thing we could do.'

'Give me back the phone, Sean.' Matt tried to grab it, but Sean held on tightly.

'Just listen to me, Matt. Please. I understand you wanting to do this. But it would be the quickest way to lose Beth and Charlie.'

Matt tried again, unsuccessfully, to win back his phone.

'You're just afraid of being implicated in all this,' Matt hit out. 'You're afraid of losing everything.'

'Maybe you're right,' Sean bristled. 'But nothing compares to the fear I feel of losing Beth and Charlie.'

They stood inches apart, not speaking, breathing hard, emotionally drained.

Sean continued, more calmly. 'Samson will know if we get the police involved. He has connections.'

'But there must be a way.'

'Ask yourself – how could the police help us right now? How could they get Charlie and Beth back?'

Matt circled the room, searching his mind for an alternative solution. He turned back to Sean, who was now perched on the arm of the sofa. 'They want all the money and drugs, so we have to give it to them.'

'But we haven't got the money or the drugs,' Sean replied.

'Then we need to find James.'

'We've all tried and tried to reach him.'

'I know.' Matt thought some more. And then it came to him. 'There might be another way. We get together the money ourselves. I don't know how much we need, but we could surely pull together enough to satisfy them. We already have the cash from the bag.'

'Yes, that's possible. But there's a problem,' Sean said. 'The money is one thing. But what about the drugs?'

Matt smiled as inspiration came to him.

'Give me my phone.'

CHAPTER
FIFTY-ONE

Harvey answered on the second ring. 'Matt, my man,' he said, his tone upbeat and friendly. 'Nice to hear from you, bruv! How are things with you?'

'To be honest, they've been better,' Matt replied. 'Look,' he continued, as his eyes met Sean's, 'I've got something to ask you, and it might – well, it will – seem a bit strange.'

'Sounds interesting. Fire away, man.'

'I need some cocaine.'

'Woah.' Harvey burst out laughing. 'Wow. Now I didn't expect that. I thought you didn't do drugs, man. I thought you was clean. You was my drug-free hero.'

'I don't do drugs. I just need some.'

'You wanna supply?' Harvey's tone was suddenly serious. 'I mean, nah, bruv – don't you get into that business.'

'It's not for supply.' Again Matt looked across to Sean, whose head was cocked slightly, straining to hear.

'Then what's it for?'

'It's for a deal.'

'What kinda deal?'

Sean nodded at Matt to tell all.

There was no easy way to say it. 'It's to get my partner and son back alive.'

'You kiddin' me, right?'

'I wish I was. Nick Samson has taken Beth and Charlie, and we won't see them again unless we deliver money and drugs to him.'

'Nick Samson, the casino guy? Shit, man. How'd you get yourself into that kind of trouble?'

'It's a long story. We just need to know if you can get us the drugs.'

There was a pregnant pause. 'I can get you drugs, yes.'

Matt's relief was palpable. 'How quickly can you get it?'

'Depends on how much you need, my man.'

'Six hundred grams.' Matt got a nod of agreement from Sean.

'Six hundred? That's a challenge. But not impossible.'

'So when can you have it?'

'How quickly do you need it?'

'Before midday.'

'Woah.' There was a tense pause. 'Hey, for you, bruv, I can do that.'

Matt felt like whooping with joy.

'You haven't asked about the cost,' Harvey said.

'It doesn't really matter. I'll pay whatever it takes.'

Harvey laughed again. 'Man, that comment *shows* you ain't no drug dealer. It's a good job you're a mate, otherwise you'd be ripe to be stung. Look, I'll get you the best price – should be around twenty-one grand?'

'That's fine.'

'Good to hear it, my man. I'll be in touch as soon as I get the stuff, bruv. You should hear from me in the next hour or so, to update you on how things are progressin'. There shouldn't be no problem, man. But if there is, I'll let you know.'

'That's great. Thanks, Harvey.'

'Pay me later, okay? And one last thing – where you wanna do the handover?'

Matt covered the mouthpiece and looked across at Sean. 'Where should we do it?'

'Somewhere where Samson and Deed won't be able to intercept it before we know Beth and Charlie are safe.'

Sean had a very good point.

'Hey, Matt,' Harvey cut in. 'I guess from the silence that maybe you're havin' trouble thinkin' of a place to take possession?'

Matt took his hand away from the mouthpiece. 'We need to meet somewhere where we know they won't be able to follow and watch us.'

'I know a place.'

'Is it okay if I put you on speakerphone?' Matt said. 'This would be good for Sean to hear too.'

'So your friend has a name?'

'Yes, sorry. I'm with Sean, in his apartment. He is – was – a work colleague. He's also Beth's brother.'

'And it's just you two?'

'Yes. Just us.'

'Put me on speaker. Okay. You need to make sure that they *are* watchin'. I give you the drugs, and you give them to Samson, at the same time and place as you get your family back, yeah?'

Matt got it. 'So you mean you'd be present at the exchange?'

'Yeah. We meet there, and only there.'

Harvey ended the call, and whistled softly through his teeth as a broad smile broke out across his face.

How could this have come together so well? Surely it was meant to be.

He pulled out the torn and faded photo from his pocket.

'I'm gonna get justice for you, bruv.'

CHAPTER FIFTY-TWO

Matt returned from the bathroom to find Sean on the phone. Sean threw him a serious look and ended the call.

'We may have a problem,' he said.

'How d'you mean?'

'I just called the bank. They won't give out that kind of money as cash. Not on the same day, at least. That was the second bank I've tried.'

'So what do we do?'

'Rob the bank? Alternatively, I don't suppose your friend Harvey can lay his hands on a lot of cash to go with the drugs?'

'I highly doubt it.'

'Then I don't know what we can do.'

'Okay,' Matt began, trying desperately to think as he spoke. 'We've got the drugs, we hope. And we've got some of the money . . . Is there enough in that bag to convince them it's all the money they've asked for?'

'No,' Sean replied confidently. 'You counted twenty thousand in the bag. Less than half of what they're expecting. And they'll know what fifty thousand pounds looks like.'

'Okay,' Matt continued, 'then what if we make it look like there's fifty.'

'How?'

'I don't know. We pad it out.'

'With what?'

Matt shrugged. 'So you're thinking it wouldn't work.'

'It's an extremely high-risk move.'

'It's too risky, you're right.'

'Do we know anyone who has thirty thousand pounds in cash to hand?'

'I wish I did.'

Sean clicked his fingers. 'Michael Thornbury.'

'Michael?'

'We need to call him, now.'

'But how d'you know he's got that kind of cash to hand?'

'Because James wasn't the only one who won big at Samson's. Michael won big, too. He had a few big wins after the Birch Grove robbery, and he told me he was keeping the money in his flat because he didn't trust handing it over to anyone else.'

Just then, Sean's mobile rang, and both of them tensed.

'It must be him,' Sean said, staring at the 'Unknown Caller' notification on the display. He looked up at Matt, as if for guidance.

'You'd better answer it, hadn't you?'

'We haven't had a chance to get our story straight.'

'Tell him what he wants to hear,' Matt urged.

'Okay, okay.' Sean took a deep, steadying breath and pressed the 'Answer' button. 'Yes, we have what you want . . . We want to meet on neutral ground, to exchange the money and drugs for Beth and Charlie . . . Absolutely, we promise, we won't try anything stupid – of course not . . .' Sean listened, then glanced at his watch. 'I think that'll be okay. We should have everything ready by then . . . Just two things . . . Firstly, we want your assurance you won't have anyone following us. Secondly, we want proof that Beth and Charlie are okay.' Sean looked over at Matt as he listened to the reply, closing his eyes briefly as he pinched the bridge of his nose.

'What did they say?' Matt said.

'He said we won't be followed on our way to the exchange.'

'And Beth and Charlie?'

'I'm sorry, mate. He didn't answer that question.'

CHAPTER
FIFTY-THREE

Michael packed quickly, making sure he had his passport and the e-tickets for the car ferry that evening. It wouldn't do any harm to get to the port early. He'd feel more secure there.

He rolled the suitcase to the front door before retrieving the three carrier bags stuffed full of cash from the back of his wardrobe. Carrying the bags outside, he hid them in the sizeable compartment in the car boot where the spare tyre was supposed to sit. They just about fitted while still allowing the panel on top to lie flat. The tyre itself he carried back into the flat and left in the hallway, deciding that if he was unlucky enough to undergo a spot check on the crossing, suspicions might be raised by seeing the tyre on display. He'd run the risk of getting a puncture instead.

He hauled the case over the front step and out on to the path, muttering a silent goodbye to his home of five years before loading the case into the boot.

Michael had two hands on the lid of the boot when a thought came to him. It was about the last time he'd used the suitcase. Last year he, Annabelle, Alex, and Rachel had headed off in this same car on a road trip to Paris. They'd rented out a private apartment right in the centre, within strolling distance of the Eiffel Tower. It had been an amazing trip, full of friendship, laughter, and love.

Holding tightly on to the boot lid, he gazed down at the case, drowning in the memories.

Then he reached down and unzipped the small front pouch. In his rush to get away, he hadn't given it a second thought. Usually he used the pouch to slip in a card with his name, email address, and telephone number, in the event of it being lost. The others had teased him about this habit, which he had picked up from his mother.

He slid his hand inside and felt for the card from the Paris trip. Pulling it out, he was surprised to see that it had been replaced by a postcard featuring several famous Paris sights: the Eiffel Tower, Notre-Dame Cathedral, and a view of the River Seine.

Intrigued, he flipped over the card. There was a short, handwritten message:

To the best of times! Friends forever!

It was signed by Rachel and Alex, with love.

Michael stood there, clutching the card, in shock at the appearance of this relic from a happier age.

He looked up at his flat, then back at the card.

Just then, his phone rang. He nearly answered it, but instead set it to silent and slipped it into the case.

He had made his decision.

CHAPTER
FIFTY-FOUR

'Here we are.'

Sean indicated right and swung across a gap in the traffic. They'd been unable to reach Michael by phone, so had set off for his apartment in Camden. 'Adelaide Terrace. Number twenty-three.'

When they got there, they cruised along the road, which was lined by imposing white Georgian townhouses.

Matt looked out for the right address. 'You really think Michael will go along with this?'

'I'll force him if I have to.' Sean's threat was disconcerting.

'I hope it won't come to that.'

'I know things about Michael that he won't want to find their way out into the wider world,' Sean said cryptically.

'Is that Michael's car?' Matt asked, nodding towards the red Audi A3.

'I think so.'

They pulled in behind it. But as Sean turned off the engine, the Audi wheelspinned and shot off at high speed.

'What the hell?' Sean said, turning to Matt. 'He was in the car.'

'Follow him,' Matt said instinctively. 'We have to speak with him.'

Sean fired the car back up and set off in pursuit.

◆　◆　◆

'Why would he flee?' Matt said. He could see Michael's Audi six cars in front as they travelled up the A40. Both their cars were limited to the speed of the other traffic, which was pretty heavy.

'Maybe he thought we were someone else.'

'Samson?'

'I spoke to Michael yesterday. Told him James had disappeared. He was pretty shocked – talked about things reaching a head. Maybe he just panicked.'

'Then we need to let him know it's us,' Matt said. 'And here's our chance.'

The lights at the junction ahead were red. Michael was at the front of the queue of traffic.

Matt unclipped his seat belt. 'I'm getting out.'

He leapt from the car, sprinting down the line of traffic. Drivers and passengers stared at him aghast as he flashed past their windows. Matt prayed the lights wouldn't change to green before he reached Michael's car.

They didn't.

Matt skidded around to the front of Michael's car, placing his hands on the warm bonnet as Michael looked on, first in horror, and then in confusion.

Matt ignored the cacophony of car horns as the lights changed to green. 'Michael,' he panted, 'we really need your help.'

CHAPTER FIFTY-FIVE

Michael powered down the driver's side window. 'You'd better get in,' he shouted.

Matt slid into the front passenger seat. 'Sorry about the dramatics.'

Michael cranked the car into gear. 'Okay, okay,' he shouted into the rear-view mirror, as several more horns blared. The car leapt forward, past the lights. 'It was you who just pulled up outside my flat?'

'Yes, me and Sean.'

'I'm sorry I bolted like that. I thought you were someone else.'

'I know the full story.' Matt peered into the side mirror to confirm Sean was following. 'I know about Samson. About the money and the drugs.'

'You know about Alex and Rachel, too?'

'Yes. Nick Samson, he's taken Beth and Charlie.'

Michael's eyes shot across to Matt, shocked. 'What? Sean didn't tell me . . .'

'We only found out this morning.'

'I'm so sorry, Matt.'

They passed through another busy intersection, and again Matt checked Sean was keeping up with the pace.

'That's why we came to speak with you. We need your help to get them back. Samson wants to exchange Beth and Charlie for the money and the drugs, at twelve noon. We've managed to get the drugs together . . .'

Michael reacted with surprise. 'James has come back?'

'No. We've sorted something else out. But it's the money we're having a problem with. We have twenty thousand that James left behind. But we need thirty more.'

'I can help with that,' Michael said, without hesitation.

Matt was taken aback by the swiftness of his offer. 'Are you sure?'

'One hundred per cent certain.'

'Wow, that's . . . well . . . fantastic. We'll pay you back, of course.'

'No need,' Michael said. 'Believe me, there's nothing I'd rather do with the cash. If it helps me to sleep better at night, then it will be worth every penny. I'm sick of all this, Matt, I really am. The lies, the money, the drugs. It's got to stop.'

'How quickly can you get it?'

'I have it already. It's in the boot. Forty grand's worth, won at Samson's casino. I want rid of it. It's blood money.' Michael threw him a smile as they pulled up to a roundabout. 'I couldn't be happier to help, believe me. You know why I'm driving around with forty thousand pounds' worth of used banknotes in my boot? Because I was about to run away. I was about to abandon everyone to this . . . this mess, and do what I thought offered me the best chance of survival. But surviving isn't living, is it?'

Matt knew just what he meant.

'I couldn't do it, Matt. I couldn't leave everyone. I wanted to see Rachel at the hospital, to say goodbye. But she'd left me a message, in my suitcase. It made me realise I *had* to stay. But I still didn't know how I could help. How I could try and make things right. But now here you are.'

Matt didn't need to understand everything Michael was talking about. But he did understand one thing: whatever his motives, whatever miracle message had convinced him to help, for Beth and Charlie it could be the difference between life and death.

It was fast approaching the agreed time for the rendezvous. Up ahead, a police car cruised from the opposite direction. Matt glanced at the two officers as it passed.

If only we had the support of the police.

But Sean had been clear, and he was right. Matt had to trust his judgement.

'Where should I be going?' Michael asked, as if suddenly snapping out of autopilot and finding himself behind the wheel without direction.

Matt regathered his thoughts as he watched the patrol car in the side mirror as it disappeared from view. 'I don't know.'

'You don't know where you're meeting for the exchange?'

'They said they'd call us, half an hour before.'

Michael checked the dashboard clock. 'So, in just under an hour.'

Matt's phone rang. It was Sean on his hands-free.

'Matt. Is everything okay?' Sean said.

'Yes, fine. I've just been explaining things to Michael. He's got the money and he wants to help.'

'That's good to hear. Have you heard back from Harvey yet?'

'No.'

There was a slight pause. 'We're running out of time.'

'I know, I know. Maybe I should give him a call. See how things are going.'

'You do that. By the way, where are you heading? You off to collect Michael's money?'

'No, he's got the money in the boot. I don't know where we're heading.' Suddenly Matt remembered. 'We need to go back to my flat and collect the rest of the cash.'

◆ ◆ ◆

Matt hardly waited for the car to stop before he was throwing the door open and sprinting up to his flat. He forced the key into the lock and retrieved James's bag from the bedroom.

Michael had followed him in and was standing at the doorway.

'You have all the money now?'

'Yes,' Matt said, clutching the bag, 'and some spare.'

Sean entered the room. 'So it's just the drugs we need.'

'Yes.'

Could they really trust Harvey? He was a thief. A robber. A drug dealer.

'And what do we do now?' Michael asked.

'Wait. We just have to wait.'

CHAPTER FIFTY-SIX

'Here we go,' Sean said, as his phone rang.

Matt's stomach lurched. Harvey still hadn't got back to them to confirm he'd got the drugs and was going to turn up. 'You'd better answer it.'

'But we *still* don't know whether we have the drugs!' Sean protested. 'What am I going to say?'

'Tell him whatever he wants to hear.'

Sean hesitated as the phone continued to taunt them with its shrill tones.

'*Please*, Sean. Just tell him we have the drugs.'

'We've got half an hour,' Sean said.

'Just do it.'

Finally, Sean answered. 'Hello.' He threw Matt a concerned glance and nodded, confirming it was Samson. 'Yes,' he replied, 'we have it all.' Another look at Matt. 'We can do that, yes,' he said, his eyes closing as he spoke. 'We'll be there for the swap. Just let us know where.' He listened for a few seconds. 'Yes, I know that place. Thirty minutes. The drugs and the money. And we get Beth and Charlie.' Then he ended the call.

'It's on,' Sean said, before blowing out his cheeks. 'Matt, I hope you know what you're doing. If we turn up without the drugs . . .'

'I know, I know.' Matt didn't really want to think about that eventuality – it brought on waves of nausea – but it would be reckless not to do so. He batted the issue back to Sean. 'If Harvey doesn't come through with the drugs, what do we do?'

'We're screwed,' Sean replied. 'There is no Plan B.'

'But—'

'No, Matt, there is no Plan B. You've got to understand that,' Sean emphasised. 'If we don't have the drugs, then we don't get Beth and Charlie back. And that's a fact. Samson won't enter into a bargain with us. He won't take some now and· the rest later. He'll punish us for not delivering what we promised. We have to get those drugs. Otherwise we most likely will never see Beth and Charlie alive again.'

Sean's dire warnings hit home. 'Then what do we do? Could you call Samson back and say we've made a mistake, that we haven't got everything yet and we need to rearrange the exchange?'

Sean dismissed the idea. 'It's too late.'

Matt put a hand to his head. He tried to think. 'There must be another way.'

'There isn't, Matt,' Sean said, softening.

Matt slipped his phone out of his pocket and tried again to call Harvey.

Still no luck in reaching him.

'Where does he want to do the exchange?' Michael asked, as Matt continued gazing down at the phone.

'On the development land, near to the Olympic Park,' Sean replied. 'It's a bit of a wasteland at the moment.'

Matt snapped out of his reverie. 'I'll just leave a message for Harvey, so he knows where he needs to get to.'

Sean nodded but didn't look convinced.

Matt left the message, giving Harvey the directions and time of the exchange.

'We need to go,' Sean said. 'We really don't want to be late.'

Matt followed Michael and Sean out of the flat, carrying the additional bag of money. He still hoped the call would come, confirming Harvey had got the drugs and was good to go. But it didn't.

'We'll go in my car,' Sean said, hurrying over to the vehicle.

Michael quickly transferred the other bags of cash from his boot into the back of Sean's car.

'I didn't spot anyone,' Sean said, as he slammed the driver's door shut behind him. 'Did a quick look around, but nothing. I'll keep a lookout as we go. I suggest we all do likewise.'

Matt was only half listening, his attention once again on his mobile, which was resting on his lap.

Please, Harvey, please come through with this. You promised you could do it.

'Just keep hoping,' Sean said, noting Matt's concentration. He eased the car off the mark before accelerating sharply as they approached the junction with the main road. 'They haven't given us much time to get there.' He zipped out between the traffic and put his foot down hard.

CHAPTER
FIFTY-SEVEN

'Here we are,' Sean said, as they approached the vast area of wasteland that was primed for a massive new housing development. 'Right on time.' He swung the car on to a gravel road built for construction traffic and slowed to a stop.

The area was totally deserted. There were no signs of life at all.

Matt looked at his watch as the time hit twelve o'clock. 'Where the hell are they?'

Sean suddenly pointed over to the far right, where a van had cruised into view.

Matt prayed Beth and Charlie were in there, safe and well.

'So what do we do now?' Michael asked.

'I'll try Harvey again,' Matt said.

'It's too late,' Sean replied flatly.

Matt felt sick as he gripped his phone. Sean was right. It was too late. If Harvey was going to pull this off, he'd have been here by now. And he'd have called to let them know.

They'd have to do this without the drugs somehow.

Sean released the handbrake and drove at a slow twenty towards the waiting white van. The car rocked and bumped over potholes and the brick-strewn ground, coming to a stop some twenty metres away from the van. The front windows of the van were darkly tinted, the occupants hidden. It had sliding doors on the sides.

'What now?' Sean said.

Matt reached for the door handle. 'We get out.' Before Sean could reply, he'd stepped out of the car and was facing the van. Something deep inside had taken control. He no longer felt fear. He just wanted Beth and Charlie back. It was an all-consuming desire.

Michael joined him, standing at his shoulder, with Sean on his own on the other side of the car. Still there was no movement from inside the van.

'We can do this,' Michael said, placing a hand on Matt's back.

Matt nodded.

They watched as the front doors of the van opened and two men climbed out. One of them Matt recognised immediately: Joseph Deed. His companion, although some way shorter than the mixed martial arts specialist, was also built like a castle keep – he might have been the guy who'd frisked him at the casino.

'You got it all?' Deed said, breaking the silence. His face was set like stone. The other man joined him, directing a hard stare at Sean.

How could Matt tell them they didn't have the drugs?

'Are Beth and Charlie alright?' he asked, stalling for time.

'They're fine,' Deed said. 'Now answer my question, before that situation changes.'

He would have to tell them the truth. No matter what the consequences.

But not yet.

'Sean, can you get the stuff out of the boot?' Matt asked.

'No,' Deed said, stopping Sean dead in his tracks. 'Just you,' he said to Matt. 'You get it. The other two, stay right where you are.'

Matt nodded, and moved around to the back of the car. He popped the boot and gazed down at the bags of money. He lifted out all four, dumping them on the ground. He paused before closing the boot, trying to eke out the process a little longer.

'C'mon. Get on with it,' Deed snapped.

'Harvey, I trusted you,' Matt muttered, as he slammed down on the boot lid. He turned to look back across the wasteland.

And then the car appeared.

CHAPTER
FIFTY-EIGHT

Matt watched as the BMW headed straight for them.

Harvey?

He looked over at Sean and Michael, then at Deed, who ominously didn't look concerned at all by the arrival of another vehicle.

Matt's hopes dimmed.

The white BMW slowed to a stop just a few metres away, its tyres crunching on the gravel. Again, Matt caught Sean's eye – he looked as tense as Matt felt.

Like the van, the car's windows were darkly tinted, so it was impossible even at close quarters to determine who was behind the wheel.

The door opened, and Harvey got out.

He smiled at Matt, but there was something unnerving about his expression. He brushed down his jacket. 'Matt, my man. Well, I said I'd be here, bruv, and here I am.'

Harvey turned and opened the back door.

Nick Samson stepped out. 'Matt, good to see you again. Sean. Michael. Well, this is quite a reunion.' He clasped his hands together and smiled.

Matt felt sick. *It's a trap. And Harvey is part of it.*

'You're surprised to see me?' Samson asked Matt.

'I just want Beth and Charlie back,' he replied. 'So let's do the exchange and we can go.'

'I know, I know.' He looked across at Sean. 'Sean, how are you?'

'Okay,' Sean said warily.

Samson's face darkened. 'You thought you could cheat me, Sean. You and your banker friends. I'm sure you now realise your catastrophic error of judgement. I'm especially disappointed in you, Sean. You've been such a close associate for these past few years. I looked out for you. Even after that most unfortunate incident, when your poor colleague fell to his death after taking that rogue batch of coke. Adam, that was his name. Hey, Matt – wasn't he a friend of yours?'

Matt looked at Sean, stunned.

'I'm sorry, Matt. I'm so sorry,' Sean whispered.

'I looked out for you on that one, Sean. Made sure you didn't get fingered. And then you betrayed me . . . You see,' Samson continued, turning back to Matt, 'people underestimate me at their peril. But I'm a businessman, an entrepreneur, not a monster. I only mess with people who mess with me. So these two,' he said, pointing at Michael and Sean in turn, 'and their friends – they messed with me big time, and they have paid the price.'

'And what did I do?' Matt asked. 'What did Beth and Charlie do?'

'Nothing. Which is why you will all be fine. As I said, Matt, I'm not a monster. But these two, now I know for certain they've been screwing me over . . . Well, I've not decided what I'm going to do with them yet.'

Matt saw Michael's face. Pure terror. He wondered for a moment whether he was going to run.

'You know, young Harvey,' Samson said, gesturing to his left, where Harvey was standing, just watching proceedings, 'he's my newest member of staff. A clever guy, as you know, Matt. We've been keeping an eye on both of you at the college. It's good to have him on board.'

Matt searched Harvey's face for some kind of explanation. But he gave him nothing.

'I trusted you,' Matt said. He hadn't meant to vocalise his thoughts, but they came anyway. 'I believed what you said.'

Harvey blinked a couple of times, but that was all.

'You have the money?' Samson said, looking at the bags still lying on the ground at Matt's feet.

'Yes.'

But what about the drugs?

'And the drugs?'

Matt looked at Harvey. 'We don't have them yet.'

Samson tutted. 'That is unfortunate. Joseph, grab them.'

Like attack dogs, both of the men lunged forward and, in a swift movement, wrapped their muscular arms around the necks of Michael and Sean, dragging them back towards the van.

Matt watched on in horror.

'Don't worry,' Samson said to Matt. 'When we release Beth and little Charlie, there will be plenty of room in the back of the van for these two.'

'I . . . can . . . get you . . . the . . . drugs,' Sean struggled to say, fighting against the pressure on his windpipe being applied by Deed.

'Too late,' Samson snapped. 'Far too late.'

'Please,' Matt tried. 'Please let them go, and we'll get you the drugs. I promise we will.'

Samson was amused. 'Matt, you really are a good guy, aren't you? How about we spare Sean's life for Charlie's? What do you say?'

'Please don't hurt my son.'

'I don't respond well to begging,' Samson said. 'What can you offer me?'

'Myself,' Matt said, without hesitation. Sean, who'd been saying something to Deed, shot him a stunned look. 'Let them go, and take me.'

Samson laughed. 'No thanks. Try again. What can you offer me?'

'How about a bullet through the head?'

Samson and Matt turned as one, to see Harvey aiming a gun straight at Nick Samson's face.

CHAPTER
FIFTY-NINE

'What the hell is this, Harvey?' Samson said. He was trying to sound his normal confident self, but for the first time he seemed unsure of what was happening.

'Tell your men to let go of my friends,' Harvey said, not taking his eyes off Samson for a second.

'You're making a huge mistake, Harvey,' Samson tried.

'You may be right,' he said, 'but just do it, yeah?'

Samson acquiesced. 'Let them go.'

The men did as requested, and Michael and Sean staggered back towards Sean's car, clutching their necks and taking in welcome lungfuls of air. They came to stand by Matt's side.

'Now,' said Harvey, with the gun still trained on Samson, 'you two. Open up the van and let Beth and Charlie go.'

Deed and his companion looked to Samson for guidance.

'Do it,' Samson ordered.

Deed yanked open the sliding door. 'Time to go,' he said. Matt watched with relief as Beth climbed out, holding Charlie. Charlie nestled his face into her neck as she rushed over to Matt.

'Thank God you're okay,' Matt said, as he placed a comforting hand on her back. Beth looked shaken and very tired, but was otherwise unhurt.

'We're fine,' she said.

'You two,' Harvey said to Samson's men, 'on the floor, face in the dirt, arms and legs spread.'

They didn't wait to be asked twice.

'And don't move a muscle,' Harvey added, 'otherwise you get a bullet where the sun don't shine – get my meanin'?'

Matt took in the scene. The two men, prone on the ground, next to the BMW; Samson, and Harvey with his gun still aimed; and then their group, next to Sean's car – Matt, Beth, Charlie, Sean, and Michael.

'Harvey, what's this all about?' Matt asked.

'That night you came to the club, they approached me, man. Wanted me to work for them, to bring you and your friends down. I said no. I didn't want no business with Samson, man. But then I found out somethin'. Somethin' about my brother Jason. You remember, Matt, I told you how he was murdered? Knifed to death.'

'I remember.'

Harvey's face hardened as he turned back to his target. 'For three years, I hunted the people who did it. I got nowhere, man. It seemed impossible. The police didn't care. The community leaders, all my contacts, they didn't know nothin'. But I never gave up. I never gave in. You know me, bruv – I'm determined. I get what I want.' He turned the gun slowly until it was side-on, but still pointing straight at Samson. 'And then, yesterday, I found out.'

'Who told you?' Samson said.

'That don't matter,' Harvey replied. 'What matters is that I hold you responsible for what happened. And I've waited a long time to get to this place – to bring justice to the man who killed my brother.'

'Don't do it, Harvey,' Matt said. 'Please don't.'

But Harvey wasn't listening. He brought the gun closer to Samson's head. But Samson didn't even flinch. 'You know, my brother wasn't perfect. But I loved him. He protected me, made sure the family was

277

looked after. Without his money, we'd have been out on the street, man. He did what he had to do.'

'I was sorry to lose him,' Samson said. 'Jason was a loyal member of my team.'

Harvey shook his head in disbelief. 'No, you're lyin'.'

'Jason was one of my best men,' Samson continued. 'Until he got greedy.'

Another headshake of disbelief. 'Jason wouldn't have worked for you. He wouldn't.'

Nick Samson smiled. 'He did what he had to do. So you see, Harvey, the money your brother brought home, keeping you in shoes, keeping food on the table for you and your family, and a roof over your head, it was *my* money.'

'You're wrong.'

Samson was emboldened. 'You know I'm not. I've been watching you for a while, Harvey. I see the potential. The spark of ruthlessness in your eyes – you remind me so much of your brother.'

Harvey was being drawn in, transfixed by the words. Matt could see his grip on the gun loosen. 'I would *never* work for you!' Suddenly the grip tightened. 'Go to hell!'

'Harvey, don't!' Matt shouted, taking a step towards them. 'Don't do this. Don't throw everything away. You're better than this. You've chosen a different path, remember?' Another step forward. 'You kill him, and you'll go to jail for a very long time.'

'It'll be worth it,' Harvey said. But there was a lack of conviction in his voice.

'Harvey, this isn't what Jason would have wanted.'

'Stop talkin', man,' Harvey said, as a tear trickled down his cheek. 'Just shut up!'

But Matt continued. 'He'd be proud you've taken control of your life, moved away from the violence.'

'It's too late,' Harvey said, his teeth clenched in anguish. 'Too late.'

'No, it's not. Did you bring the drugs?'

There was a momentary pause, as if he didn't want to answer, and then Harvey said quietly, 'Yes.'

'Then give them to him.'

Matt now addressed Samson. 'That's my offer. You have the money and the drugs. And you leave us alone. Never come near us again. Harvey included.'

Samson twitched, then smiled. 'Deal,' he said emphatically.

Harvey laughed in disbelief. 'You're jokin', right?'

'No, I'm not,' Matt replied. 'It's got to end here, Harvey.'

'You have my word,' Samson said.

Harvey threw Matt another look, and Matt nodded.

'Just go,' Harvey said, gun still raised. 'Get in the van and go.' He slid his hand into his jacket and pulled out a large packet of coke, throwing it over towards the van.

Samson, Deed, and their companion grabbed the drugs and bags of cash, and then retreated to the van. Samson turned at the door. 'I'm sorry about your brother, Harvey. Such a waste.'

Harvey gestured with the gun. 'Just leave, before I change my mind.'

And with that, the van door closed. The wheels of the vehicle spun on the gravel, kicking up dirt, and it sped off across the wasteland.

Harvey joined the others, gun now hanging limply at his side. 'We were on top, man,' he said, as the van disappeared in the distance. 'We could have won.'

Matt placed an arm around Beth as Charlie emerged from her protective embrace. 'We have won, Harvey. We have won.'

CHAPTER SIXTY

James Farrah paused the Liam Neeson movie on the television and went into the kitchen to refill his glass of red. He considered his next move. He'd stay for at least a week in the lodge, deep in the New Forest, before crossing the Channel on the ferry and then tracking down through France and Spain to Portugal.

He'd already identified a few suitable apartments in the Algarve. Looking right on to the Atlantic Ocean. Expensive, but he could afford it.

There was plenty of time to decide what to do after that. Maybe he'd just stay there until he got bored.

He'd enjoyed the two nights here, hidden away from everyone and everything. When he'd purchased the state-of-the-art lodge twelve months ago, he'd vowed to keep it his own little secret. It would be his bolthole.

Only one other person knew about it.

He smiled as he took a glug of wine.

He'd never expected the lodge would come in so useful.

James moved to the window. Total blackness outside. With the lodge silent, the woodland creatures made their presence felt. An owl hooted, and there was the caw-caw of a crow.

It was a pity Beth couldn't be here with him. But one had to make choices in life.

James returned to the sofa and resumed the movie.

Liam Neeson was firing off half a dozen rounds at an Eastern European gangster when James thought he heard a noise at the window.

A knock?

He stiffened, but shook it off as a trick of the mind.

Neeson was now pursuing his target across Rome on a moped, zipping across piazzas, narrowly avoiding tourists.

There it is again!

James moved over to the window. Nothing.

Is that scratching at the door?

He put his eye up to the spyhole just as the knock sounded out. He backed away from the door.

Had they managed to track him down?

He ran over to the kitchen area and grabbed the biggest blade from the knife block.

Knock knock!

He couldn't pretend he wasn't in. The lights were low, but detectable. His car was parked outside. He searched for options, gripping the knife so hard his knuckles ached. He wouldn't stand a chance against the men Samson had sent.

They would kill him.

It wasn't supposed to end like this.

Knock knock!

'I'm sorry!' he shouted, before he'd really had a chance to think about what he was going to say. 'I'm really sorry. You can have the money back!'

But maybe it wasn't them after all.

Once again, he moved towards the door, his face right up to the spyhole. 'Who is it?'

'It's Matt Roberts,' came the voice.

CHAPTER
SIXTY-ONE

Matt held his nerve in the cool darkness of the forest as he waited for James's next move. A twig snapped underfoot as he shifted on the spot.

There was no way of predicting his reaction. Coming here was most certainly a risk.

The lock clicked from inside, and Matt stood face-to-face with James Farrah. He looked relieved, and Matt knew why – from his shouts, it was clear he had feared a much more dangerous visitor. 'Sean told you,' he said, holding on to the doorframe, one arm out of view.

'Yes. He remembered, yesterday.'

James smiled tightly. 'He was the only one I told about this place. Not even Beth knows. I suppose you'd better come on in. Welcome to my humble abode.'

The first thing Matt saw upon entering the lodge and turning sharp right was a six-inch carving knife on the kitchen worktop.

James noticed him spot it, but didn't offer an explanation. Instead he picked up a remote and turned off the television in the corner. 'Please, take a seat,' he said, as the movie gunfire fell silent.

Matt lowered himself on to one of the comfy chairs in the living area. He looked around. The place was all wood panelling, ceiling and floor, with a strong smell of beech. The furnishings were bachelor-pad staples – Bose audio system, Apple Mac, flat-screen television. It reminded Matt of Harvey's place, with his malfunctioning electronic curtains, and the memory helped him relax a little.

'Like it?' James smiled.

Matt ignored the question. 'How could you do it?'

'Excuse me?'

'How could you leave Beth and Charlie at the mercy of Nick Samson?'

'I don't know what you mean.'

Matt fought to control his anger. He wanted to launch himself at this man, who hadn't only taken everything from him, but had then played so recklessly with the ones Matt loved the most. 'Oh, I think you do.'

'I do care about Beth,' James said. 'And she cares about me, as much as you don't want to believe it. We had something good together.'

'And you chose this instead,' Matt stated, gesturing at the lodge.

James shook his head.

Again Matt forced himself to remain calm. Losing his cool would be extremely counterproductive. 'Don't you even want to know how Beth and Charlie are?'

'I got her message,' James said. 'I know she's okay.' His choice of words was deliberate.

'You also know it's over then.' Matt knew Beth had called him, to tell him it was finished and to vent her fury at how he had risked not only her life, but Charlie's too.

James held up his palms. 'What can I say – I had to make a choice. I'd prefer Beth to be here with me, but sometimes you can't have everything.'

'I never thought I'd hear you say that.'

'You must be loving this,' James said. 'I bet you couldn't wait to get back into her—'

'Tell me about Alex McKenzie,' Matt cut in.

'Alex McKenzie?' James seemed bemused. 'What about him?'

Matt held on to his emotions. This was the point of no return – a step into the unknown – and he needed to remain focused. 'Tell me why you killed him.'

'What?' James laughed off the insinuation as preposterous. 'Are you alright in the head, Matt? Alex was killed by—'

'Nick Samson. Or one of his men. They ran him down to send a warning to you all, to turn up the heat and get you to admit you'd stolen money and drugs from under their noses. At least that's what you wanted Sean and Michael to believe. It was the perfect cover, wasn't it?'

'You're crazy.'

Matt pressed on. 'The police believed they were looking for a routine hit-and-run. Sean and Michael feared it was Samson. But you knew differently, didn't you?'

'Maybe you should go back and enjoy family life, Matt.'

'I read the news reports. Alex wasn't wearing a helmet at the time of the crash. And yet his colleagues, fellow cyclists at UGT, said he always wore a cycle helmet.'

'So?' James was flushing. 'He forgot the helmet on the day he needed it. Sometimes life just isn't fair.'

'I didn't see it at first,' Matt continued. 'Not until yesterday. It was in the slide-out drawers under Charlie's bed. Alex's cycle helmet. He'd written his name underneath the fabric.'

James looked on, not speaking.

'It was you, wasn't it, who Charlie saw at the top of the stairs? He called you the "naughty man". What did you threaten him with not to name you?'

Again, James said nothing, his tongue pushing against the inside of his cheek.

'You decided to flee and abandon Beth and Charlie, Michael and Sean to their fate. But then you remembered you'd left the helmet in the top-floor office, and rushed back to retrieve it. Except in the meantime, Charlie had found it first, taken it down to his bedroom, and hidden it away. When Beth came home in the middle of your frantic search, you waited upstairs, but Charlie saw you and you ran, without the helmet and without the bag of cash you'd left in the storage space.'

James surprised him by smiling and slow-clapping. 'You know, Matt, I underestimated you.'

'Why did you kill Alex?'

'I tried to convince him not to go to the police. We were handling it okay. All we had to do was stick to our story, and Samson would get bored and walk away. He couldn't be sure about what we'd done. We were doing fine. But then Alex lost his nerve and penned a letter explaining everything, thinking the police would offer protection. It would have brought us all down with the fool. Fortunately, I managed to stop him sending it.'

'By killing him.'

'I tried to reason with him.'

'And what about Rachel Martin?'

'I couldn't be sure Alex hadn't told her what had happened.'

'But you didn't push her in front of that Tube train. The person who did it was picked up on CCTV. Who is he?'

'Someone I hired. He also was driving the untraceable four-by-four that so effectively dealt with Alex. You make a lot of useful contacts in the drugs trade.'

'You stole Alex's cycle helmet that day at work to make sure he wouldn't survive the impact. And your hired hand did the rest.'

James just grinned.

'The same person – you also hired him to follow me.'

'Possibly.'

'He was seen following me on the Thames, and at the leisure centre.'

'He followed you pretty much everywhere, Matt,' James stated. 'I needed to be sure Sean wouldn't tell you what was going on. I knew how you'd delight in ruining everything for me if you were to find out. So I arranged for him to keep a close eye on you.'

'You sound paranoid.'

'Just careful,' James replied. 'Tell me, have you told the police about all this?'

'Not yet.'

'Not ever, I bet.'

'How can you be so sure?'

James smiled. 'Because you can't tell the police about me without incriminating Sean – and I know you wouldn't want to do that, would you, Matt?'

'Sean didn't commit murder.'

'No, but he *is* a drug dealer. He'll face jail, and his career will be as dead as Alex McKenzie.'

'You're right. I don't want to incriminate Sean.'

'Then what the hell are you here for, Matt?'

'I met with Jessica.'

'Oh? Thinking of rekindling that old romance?'

'She explained how you set me up.'

'I thought she would. She's a bitter, rejected woman, out for revenge.'

'She also told me about your anger-management issues.'

'Oh really?'

'She showed me the marks on her neck from where you throttled her. And it isn't the only time that's happened, is it?'

'I'm not sure where this is going, Matt. But please, do hurry up, I need to finish the movie.'

'She's going to the police,' Matt revealed. 'She's willing to testify you physically assaulted her, on numerous occasions.'

'It's her word against mine,' James said dismissively.

'If the jury believes her, your career will be over. And even if there isn't a conviction, the police investigation, the trial, will derail your hopes of a quick getaway.'

'It that *all* you've got? She's bluffing. She won't go through with it.'

'She won't have to,' came a voice from the doorway.

CHAPTER
SIXTY-TWO

Matt looked across at his friend. 'Sean, I told you to wait in the—'

'She won't have to go through with it,' Sean repeated, meeting first Matt's, then James's gaze. 'Because I've told the police everything – Michael knows too, and he'll support the story.' He looked over at Matt. 'I called them on the way here, when we stopped at the services. They've just arrived.' He looked back at James. 'I couldn't let you get away with what you did.'

'You idiot!' James lunged for the knife. But before he could lift the blade from the worktop, a shout rang out.

'Police! Down on the floor. Now!'

James sank to his knees, head bowed, as six uniformed officers pushed their way into the lodge and surrounded him.

'James Farrah,' one of the officers said, as he handcuffed him, while another held him by the shoulders, 'I'm arresting you in connection with the death of Alex McKenzie.'

Matt watched on, but James didn't lift his head.

CHAPTER
SIXTY-THREE

'Harvey – good to see you.'

Harvey looked up from the bench as Matt approached. The sun was shining by the River Thames, just down from Westminster. It was two weeks since the events that had seen Matt reunited with Charlie and Beth, Harvey sparing Nick Samson's life, and James arrested.

'Hey, man, great to see you!'

Matt took a seat. 'I did wonder whether you'd show when I didn't hear back from my text. I thought you might still be angry about what happened.'

'I was angry for a few days,' Harvey admitted, 'but not with you. With myself, I guess. I had to get my head round lettin' Samson go – but I know now, shootin' him wasn't the right way to do things. Once I got that clear, things have felt a lot better.'

'That's great. Really great.'

Harvey looked off towards the river, where a rowing boat skimmed past. 'You know, I've decided, I'm goin' to enrol for a degree. Graphic design. I've looked into it. Spoken to someone. They've got grants I can apply for.'

'That's fantastic, Harvey, it really is.'

'How about you, bruv – you not changed your mind, gone back to the bank?'

'I'm starting my teacher training course in September.'

'Good on you, man. I bet Amy is stoked.'

'She is.'

'And your family?'

'They're happy too.'

'I meant you and . . .'

Matt caught his drift. 'Beth and I, we're going to make a go of it.'

'Ha ha!' Harvey said, slapping Matt's back with some force. 'Amazin'!'

'It's early days. But I think we'll be okay.'

'I'm sure you will, bruv. So, heard any more about James Farrah?'

'No.'

'He'll go down for his crimes, man! Big time. Oh, I meant to ask about the girl, Rachel. She okay?'

'They brought her out of the coma. She seems to be doing well – sitting up and talking. The doctors are very hopeful.'

'So all is well,' Harvey said.

'Pretty much.' But everything wasn't well. 'Apart from Sean.'

'I don't think you need to worry about Sean. The police will drop the drugs investigation, believe me.'

'How so?'

''Cos Nick Samson will have a word with his friends high up in the force – there's no way he'll want people pryin' into his business.'

'As much as I'd like to see Samson brought to justice, I hope you're right.'

'I am right, bruv. But don't you worry, man, one day Samson'll get what he deserves. How are things with you and Sean?'

'I really don't know. Knowing he was responsible for what happened to Adam, and he never said . . .'

'If I can let Nick Samson live, you can move on with Sean. You just gotta do it.'

'Maybe.'

'The hate and anger I felt about Jason's death, and my dad runnin' out – holdin' on to that, lettin' it consume me, I realise now it was all about protection. I was protectin' myself from having to face the fact Jason was dead, and Dad was gone. But you know what?'

'What?'

'Now I've let go, bruv, it feels liberatin'.'

CHAPTER
SIXTY-FOUR

Five Months Later

'How do I look?'

'Very smart, Mr Roberts,' Beth said, as she moved across the bedroom towards Matt and straightened his tie, before brushing off some fibres from the shoulders of his suit jacket. She kissed him on the lips. 'How d'you feel?'

'Nauseous.'

'Oh,' she said. 'I wish you'd told me that before I kissed you. Could have been a nasty start to the day.' She smiled sympathetically. 'Do you really feel that bad?'

'Been up since five. Reading through my lesson plans.'

'You'll be fine,' Beth said. 'It's understandable, being nervous for your first lesson on the first teaching placement. But after the way you handled Harvey and co., you should have no worries.'

'After those first few weeks of class observations, I'm starting to think thirteen-year-olds in an inner-city London comprehensive are more challenging than ex-offenders,' he joked.

'I think you might be right. But I have every confidence in you. And so does Charlie. Charlie, you can come out now.'

'I thought he was downstairs watching TV . . .'

Beth smiled as Charlie entered the bedroom, brandishing a piece of paper.

'This is for you, Daddy,' he said, handing Matt the drawing. It was of a man with a huge head, holding a pen, in front of lots of smiling faces.

'Is that of me, Charlie?'

'Yes. Doing your teaching!'

'Oh, that's lovely.' Matt crouched down to take a closer look. 'Thank you so much.'

'I did it for you, Daddy. I know you'll be *great*!'

Matt stroked his hair. 'You're too sweet.'

'Can I watch TV now?'

'Of course.'

As Charlie raced back downstairs, Matt turned back to Beth. 'I've got a confession.'

'Go on . . .'

'The teaching isn't the only reason I'm nervous.'

'Oh, right. It's about yesterday – about what you asked?'

Matt nodded.

'I just need a little more thinking time.' She watched Matt for his reaction. 'You know I love you, don't you?'

'Of course I do.' Matt smiled.

'It's just that, you know . . .'

'Don't worry. Take your time.'

'It's not that I don't . . .'

'If you decide it doesn't feel right, I promise I'll let it drop and we'll be fine, absolutely fine. Oh, I'd better go,' he said, realising the time.

He gave Beth a goodbye kiss.

'Wait,' she called, as he made for the stairs. Her voice was nervy. 'I'm scared, Matt.'

Matt moved back towards her. 'Scared?'

She smiled sadly. 'I'm scared it'll change things.'

'I know.'

'You promise it won't?'

'I promise.'

She visibly gathered herself. 'Then the answer is yes.'

'Are you sure?' He moved closer, hardly daring to believe his ears.

'Yes,' she smiled, relaxing into the decision. 'I would *love* to marry you.'

Matt was lost for words as they embraced.

'What's wrong?' Charlie said, having returned from downstairs to seek out company. 'Is something the matter?'

'Everything's fine,' Matt said, as he and Beth parted. 'You know how much you like parties?'

Charlie nodded excitedly.

'Well, there's going to be a really special one very soon.'

'Will there be cake?'

'Oh yes,' Matt said, as mother and father cuddled their son. 'A really big cake.'

ACKNOWLEDGMENTS

I'd like to thank all the people who have helped me during the writing of this novel. First of all, the Thomas & Mercer team, in particular Emilie Marneur. Special thanks to my editor, Mike Jones, who worked so hard on the initial drafts and challenged me to make this the best book it could be, and to my copyeditor, Monica Byles, for all her hard work in the latter stages. Thanks to my agent, Jon Elek, for his advice and support. I've been very fortunate over the past few years to have had amazing support from my readers, particularly those in my Facebook group. It's a pleasure to know every one of you. A special mention goes to those readers who took the time to read and comment on the draft of the novel: Toni Holmes Ray, Christal Worth, Robin Shulman O'Kane, Jennifer Moore, Elsi Gabrielsen, Ailsa Wood, Bonnie Sue Foley, Jan Settle, John-Paul Coe, Yvonne Pearson, Kristal Ginn-Farrar, Cara Gunia, Marje Hirst, Kimberly Daigle, Patty Younts, Gayle Valentine, Stella Ash, Eileen Mintonye, Pat Field, Patricia Cheshire, Anca Andronic, Vicky Larios, Patricia Northall, Angela Casbeard, Rebecca Casbeard, Tracey Silvestri and Jennifer Olow. Last, but definitely not least, I want to thank my wonderful family for their support and love.

ABOUT THE AUTHOR

Known for his fast-paced thrillers and mysteries packed with suspense, twists, turns and cliff-hangers, Paul Pilkington is a British writer from the north-west of England. He is the author of the Emma Holden suspense mystery trilogy, the first of which, *The One You Love* (2011), was number one in *The Bookseller* Fiction Heatseekers Chart. The second in the series, *The One You Fear* (2013), was named as one of the Best Kindle Books of 2013 (UK Kindle Store Editor's Choice). The final instalment, *The One You Trust* (2014), has helped the series to achieve over 4,000 five-star reviews on Amazon. He is also the author of standalone mystery thriller *Someone to Save You*, which is a Kindle number one bestseller in the UK and Australia.

Paul loves hearing from his readers. You can find him online at www.paulpilkington.com, chat with him at www.facebook.com/paulpilkingtonauthor, or tweet him at www.twitter.com/paulpilkington.